WHO BROUGHT THE DOG TO CHURCH?

Kindness heals hearts. Tracy

WHAT OTHERS ARE SAYING . . .

Who Brought the Dog to Church? by Tracy L. Smoak is a delightful contemporary Christian novel about community, care, and friendship. There is the difficult topic of domestic violence which is sensitively portrayed by Tracy. Her style of writing enables the reader to easily picture the victim and the abuser as we get inside their heads. There is also the theme of loss as women struggle with grief after losing their husbands. Tracy L. Smoak writes in an easy, personable style. Although there are serious themes, her style is easy-going and peppered with humor. Tracy L. Smoak is a new author to me and certainly one that I want to read more from. Her story tackles serious, relevant issues in an easily relatable way while revealing the heart and love of God for His children. *Who Brought the Dog to Church?* is a charming tale that I can highly recommend.

—JULIA WILSON
BLOGGER AT WWW.CHRISTIANBOOKAHOLIC.COM

In *Who Brought the Dog to Church?*, Tracy L. Smoak has done something remarkable—she's woven serious topics such as death, immigration, and domestic violence, with the laugh-out-loud antics of a bunch of small town church ladies to produce a funny, heartwarming, and thought-provoking tale. The relationships between Betty, Letitia, Ida Lou, and Elizabeth are darling! Fun connections and revelations sprinkled throughout the book make it a page-turner not to be missed, and the whole story wraps up in wonderfully satisfying and sweet conclusion. This book gives readers hope for abundant joy, even in the midst of pain, and, most of all, points us to the unfailing love of the Savior.

—HEATHER NORMAN SMITH
AUTHOR OF *SONGS FOR A SUNDAY, WHERE I WAS PLANTED, NEW WINE TRANSPORTATION COMPANY,* AND OTHER INSPIRATIONAL SOUTHERN FICTION

WHO BROUGHT THE DOG TO CHURCH?

a novel

TRACY L. SMOAK

Ambassador International

GREENVILLE, SOUTH CAROLINA & BELFAST, NORTHERN IRELAND

www.ambassador-international.com

Who Brought the Dog to Church?

Paperback ISBN: 978-1-64960-422-4
eISBN: 978-1-64960-470-5
Library of Congress Control Number: 2023936440

Cover design by Hannah Linder Designs
Interior Typesetting by Dentelle Design
Edited by Martin Wiles

AMBASSADOR INTERNATIONAL
Emerald House
411 University Ridge, Suite B14
Greenville, SC 29601
United States
www.ambassador-international.com

AMBASSADOR BOOKS
The Mount
2 Woodstock Link
Belfast, BT6 8DD
Northern Ireland, United Kingdom
www.ambassadormedia.co.uk

The colophon is a trademark of Ambassador, a Christian publishing company.

Jesus said, "Blessed are those who mourn, for they will be comforted."

Matthew 5:4

CHAPTER ONE

EVANGELISM GONE TO THE DOGS

A little brown dog, of all things, reclined on the church pew to the left of Betty Herndale. The pooch wore a polka-dot bow in its topknot, and its cotton-candy tongue lolled on the plush seat cushion. Betty couldn't believe modern manners had slipped so low.

Some people might not have a problem with a dog in the sanctuary, particularly since members of The First Church in Prosper, Virginia, valued evangelistic efforts. But Betty minded—a lot.

Bringing a pooch to church violated the notion of hospitality. God loved all creatures, great and small, but even He didn't invite hairy dogs to sit on new pew cushions during a Good Friday prayer vigil. What would members of the ladies' auxiliary do if they saw that terrier seated on the purchase from their many bake sales?

And what if the mutt had mange? Betty scratched her forearm. Then, she adjusted her floral dress to cover her knobby knees and tightened her disapproving lips as she stared at the dog's owner. This middle-aged woman named Ida Lou-something-or-other attended last week's Bible study as a new visitor. The guest said little about herself, except she'd recently relocated from a larger city. Perhaps Ida Lou came from a church that allowed pets. Well, Betty would quickly squelch that notion.

However, Betty couldn't figure out how to alert the newcomer regarding the impropriety of including a dog in this night's holy petitions without breaking the silent vigil. The two other people, praying with heads bowed in the back of the church, didn't seem to notice anything. Perhaps they also sought Divine guidance on how to handle this delicate situation.

Ida Lou, a classic blonde beauty in a butter-yellow jumpsuit and leather sandals, sat across the aisle, apparently enthralled by the stained-glass windows and oblivious to Betty's displeasure.

If she'd noticed the dog as soon as she entered the church, Betty would have sat elsewhere. Now that she was settled, she couldn't very well get up and move without making a scene and disturbing others in the peaceful quiet.

The four-pawed source of conflict sat up, cocked its head, and wagged its tail—as if hoping to declare a truce. Betty glared. The pup took the hint, crawled over the blonde's lap, and hid on the opposite side.

Although the pet's owner must have been twenty years her junior, Betty thought the newcomer should have known better. "Some people are allergic to animal hair," Betty whispered just loud enough for Ida Lou to overhear. But the noise of others opening doors and entering the dim sanctuary must have drowned out her comment.

Sensing a sneeze coming on, Betty dug through the handbag on the pew beside her, searching for her travel pack of tissues. However, her usual allergic reaction to pets didn't materialize—at least not yet. Thank goodness. She had enough to worry about without that.

Someone should vacuum that pew before Sunday services. Imagine unsuspecting Easter pilgrims sitting on the cushion, only to stand an hour later with hairy bottoms. Betty's memory conjured up museum images of Neanderthals.

Betty shifted her substantial frame to a more comfortable position that favored the left hip. The wooden bench squeaked in protest, but Ida Lou didn't glance over.

Inhaling the fragrance from Easter lilies arranged around the chapel, Betty sought calm. The new Hammond organ sat silently in the choir section. Its antique predecessor had piped her wedding processional fifty years ago when she had carried a white rose bouquet down this center aisle. Donovan had waited for her at the altar, tall and debonair in his black suit.

She nestled against the row's end and pretended he sat next to her with his heavy arm draped protectively around her shoulders. *Lord, why couldn't Donovan stay longer?*

There was no answer. Figured. Silence was the only heavenly communication she got lately. Slouching down and leaning her head against the pew back, she studied the oak beams of the arched ceiling. Donovan's farming family had crafted them with the same skill they'd used to construct their barns. A sigh escaped her lips. History everywhere around her, but not much future. Not anymore. If only she'd noticed the warning signs about Donovan earlier. Maybe he'd still be with her.

Life in Prosper tick-tocked as steady as gears in a grandfather clock. Once, Betty had been at the heart of all the goings-on in the church and community. Now, seconds measured as though they were eons. Grief had become her constant companion. Could she have done anything to prevent the tragic outcome? Who was she without her husband?

No sense whining about what couldn't be changed. But every so often, as when she sat in church and nothing seemed altered, she pretended for a moment Donovan would soon slide beside her on their pew, and she would reach out to hold his work-calloused hand.

Aching loss threatened to overwhelm her again. *Dear Lord, please hold me close to keep the loneliness at bay.* She would *not* cry. That showed weakness. Betty inspected what the others in the sanctuary were doing.

Was there a Scripture about having a dog in attendance? The only one that came to mind was something about dogs eating crumbs under the master's table. She didn't want to quote *that* to Ida Lou. Imagine if the clueless newcomer brought her mutt to the next potluck.

Betty redirected her thoughts to the task at hand and looked at the prayer requests written on white index cards. Blue veins stood out on the top of her hands, and arthritis knobbed her knuckles. How could her body look old when she felt as though she were thirty? She squinted at a child's uneven scrawl: "Please pray for my little brother's ear to heal." She offered up that petition, then flipped to the next card.

At the sound of scratching, she swiveled to the side and gaped at the Yorkie, scraping its pink painted toenails along its midriff. Betty pictured fleas with parachutes on their backs jumping out of the swirls of fur to make residence on the very spot where Elder Stan Stout and his wife, Melissa, sat every Sunday.

She cleared her throat, hoping Ida Lou would notice and make eye contact so Betty could send her a disapproving look. But the woman simply gave her dog's head a gentle pat, staring toward the front of the church with a distracted expression.

Betty uncrossed her ankles and tapped her polished ankle-high boots on the hardwood floor, thinking that noise might get Ida Lou's attention. No such luck. How had Christ put up with pesky people and their indiscretions?

Betty watched the tan dog crawl back into Ida Lou's lap, circle around once, and then curl up to sleep. Then, stifling a sneeze, she forced herself to study the next card: "Dear Lord, thank You for my friends and family."

She slapped that prayer card face down on the bench. No sense praying something she didn't feel. Anger vied with guilt. Shouldn't she be grateful for what remained? What was it Job had said when he lost everything? Something like, "The Lord gave, and the Lord took away. Praise His Name." She wasn't going to be a hypocrite and start singing hallelujah. No sir.

She wasn't happy with God. He hadn't answered *her* prayers. Yet she tried to be faithful during the last year and accept her circumstances. Her heart hurt, and nothing seemed to take away the raw ache of loss. She had focused her life on being a good wife and raising their son, Ben. Did she have a life purpose anymore?

Loud snores reverberated across the front row. Glancing over, Betty saw the dog's little chest rise and fall with even, deep breaths. No peace tonight in church with that mongrel present.

Fed up with the dog, God, and everything else, Betty grabbed her purse, heaved up to standing, and stomped her brogans down the center aisle toward the rear of the building.

As she barreled out the back double doors, a series of gale-force sneezes stopped her in her tracks. Good thing she'd had the decency not to succumb to them during the silent prayer vigil. Then again, a good sneezing fit might have caught the attention of the cause of her discomfort.

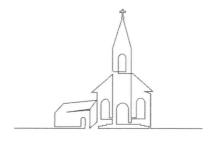

CHAPTER TWO

SEEKING SANCTUARY

Slamming church doors startled Ida Lou Besco. She stiffened, almost knocking Sweetie from her lap. Comforting her pet, she bowed and prayed that whoever had such a bad cold would recover soon. She knew the importance of good health.

She'd left her husband's side at the hospital twenty-eight minutes ago. Though he hovered on the edge of death following a massive heart attack, she had to hurry home to take care of Sweetie when evening approached. She knew no one else to ask for help.

While walking her dog, she'd followed an impulse to duck into her new neighborhood's church. The quaint, brick building invited her to hide from the hospital's antiseptic, white walls. She hoped no one would mind her bringing a seven-pound Yorkie into the sanctuary.

Ida Lou grabbed the hymn book from the pew in front of her and opened it. She smiled for the first time in hours as she focused on the lyrics to the familiar song. She needed a friend who understood her sorrows and offered hope.

She stroked Sweetie's long, silky fur—in much the same way as when her daughter was young and she'd spent hours brushing her fine dark tresses. That was before she'd lost her precious girl. Three years had passed since that tragic day at the graduation ceremony, yet the pain lingered. Now, she might lose Richard, too.

Ida Lou envisioned the pale, thin shell of her burly husband, whose few movements the hospital ventilator commanded as it emitted intermittent beeps. She'd fled the cold environment for a short break—not only to walk the dog but also to seek hope. Fear clung even as hospital smells permeated her clothing.

The stained glass at the front of the church revealed a purplish-blue sky behind brilliant light with Christ's hand extended toward her. She imagined a rich, bass voice comforting her with the Bible passage from John 10:27-28 memorized years ago: "My sheep listen to my voice; I know them, and they follow me. I give them eternal life, and they shall never perish; no one will snatch them out of my hand."

Surely, God would show mercy this time. Hadn't she been faithful to Him even after the loss of her child? Only her hope in eternity kept her from going mad with grief.

She missed simple things most. Like hearing her daughter and husband debate in the kitchen over whether mint chocolate chip or butter pecan was the better ice cream. Or watching her husband throw a gently spiraling football into their daughter's giggling embrace.

Then tragedy struck again. One minute Richard was sitting in his worn armchair, waving his unlit Half Bent Billiard pipe as he argued what word filled the seventeen-down column of the crossword puzzle. The next moment, he had dropped the pipe and was clutching his chest. Then he crumpled onto the carpeted floor of their living room.

She cried out his name and leaned down to touch him. He didn't respond. Frantic, she'd dialed 911. In the following blur—hearing sirens, seeing flashing red lights, and smelling singed flesh from the defibrillator's shock—Ida Lou wanted to believe in miracles. But as each hour ticked by without any sign Richard would regain consciousness, faith dwindled. White-coated doctors talked in hushed tones, and she had difficulty following their technical jargon. She shivered at the real possibility of widowhood. Tears stained her blouse. Sweetie sensed her distress and caressed her cheek with a rough tongue.

Ida Lou had to get back to her husband. She picked up the large designer bag at her feet and nudged Sweetie into it. Her fingers gripped the handles, and she tiptoed toward the back of the church. No one looked as she passed. She wanted to shout, "Hey! My husband is dying! Can you help me?" But pride kept her from disclosing such vulnerability to strangers.

She picked up a pen and a blank index card at the room's rear. In a jagged script, she wrote, "Please pray for my husband, who had a heart attack last night. He's in intensive care at Memorial Hospital."

After signing the card and placing it on top of the stack, she stepped outside to the parking lot. She would tuck Sweetie in for the night at home before returning to the chair in Richard's hospital room. No way was she going to leave him alone for long. Richard was all she had left—and her memories of their daughter.

CHAPTER THREE

CARRYING THE CROSS

The cell phone's shrill ring interrupted Betty's Saturday breakfast as she was about to take the first bite of peanut butter on rye. Caller identification showed the church office. Irritated, she set down the toast.

This better not be another last-minute plea for me to organize the auxiliary's annual fundraiser. Last year, six unruly teenagers, who were supposed to be helpers, "accidentally" locked themselves in the sanctuary loft for four hours. She'd solved the problem by hiring a locksmith to free them. Never did get her personal expense reimbursed.

Betty picked up, halfway hoping the other party would apologize for a wrong number. "Hello."

"Mrs. Herndale? Pastor James here. How are you this fine morning?"

"Other than my bunions acting up, I'm fine. Thank you for asking." Trivial comments about the weather annoyed her.

"Is this a good time to talk?"

That depends on what you've got in mind. "Sure." She held her breath, gearing up for whatever Pastor James might say next.

"It's about our church family standing together."

Betty groaned inwardly, sure he was going to ask her to counsel Letitia Larrimore again about imbibing too much wine. That woman had experienced a couple of embarrassing incidents that would best not be repeated. The church used only juice now for communion so as not to cause difficulty for anyone.

"You know, we need to look out for one another."

That man didn't know when to stop. Sometimes, his sermons went over ten minutes and made people late for lunch reservations.

"We certainly do." But there were limits! Just because Letitia was her best friend and next-door neighbor didn't mean Betty should be saddled with the responsibility of making sure Letitia controlled herself. As though anyone could manage that task.

"I think we can do much more."

Oh boy, here we go again. Last month communion almost ended in a panic when the juice ran out. Good thing Betty found the leftover purple Kool-Aid mix from Vacation Bible School. The elders better make sure they have a sufficient supply next time. She was tired of cleaning up everyone else's messes.

"Go ahead, Pastor James. I'm here to serve, as long as the Lord gives me strength." She hoped that little reminder of her vulnerability would make him think twice about making more requests.

"There's a woman in our church who's hurting a great deal. I was hoping you'd talk with her."

She plunged her knife into the peanut butter jar. She was going to wring Letitia's neck. "How can I help?" she cooed.

"One of our new visitors, Ida Lou Besco, filled out a prayer card last night at the vigil. She indicated her husband had a massive heart attack Thursday evening."

"How horrible!" This was worse than Betty imagined. How could the pastor bring up such a tragedy to her? Didn't he remember this week was the anniversary of Donovan's death?

"Do you think you could go to the hospital and sit with her this morning?"

No, he did not just ask her to do that. Betty gulped. Prosper Memorial Hospital held powerful memories for her, and none of them were good.

"I hate to ask you to go, but you are very discreet and have a quiet strength that others can depend on in a crisis."

A crow outside her kitchen window cawed loudly. Her morning devotion had been about a rooster crowing when Peter denied knowing Jesus. Peter had been more concerned about his convenience than doing the right thing. She didn't want to make the same mistake.

"I could be there in ten minutes." Her voice came out so softly that she wasn't sure he heard it.

"Thank you, Betty. I'm officiating at the Smith wedding shortly, but I'll stop by the hospital as soon as I finish. Should be around noon."

Betty gritted her teeth and willed her beating heart to slow. "Should I start the prayer chain for Ida Lou and notify the team of her situation?"

"Good idea. I knew I could count on you."

Betty disconnected. Remorse filled her for how she had judged the woman last night at church. If the pastor only knew how hard her heart was, he'd never trust her with anything.

She hit speed dial for her best friend.

"*Buenas tardes.*" Letitia giggled.

Betty sighed. "My dear, I do not have the time to listen to you butcher a language you're only learning so you can flirt with the gardener."

"I was only trying to wish you a good morning. You don't have to be such a grouchy grump."

"But what you actually said was, 'Good afternoon.'"

"Oh. Sorry. What's up?"

"I'm calling to activate the prayer chain for an emergency. And if we keep jabbering on and on, it will *be* afternoon by the time we get this launched."

"What's the prayer request?" Letitia's tone became curt.

Betty kicked off her bedroom slippers and looked for her boots. "I'm on my way to the hospital for Pastor James."

"The pastor's in the hospital?" Letitia shrieked.

"No, dear. Mrs. Besco filled out a prayer card. Her husband had a heart attack Thursday night. Will you make the next call for the prayer chain?"

"Of course."

"I'll send a group text message, but please follow up with the personal calls like we agreed to ensure everyone stops to pray."

Before Letitia could launch into a series of questions Betty had no answer for, Betty slammed down the receiver. She turned away from the breakfast table, leaving her cold toast untouched. Her stomach lurched as she stepped to the foyer, dreading the task she'd agreed to handle.

She removed the hair rollers and placed them on the little, round table. Gazing into the mirror, she fluffed her soft, white curls. After putting on her boots, she pulled a red sweater from the coat closet. She shivered, dreading the frigid hospital waiting room.

Collecting her purse, she headed out the front door, determined to stand with Ida Lou in her time of need. Wasn't that what the Lord asked of His faithful—to pick up and carry the cross, no matter the cost? Betty hoped courage wouldn't fail her when she reached the hospital.

CHAPTER FOUR

PRAYER CHAIN MISHAP

Letitia Larrimore stared at her phone screen a moment before setting it down on the table, leopard-print case up. She loved Betty like a sister, but their temperaments were as different as night and day. They'd become best friends in middle school, but Betty's holier-than-thou attitude still irked her. Betty's fun meter generally registered zero unless Letitia helped her along. The thought teased out a smirk. What prank could she pull next?

Letitia dug through a haphazard pile of papers on her kitchen desk. She shoved aside an old chocolate bar wrapper and retrieved the prayer chain list from under a pizza coupon that had expired two months ago. Betty insisted on back-up systems for every process and faithfully mailed paper copies of the people who offered to pray every month. Letitia loved the excuse to chitchat when time permitted. AnnMarie was next to call.

After a few rings, her voicemail came on. Letitia paused. Betty said the man in the hospital was married to that newcomer. What was her name? Tapping her fingernails on the counter, Letitia tried to remember. Mrs. Bess Something-or-other? Or was it Melissa? She was terrible with names. Besides, who could keep track of all the new people who visited their church or Bible study, attended once or twice, and then stopped coming?

Frowning in concentration, Letitia remembered the husband of the only Bess she knew had gotten a job delivering the morning's newspaper. And today's edition was sitting on her kitchen table above her yoga mat and exercise clothes. She breathed a sigh of relief. No problem there, then. The only Melissa she knew was Elder Stout's wife. Although Melissa could be stuffy, she hoped Stan was okay.

At the tone, Letitia left a message for AnnMarie that Melissa's husband had suffered a heart attack. Following prayer chain rules, Letitia kept moving down the list of prayer volunteers until she got a live connection. "Robin, there's a prayer-chain emergency. Melissa Stout's husband had a heart attack Thursday."

"That's awful!" Robin exclaimed. "I'll call the next person on the list."

Letitia disconnected, then checked her watch. She'd completed the first round of prayers in less than three minutes. When Betty's son Ben had experienced trouble with his appendix last month, it had taken thirty minutes to call all twenty names—mainly because AnnMarie got chatty. Betty often timed them to make sure they stayed on task. The prayer team could set a new record if everyone else did as well as Letitia had today.

Grabbing her bottle of metallic-blue nail polish, Letitia lifted her bare foot to the kitchen chair to paint her left toenails. Then she realized she hadn't prayed. Feeling a stab of guilt, she dabbed on the polish, then hurried—as much as possible without messing up the polish—to her special "prayer chair," the recliner in the corner of the living room. She prayed fervently for Melissa Stout and her poor husband.

To distract herself from the sad circumstances of the prayer request, she looked out the window to see if that handsome Juan had started working on the grounds yet. She scanned the manicured lots of her retirement community and looked for his friendly face.

Rats. Might as well keep practicing her Spanish. What had Betty said about her greeting? Oh, yes. Well, she probably wouldn't see Juan till afternoon, anyway. So how did that phrase go? *Bones tardy?* Something like that. She smiled, thinking about making a new friend.

CHAPTER FIVE

UNDER ATTACK

Sarah McAdams cowered in the corner of her bedroom in Summit, North Carolina, holding her knees as a shield. Prayers for help screamed from her silent throat.

"This pigsty better be spotless before I get back for lunch," her husband yelled, stabbing a finger toward the bed linens he'd just ripped from the mattress and tossed onto the floor.

Sarah bent her head, allowing her long, dark hair to cover her face. Looking at him when he was in a tirade only infuriated him more. She studied a crack in the drywall and tried to ignore the fissure widening in her heart.

Charles stomped to the dresser. In one quick swipe, he sent knickknacks and picture frames flying. They crashed on the pale-blue shag carpet like jetsam from a shipwreck.

Hoping the commotion hadn't awakened their two-year-old, Sarah refused to cry out. Her husband approached the one item left standing on the dresser: her jewelry box.

He opened one of the little drawers and took out her favorite necklace—the slim gold chain with three pearl pendants her parents had given her as a college graduation present three years ago. He leered at her and dangled it inches from her face. He snapped it in half without a word, then dropped the two sections to the ground. The pearls scattered and rolled away.

"Why . . . " Sarah sputtered. "How could you—"

"That's for not answering your phone when I called."

She should rise and defend the prized possession, but her limbs were like gelatin.

Every time Charles attacked her, Sarah hoped it would be the last. But as his violent episodes continued, she learned to disassociate mind from body. Mentally withdrawing to an aqua cloud far away was the only way she could escape without abandoning her child.

Charles grabbed a handful of Sarah's hair and yanked her head back. Pain seared her neck and scalp. He stared deep into her eyes. "Today's lunch better have more flavor than yesterday's junk."

His breath smelled terrible. She swallowed with difficulty, not bothering to mention he'd instructed her to prepare tuna salad yesterday. How was she supposed to know he preferred the canned tuna in water to the one in oil?

Sarah found it impossible to predict what would set him off. The more she tried to please him, the irater he became. But she knew better than to pass off the blame on him.

"You're right, honey. I'll work on a better recipe for your sandwich. Maybe add some apple chunks and celery?"

Charles raised his free hand. Sarah flinched. But instead of hitting her, he released the knot of hair in his other fist, then used his thumb with tenderness to wipe a teardrop from her cheek. The unexpected kindness sparked a hint of hope in her heart. Maybe his fit was over, and she could start cleaning up the damage.

Charles glanced at his wristwatch. "I'm going to be late for work." He kissed her swollen lips, then turned toward the door and grumbled, "I wish you wouldn't make me mad."

Sarah pushed tangled strands of hair off her forehead and focused on slowing her breathing. She'd survived another episode . . . and her little boy hadn't seen it.

As Charles passed the dresser, he picked up his police hat. His elbow knocked over the jewelry box, and it landed with a loud clatter, spilling its remaining contents.

He pulled the hat down over close-cropped, auburn hair and aligned the bill over his nose. "If you had plans to use the car today, forget it. I'm taking the keys."

Sarah stifled a gasp. How was she supposed to get groceries if he had the car? Did he expect her to push Ricky in the stroller and carry bags of food home?

Charles looked in the mirror and used the sleeve of his uniform to polish the badge over his heart. Then he left the bedroom without a glance.

After the front door slammed, Sarah waited a few minutes, in case he came storming back in to catch her doing something else wrong.

Outside, the car engine turned over and purred. Then the sound drifted away. Sarah tested one foot to see if she could stand. Painful, but not impossible. With shaky arms, she pressed her hands against the floor and crouched on her heels. She stood slowly, then gazed at the ruined pictures and jewelry on the carpet. She'd pick those up later— and look for the cherished pearls. But she couldn't face that task now.

Sarah headed to the bathroom and stood at the mirror over the sink. Hair like Medusa's framed a pale face. A gash high on her right cheekbone promised to turn blue later. She splashed cold water over the blood around her lips, then brushed through her matted hair. The left side of her face throbbed, and her throat burned when she swallowed. *I can't live like this anymore. I just can't!*

Today was the first time Charles had choked her. Each horrible attack consolidated his power and crushed her defenses. If she didn't do something now, she might not get another chance.

She needed to protect her precious two-year-old, no matter what. But if they split, Charles might get custody. Then who would shield her son? She slipped on a housecoat, then went to check on Ricky.

When she entered his room, she saw her red-haired toddler sitting in the middle of his car bed, sucking his thumb and clutching a threadbare teddy. His wide blue eyes stared at her. His slurping noise was the only sound in the room.

What was she thinking? She couldn't protect herself, much less her son. She moved to the bed and hugged him gently. "Mommy loves you," she crooned. "Everything's going to be okay." She tousled his hair and patted the teddy on its silky ear.

Sarah thought about the escape plan she'd been discussing for weeks with Wilma, an advocate at Family Matters. The agency helped victims of domestic violence. Could she go through with it?

How could she *not*?

"After breakfast, let's go to the park for a picnic." Sarah kept her voice bright and cheerful for her son's sake.

A little pop sounded as Ricky withdrew his thumb from his lips. He sat up straighter and studied her face. Then he raised his arms for her to pick him up, still clutching the stuffed animal in one small hand.

CHAPTER SIX

RESOLUTION TESTED

At 8:25 Saturday morning, the double glass doors of Prosper Memorial Hospital swooshed open, mussing Betty Herndale's white hair. Sweat dampened her palms in the atrium. Despite beautiful artwork on the walls and the scenic garden overlook, dread lurked beyond the appealing entryway. Memories threatened to overwhelm her, but she clenched her jaw and moved to the information desk.

"Good morning, Mrs. Herndale," said Kara, sporting the classic pink jacket the hospital required volunteers to wear.

Betty smiled at her former Sunday school student. "I'm glad you're on duty this morning. I need to go to ICU. Pastor James sent me over to see someone."

"I'll phone ahead so the nurses will let you in."

Having been a part of First Church for seventy-one years certainly had advantages. "Thank you." Betty waved and continued toward the elevators.

Her stomach fluttering, she followed corridors without hesitation and pushed the button for the second floor. How could it be that she stood here for Donovan one year ago?

With a ding, the polished doors opened. The long hallway and sparkling white floors looked the same. The faint echo of her brogans mixed with the hustle and bustle of footsteps as medical staff hurried to care for patients. She pulled on the sweater as the frigid air hit.

She picked up the phone at the ICU entrance and dialed the nurses' station. Within seconds, she heard a click as the doors swung open. She walked toward the waiting room, her head held high to hide the ache in her heart.

"Could you please tell me which room is Richard Besco's?" Betty asked a nurse.

The petite uniformed lady pointed toward the corner. "He's in 1202."

Betty nodded thanks and approached the room. She hesitated before peeking around the white curtain pulled halfway across the opening. Not wanting to violate anyone's privacy, she gave a tentative double knock on the wall.

"Come in," called a woman's soft voice.

Betty stepped around the curtain. Beyond the still form on the bed, she saw Ida Lou Besco sitting on a chair. Purplish circles of fatigue darkened the skin under her blue eyes, and tears clung to her long, dark lashes.

"I don't know if you remember me, but we met at the Bible study on Tuesday. My name is Betty. May I come in?"

Ida Lou nodded. "Of course."

Betty edged around the patient and headed toward the wall near Ida Lou. She kept her eyes on the woman so the bed and medical equipment wouldn't trigger flashbacks and cause her to falter in her mission.

"I wasn't expecting visitors." The blonde tugged on her red plaid top, which clearly mismatched lime green slacks.

"Pastor James got the prayer card you filled out at the vigil. He asked me to stop by. He'll be here as soon as he finishes the Smiths' wedding." Betty looked around the room for any telltale signs of the hairy dog.

Ida Lou pointed toward an empty chair in the corner by the window. "Please, have a seat."

Betty detected a faint scent of rose as she passed Ida Lou, contrasting with the medicinal smells.

After Betty sat, an awkward silence ensued. She didn't know what to say. Nor could she bring herself to look at the man hooked up to machines, so she focused on Ida Lou's stylish haircut and silvery highlights.

"What—" Betty cleared her throat, and the sound practically echoed in the small, quiet room. "What happened to your husband?"

"Richard seemed fine Thursday morning, other than complaining of heartburn. But that night, he collapsed in the family room. I called 911. Paramedics started CPR as soon as they arrived. They had to use an AED to shock his heart." A tear dropped from her eye.

Betty ached. She remembered the trauma of seeing the man she loved collapse. She reached into her purse for a tissue and offered it to Ida Lou.

"He's been like this for more than thirty-six hours. The doctors say all we can do is wait. The blood work showed elevated tropo-somethings, which confirmed a heart attack."

Betty arched an eyebrow at the unfamiliar terminology but didn't ask for clarification.

Ida Lou grasped her husband's inert hand. She stroked his fingers, careful not to disturb the taped section covering the IV port.

Seeing the sheet over the patient's chest rise and listening to air hiss through the breathing tube made Betty's mind flash to scenes she'd tried to forget.

"I feel helpless." Ida Lou shivered.

Betty wanted to encourage her, but a glib reassurance might be offensive. She took off her red sweater and wrapped it around the young woman.

"Aren't you cold?"

"Don't worry about me. I've got plenty of insulation." Betty laughed, patting her girth.

Ida Lou smiled slightly as she cuddled into the warm cardigan. "It's nice of you to come. I was getting lonely. The nurses are sweet, but they have so much to do."

"I'm here for you." Betty got out of her chair, then took Ida Lou's other hand. "Is there anybody you want me to call?"

Ida Lou's beautiful face clouded. "No. There's no one else. It's been only the two of us for three years."

Betty wondered about the woman's reference to three years. Ida Lou was middle-aged. Had she and her husband married late in life? Did neither of them have children? Curiosity nudged her, but this wasn't the time to pry.

A gentle knock sounded, and a nurse appeared by the curtain. "Mrs. Besco, we need to check your husband's vitals and take blood. Would you mind stepping out for a few minutes?"

Ida Lou stood stiffly and stared at her husband's statue-like countenance.

Betty gave her hand a gentle squeeze as she led her toward the hallway. "Have you had breakfast?"

"No. I don't think I can eat. My stomach is churning."

"You've got to take care of yourself. Let's go to the cafeteria and see if they have oatmeal or yogurt. Those might help settle your tummy."

Ida Lou glanced over her shoulder toward the closed curtain. "Guess I can't do anything here right now."

Betty walked beside Ida Lou as they headed down the hall. She hoped everything turned out well for the woman and her husband, but she didn't want to offer false assurances. Betty knew religious platitudes could cut to the marrow of a person's faith. She'd promised herself that, given a chance, she'd be honest instead of raising false hopes or murmuring clichés.

As she escorted Ida Lou toward the cafeteria, Betty recalled well-intentioned but misguided phrases people had said to her one year ago in this hallway. An elder had said, "Trust God. He'll deliver if you pray hard enough." Yeah, right. So much for her resolution.

Another congregation member knocked her for a loop by asking if she needed to confess a secret sin so God would remove His hand of judgment. The echo from that self-righteous comment haunted her.

Betty determined to hold her tongue and not burden Ida Lou Besco with more weight than she already carried. If God needed to tell the young woman something, He'd have to do it Himself.

CHAPTER SEVEN

STEPPING OUT

Sarah balanced Ricky on her hip as she carried him to the kitchen. She set him in his booster seat, grabbed a box of Cheerios from the pantry, and poured them into his favorite Superman bowl.

Adding slices of banana to the mix, she said, "Mommy's going to pack yummy peanut-butter-and-jelly sandwiches for our picnic."

"I wanna watch a show." Ricky wriggled in the seat as though to get down.

She didn't need any pouting this morning. She set the bowl of dry cereal and banana in front of him, then kissed his forehead. "How about breakfast and Big Bird?"

He clapped his hands in delight and swiveled his head toward the television. She turned it on.

Moving toward the refrigerator, she opened the bread bag. Seeing only half a heel in the bottom, she sighed. "I shouldn't have to scrimp to buy bread." But Charles gave her only eighty-five dollars weekly for groceries, and she had to account for every penny with receipts. Even going to the local food pantry didn't leave much margin for setting aside emergency cash.

Deciding to make do with what she had, like always, Sarah took a large, blue canvas carryall out of the pantry and put in a box of crackers, two green apples, three juice drink boxes, and four slices of American cheese. After packing napkins in the side pockets, she checked on Ricky.

She wiped off smashed banana from his hands and chin, then lifted him from the booster seat. "I'm going to go change clothes. You can watch television in the living room, okay?" She helped him down from the seat and watched him scamper to the couch.

Still holding bits of cereal in his hand, Ricky leaned around her to get a better view of singing puppets on Sesame Street.

Sarah returned to the bedroom. Knickknacks and picture frames dotted the soft carpet like a minefield. But she couldn't return them to their rightful places on the dresser until she put away the contents of her upended jewelry box.

After setting the hand-carved wooden box upright, she picked up the bracelets and earrings. Charles had purchased these colorful pieces of costume jewelry for her after their many fights. She returned the items to their proper drawers.

Then she got down on her hands and knees to scoop up items on the floor, including the two halves of her gold chain. She checked everywhere for the three little pearls. They'd rolled too far under a piece of furniture for her to see, much less reach.

Sarah caressed the gold links lying in her palm. Maybe someday, she'd figure out how to repair the broken necklace. Perhaps eventually, she'd fix her own brokenness.

She set the two chain halves on a strip of black velvet in the jewelry box alongside the only pieces of any monetary value. Charles had given her an opal ring and a diamond tennis bracelet after two nasty fights.

Wondering how much they might be worth at a pawn shop, Sarah took them out and set them on the dresser. Then she arranged the remaining items in neat rows to camouflage any gaps. Charles would have to look carefully to notice anything was missing.

After a quick shower, Sarah dressed in jeans and a faded t-shirt. With methodical discipline, she made the bed and arranged the pillows in the precise pattern Charles preferred. Then she picked up his dirty clothes and her nightgown and tossed them into the hamper.

If by some miracle she managed to escape today, leaving the house in good order would allay suspicions Charles might have—at least for a little while. If she failed to get away, he would be pleased she'd cleaned the house.

She took the opal ring and tennis bracelet to the kitchen, putting them in a zippered interior pocket of the blue satchel. After setting it on the floor next to the garbage can, she lifted the white plastic bag full of kitchen refuse and reached underneath for the small, crumpled brown paper bag she'd placed there two weeks ago. Inside was the cell phone Wilma had given for emergency use. Charles couldn't monitor calls made on this.

A slight popping sound made Sarah jump. Ricky stood in the doorway, his thumb shiny with saliva. "Mommy, what you doing?"

"I lost my phone." Like a magician performing a trick, she pulled the small object out of the paper bag. "Look, here it is!"

Ricky stuck his thumb back in his mouth and watched her drop the plastic trash bag into the container. Then he returned to the living room dragging his old teddy bear.

The tuna cans and eggshells in the kitchen trash would no doubt stink by the end of the day. *Maybe I should take out the garbage before I leave.*

She stared at the phone in her hand. "I'm sick of cleaning up Charles' trash," she said.

Sarah moved to the far end of the kitchen so Ricky wouldn't hear her, then jabbed memorized numbers on the keypad. She held her breath until she heard Wilma's voice.

"Thank goodness you answered," Sarah whispered. "Charles got crazy again this morning."

"Are you safe right now?"

"Yes. But I need a ride. Can you meet me in fifteen minutes at our prearranged spot?"

"Absolutely."

After hanging up, Sarah wiped sweaty palms on her faded jeans. Charles got mad if she texted him at work. Unless he reached out to her first, she could communicate only if there was an emergency. He didn't want to be distracted while on patrol.

She needed an alibi to buy time in case he came home early. A note on the kitchen counter might work. She picked up a notepad and pencil and wrote.

Charles,
Ricky and I are going to the park for a walk. Be back soon.
Love, S

With Ricky engrossed in the program and hugging the teddy close, Sarah hurried to the bedroom and grabbed the old clothes she'd tucked away in the bottom drawer of the dresser for herself and her son. Then she tidied the remaining items, so nothing looked amiss.

She glanced at her wristwatch. Six minutes had passed since dialing Wilma. Nine minutes to go.

Fearing losing her resolve, Sarah rushed to the kitchen, stashed the clothing in the satchel, and wrapped the phone inside Ricky's t-shirt. She twisted her wet hair into a knot at the top of her head, wincing at the tender scalp, and then tucked it under a baseball cap. She donned sunglasses, hoping to cover the injury Charles had given.

"Time to go, honey." She turned off the television and pointed toward the hall for the stroller.

He pitched a fit and threw himself on the floor. "I don't want to!"

She didn't have time for this. "Ricky, you need to get up now. We have to go."

She grabbed his hand and led him toward the stroller. He clutched the bear and didn't resist. Sarah slung the canvas strap over her shoulder and grabbed her purse. Out of habit, she picked up the old-model smartphone from the kitchen counter near the charger. Charles required she carry it with her at all times, so he could reach her immediately if he called or texted.

She stared at the phone as though it were a serpent. Not answering it quickly enough yesterday had set Charles off this morning. She needed to answer if he called before she reached a safe place. Sarah cupped it in her hand, not wanting to take a chance of being unable to retrieve it fast enough.

She and Ricky headed outside into the bright, sunny day. They barely passed their front lawn when the next-door neighbor, Mrs. Connell, approached, carrying the daily newspaper.

"Good morning, dear. You two are out and about early." The elderly woman leaned over to give Ricky's chubby cheek a gentle tug.

Kicking his feet, Ricky said, "I want to swing."

Sarah pushed the sunglasses tighter on the bridge of her nose, hoping they hid the mark on her face.

"Off to the park, are you? What fun." The top row of Mrs. Connell's dentures protruded, giving her face a horsey look.

"We're going to ride the new merry-go-round." Sarah put on a big smile, not wanting her nosy neighbor to suspect anything.

Mrs. Connell looked at her. "I bet your wonderful husband would put a swing set in your backyard if you asked him. He did a tremendous job repairing my wood deck last week."

"I'm sure he would," Sarah hedged, "but I hate asking Charles to work when he's home. You know what long hours he puts in for the force." Charles hardly lifted a finger at home. He said she could take care of the house since he paid all the bills.

"Indeed. And this city is a lot safer because of his vigilance."

Sarah looked down to hide her grimace. If only that woman knew the real deal.

"Well, you two have fun at the playground." Mrs. Connell shuffled toward her front door.

Sarah pushed the stroller away, conscious not to move too quickly. She wanted to blend into the landscape like any other mother.

Three minutes to make the rendezvous.

CHAPTER EIGHT
SHADOWS CROSSING

Betty and Ida Lou lingered over breakfast in Prosper's hospital, nibbling on small spoonfuls of oatmeal sweetened with brown sugar and golden raisins. They rested in the sunlit cafeteria and listened to murmurs of others' conversations while silverware tinkled on plates. The aromas of fresh-brewed coffee and baking blueberry muffins wafted across the dining area.

Betty made idle chitchat about gardening and favorite recipes, hoping to give Ida Lou respite from her frightening situation. She knew the difficult decisions looming if Richard didn't regain consciousness.

When they returned to room 1202, Betty turned on the television, and the two talked about the day's news headlines. Ida Lou looked at her husband often, saying things like, "Richard, when you get out of here, won't it be fun for us to do such-and-such?"

Betty's heart sank each time she gazed at the unresponsive man. She understood Ida Lou's brave belief that her man might be able to hear her, even if he couldn't respond. But that didn't make it any easier to listen to the gut-wrenching one-way conversation.

What would Pastor James want her to say to comfort Ida Lou? And what would she do if Richard's condition deteriorated during her watch? The pastor needed to wrap up that wedding and soon. Perhaps she should try to prepare Ida Lou for what might come. She wished someone had done that for her, instead of letting her cling to false hope.

Pastor James' voice echoed in the hallway, inquiring about the Besco patient's location. Betty bolted out of her chair, hurried to the curtain, and swung it aside. "Psst, Pastor. In here." She waved him over.

"Hello, Betty." He smiled and gave her shoulder a gentle pat as he entered the room. "Ida Lou, I see you're in good company."

"This woman has been such a blessing," Ida Lou said without leaving the bedside chair. "I can't thank you enough for sending her to be with Richard and me."

Pastor James walked up to Ida Lou. The bushy eyebrows that framed his hazel eyes resembled outriggers on a deep-sea fishing boat. But Betty liked most the way the skin around his eyes and mouth crinkled in well-worn smile creases. That preacher's skinny frame could barely hold his huge heart.

"Guess I'll be going," Betty said, eager to slip away and leave him with the responsibility of comforting the young woman. "Ida Lou, I'll pray for you and your husband."

Tears welled up in Ida Lou's blue eyes. "You've met me only once, but you spent hours in the hospital with us. That means so much."

"Just doing what Jesus wants us to do for each other." She wasn't sure how to fill the awkward silence. Maybe, just maybe, God was answering her prayer about purpose.

"If not for you, I would've been here alone." Ida Lou wrung her hands in her lap.

"We're never alone," Pastor James said gently. "God is present in every situation, and He will be our Strength."

A shadow crossed Ida Lou's face.

Betty edged toward the curtain, not wanting to get caught in a lengthy theological discussion. "Ida Lou, is there anything else I can do?"

"No, thanks. You've already done so much." She played with the hem of her shirt for a moment. Then she looked up with a wistful expression. "Actually, there is one thing. Do you think you could take Sweetie for a walk? She didn't get out much yesterday."

Oh no, anything but that! Hadn't she done enough, sitting in a hospital for hours on end and staring at a dying man?

Betty pictured angry red welts on her arms from allergic reactions to touching the dog's fur. Her nose itched at the thought of being in a home with pet dander everywhere.

"I don't know much about dogs, I'm afraid. But my friend Letitia is great with them. Is it okay if she helps?"

"Sure. Sweetie loves company."

Well, now she was committed. Better stop by the pharmacy in the hospital lobby to stock up on over-the-counter antihistamines.

"Our villa is in Horizon Vista, number 467 on Begonia Lane. That's on the corner of Fifth Street. Do you know where that is?"

"I sure do. It's the section right behind me."

Ida Lou's face beamed. "What a coincidence! I'm so glad we're neighbors." She pulled a small spiral notebook from her purse. "I'll write the garage code so you can get in."

Betty watched her scribble. "Are you sure you're comfortable giving me that information?"

Ida Lou ripped out the page from the notebook. "Of course. You've been with me all day. And Pastor James trusts you." She handed her the slip.

Betty looked at the pastor and shrugged. He nodded for her to proceed.

"I'll come back later to give you an update on your dog." *And it'd better not poop in my yard.*

Betty tucked the paper into her purse and turned to leave. As she slipped past the privacy curtain, Pastor James asked Ida Lou if she'd like to pray.

Why hadn't she thought of that? Betty felt a need to pray, too—before she killed herself trying to do good deeds.

CHAPTER NINE
FRITO LAY TO THE RESCUE

Ricky's stroller clattered along the sidewalk as Sarah pushed past the Shady Oaks neighborhood and headed toward the park. She'd have to hustle to meet Wilma by nine o'clock.

At the end of the street, Ricky started bouncing in the buggy. "Swing!" His chubby, little hand pointed toward a jungle gym. The prefabricated castle painted in primary colors had a turret to climb. A moat of thick mulch surrounded the structure. How would she get around her promise to let him enjoy this place? She couldn't relax until she and Ricky were safely away.

She leaned to look him in the face. He had tiny freckles on his nose. "Sweetie, Mommy has to go to the store first. Then we'll go for a ride."

Ricky's bottom lip poked out. "Want to swing right now, Mommy."

Sarah's shoulders tensed in anticipation of him crying and making a scene. "We can get chocolate milk at the store."

She hated luring him with the promise of a treat. But her head pounded, and the cut on her cheek burned. If she didn't find refuge today, she might not live to get another chance. Then who would take care of her child?

Ricky hunched down in the stroller seat and tugged on the ear of the teddy. "Okay."

A sick feeling washed over Sarah. Would her son ever have a normal life? Would she?

Moving ahead steadily, she gazed at the swing set by the castle. A smile tugged at her lips as she remembered her dad pushing her higher and higher when she was little. She'd loved how the wind lifted her hair, and her toes touched white fluffy clouds. If only her dad were here.

But no. That door slammed shut years ago.

The stroller bumped an uneven concrete section and jarred her from her mental fog. Didn't Ricky deserve the opportunity to grow up with two parents in a stable home? But how would he be affected if she left Charles? A bead of sweat dripped down the side of her face.

She headed for the convenience store past the park. Here goes. If Charles happened by, she could honestly say they needed bread.

In the convenience store's parking lot, Sarah crouched down to pat Ricky's knee. "You'll have that chocolate milk in a minute, buddy."

A truck hauling a trailer full of lawn equipment rattled up to the island for gas. Other vehicles parked, and drivers and passengers exited. Sarah tensed, looking for Wilma's familiar face. She had no one else to call because she had severed ties with everyone, even her college roommate Terri. Juggling Charles' jealousy made having other friendships impossible.

She'd arrived precisely at nine o'clock. Where was her rescuer?

With precious seconds passing, Sarah pushed Ricky into the store and down an aisle toward the cooler for a pint of chocolate milk. She would have liked a bottle of water but opted to save what money she had.

She wheeled Ricky to the register and set the carton on the counter. Her peripheral vision caught a flash of movement as she looked in her purse for the wallet. A blue-and-yellow Frito Lay panel truck zoomed around to the store's side. Finally!

After throwing a couple of dollar bills on the counter, Sarah shoved the stroller toward the door.

"Hey, lady, you want your change?" the cashier called out.

"No, thanks. Keep it."

As she hurried outside, Ricky craned his head around the backrest and held out his hand. "Can I have my milk?"

"Sure, baby. Here you go." Sarah paused a moment to open the carton and put it in Ricky's hand. Then she hurried around the building's corner, where a sign read "Deliveries in Back."

Glancing behind at uninterested motorists filling their gas tanks, Sarah pushed Ricky's stroller beside a large, green dumpster that hid them from passersby.

"Stinky." Ricky held his nose, spilling chocolate milk on himself.

Patting the drops on her son's arm, Sarah checked behind to make sure no one was watching before approaching the open driver's side window of the parked Frito Lay truck.

Inside the cab sat a woman with dark brown skin and hair styled in tight curls, reading a sheet of paper on a clipboard. She turned toward Sarah. "Sorry, I'm late."

"I was worried."

"Hey, I got ya, girl. Just have to unload a couple of boxes, and we'll be on our way." Wilma opened the door and slid out of the cab. "I backed in so no one can see inside the truck."

She walked around the side, then pulled on the latch. The door slid up, revealing rows of cardboard boxes. Wilma yanked out a ramp, which hit the concrete with a metallic clang. "Go ahead and put Ricky behind that stack of Cheetos."

While Wilma went through the store's back door, Sarah angled the stroller between the trash receptacle and the truck. As she skirted the rusty edge of the metal container, Ricky lifted his empty milk carton. She grabbed it and tossed it into the dumpster. Then she paused, thinking of something else.

Well, why not? She was sick of Charles' summons and didn't want to be leashed to him anymore. She pulled the phone out of her jeans pocket and chunked it into the trash. "So, Charles, can you hear me now?" she muttered as a smug smile twitched at her lips.

After rounding the truck's fender, Sarah wheeled Ricky's stroller up the ramp.

"Mommy, where are we going?" Her little boy's brow puckered in confusion.

"Remember I told you we'd go for a ride?"

He smiled, revealing a dimple.

"We're going for one now with Miss Wilma."

"Yippee!"

Sarah kissed her son's forehead and unbuckled the strap around his waist. After helping him stand beside her, she folded the stroller and set it by a box of chips. She squeezed into a small space between the cases, sat cross-legged, and pulled her son onto her lap.

Ricky clapped his hands. "Let's go!"

"We will, honey. Just as soon as Miss Wilma gets back."

So far, so good. But what was ahead? She stroked Ricky's red hair. Could she pull off this escape? Her stomach roiled with tension. What would she do if Charles used his police connections to hunt her down?

CHAPTER TEN

PEANUT-BUTTER JAM

Betty gasped at the apparition before her. Clad in hot pink bicycle shorts and a purple polka-dot tank top, Letitia stood barefoot at her front door. From the blue-polished toenails to the salt-and-pepper hair pulled back in a rhinestone headband, Letitia always made a fashion statement—but rarely a good one. What was Betty to do with her free-spirited friend?

"Come on in," Letitia said. "You're in time to see Hugh and Lacy get back together. After she had the baby, they broke up because Hugh messed around with another woman. But Lacy wanted him to have a relationship with their child, so she decided to forgive him and—"

"Letitia, what on earth are you wearing?"

She looked down and giggled. "This is my new yoga outfit. We're having a contest at Silver Sneakers, and I figured wearing the right clothes would motivate me."

"Women our age are not meant to wear tight shorts and tank tops."

"Honestly, you can be so uptight." Letitia grabbed Betty's arm and pulled her inside the house. "You need to learn relaxation techniques."

"Letitia." She raised her voice over Hugh's contrite confession on television of how much he adored Lacy. "There's a cute Yorkie around the—"

"Shh." Letitia held her forefinger to her mouth and focused on the blaring screen.

When a commercial for laundry soap came on, Betty seized the opportunity. "Will you help me walk the new neighbor's dog?"

"I'd love to! Is it a boy or a girl?"

Betty scratched her forearm. "A girl. I think. Name's . . . Sweetie. Dumb name for an animal."

"How adorable! Let's go. It's beautiful outside."

"What about Hugh and Lacy?"

"Oh, they'll be just fine." Letitia winked, pointing to the starlets engaged in mouth-to-mouth resuscitation. She slid on flip-flops, then followed Betty outside.

They walked past their red-brick duplex and headed toward the adjacent unit, where Letitia waved at the Adonis-like landscaper with broad shoulders and narrow hips. "*Hola*, Juan!"

The muscular man swept off his straw hat, revealing thick, glossy, black hair. He placed the hat over his heart and gave a slight bow.

"Lovely day, isn't it?" Letitia simpered. "And those are gorgeous purple verbena you're planting."

Betty wanted to put her finger in her mouth and gag. But instead, she quickened her pace, hoping to stem Miss Hot Pants' soliloquy and prevent Letitia from butchering more Spanish phrases.

When Letitia didn't follow, Betty grabbed her arm and pulled. Juan put his hat back on and grabbed a shovel.

"What do you think you're doing?" Betty fussed as they walked. "That young man is probably barely out of his teens."

"Can't blame a gal for trying." Letitia waggled her eyebrows. "Betty, don't be uptight. A harmless flirtation won't hurt anyone."

"Good grief." Betty released her hold on Letitia now that Juan was out of sight behind the azalea shrubbery.

Betty approached the garage security pad and keyed in the numbers Ida Lou had given. Then, with a quiet hum, a motor raised the white metal door.

Inside the garage, Betty heard shrill yaps and tiny scraping toenails. She turned the knob and opened the door. A puff of brown sailed past her into Letitia's waiting arms.

"Hello, cutie pie." Letitia nuzzled the dog's squirming little frame and cradled her against the purple tank top. "She's adorable!"

Betty's nose itched. "C'mon. Let's see if she had any accidents."

As they entered the home, Betty gasped. The family room looked like a tornado had hit. Newspapers were scattered everywhere, and muddy boot tracks stained the cream carpet. Couch cushions sat haphazardly on the floor. A lamp with a damaged shade lay on its side. Betty smelled urine and looked down at the carpet, where a small, yellow puddle made her cringe.

"This place makes my house look like a feature out of a magazine," Letitia quipped.

"Shush. This is Ida Lou's house. She's the one whose husband had a heart attack Thursday."

"Well, why didn't you say so?" Letitia hung her head.

"This must have happened when the EMTs came in." Betty started picking up cushions and arranging them on the couch.

Letitia's fingers stopped stroking the little dog's head. "Wait. Did you say *Ida Lou's* husband had the heart attack?"

"Yes. That's the one I called you about this morning for the prayer chain."

Letitia nibbled on her lower lip. "I think Sweetie needs a potty break. I'm gonna take her out for a quick walk." She grabbed the leash hanging on a coat rack near the back door.

Betty let her go and continued straightening. The kitchen wasn't much better—a dirty skillet sat on the stove, and two plates with dried cheese omelets remained on the table. She opened a window to let in the fresh air. Then she cleared the table, scraped the plates, and filled the sink with hot water. A few drops of green dish soap added bubbles and an apple scent. If only tidying up her emotions were this easy. What was it the Lord wanted her to do with her life?

She'd washed a few pieces of silverware before Letitia cried out, "Help!"

What now? Betty looked out the window and saw her friend in hot pursuit of Sweetie, the leash trailing behind. They were chasing something with a bushy, ringed tail and a round, plastic head.

The odd-looking creature crashed into the crape myrtle and careened toward the bird bath. Sweetie barked, and Letitia zigzagged behind with one bare foot and a sandal flapping on the other.

Before Betty could figure out what to do, Juan came into view with a box of annuals. He placed the flowers on the ground and raced toward the animals.

Dashing outside to help, Betty saw Juan trap the other animal by covering it with the large cardboard box. Her chest heaved with the exertion.

"What is that thing?" Letitia asked, voice shaking.

"It's a young raccoon with a jar of peanut butter stuck on its head." Betty tried not to laugh at how silly that sounded.

"What should we do?" Letitia asked while Sweetie continued rumbling threats.

"We call animal control. That thing might have rabies." Betty pulled out her phone and dialed the number.

Fifteen minutes later, a lady in a tan uniform arrived. Her hip holstered a revolver.

"Folks, could you please step aside?" Once the gathered crowd complied, she put on heavy work gloves and pulled a wooden rod with a noose at the end out of her toolbox.

"You're not going to kill the poor thing, are you?" Letitia looked near tears.

"I hope not, ma'am. Now, if you'll all give me some room . . ."

They backed up but stood close enough to see the little raccoon poke its head out from the box where it was cornered, staring past globs of peanut butter inside the jar. The little thing's sides heaved. How long had it been running around in terror?

"Bet that creature rues the day it raided the trash bin," a bystander commented as the animal control officer slipped the noose over the raccoon's head.

After tightening the rope to immobilize the animal, the woman reached down with her other gloved hand and loosened the jar in a gentle clockwise motion. Enough peanut butter remained inside the lid to grease the movement. The jar came off with a pop. The raccoon, still dangling from the rod, lunged toward the woman, clamping its jaws on air.

"That's gratitude for you," commented another bystander.

"The little guy's just scared," the officer said.

The raccoon looked up with shiny, black-button eyes, a dab of peanut butter stuck on its nose.

"He looks fine. No sign of rabies. I'll load him up and relocate him in the woods." The officer stood and turned toward her truck.

"Thank you very much," Betty said. What was it about Letitia that attracted crazy adventures? They only had to walk a neighbor's dog. Should be simple. Shouldn't it?

As the neighbors dispersed, a bald guy whistled at Letitia's pink shorts.

"Why don't you go back to the house and give Sweetie some water," Betty suggested. "I'll stay here and help Juan pick up the flowers."

Her friend opened her mouth, no doubt to protest, but she didn't argue. She swung her pink hips in an exaggerated motion and sauntered around the corner.

Betty followed Juan to the dropped pansies.

"*Muchas gracias,*" he said as they retrieved plants and finger-raked dark potting soil back into scattered containers.

"Thank you," Betty said. "You saved the day."

He scuffed the toe of his worn work boot into the dirt. What a nice young man. Betty made a mental note to get to know him better. How to do that without Letitia tagging along would be the trick.

CHAPTER ELEVEN

CARDIGAN AND KISSES

Ida Lou stood to stretch her cramping legs. The uncomfortable hospital chair left much to be desired. The Spanish Inquisition could have used it as an instrument of torture. She massaged her lower back with one hand.

Machines behind Richard's bed clicked, whirred, and beeped, yet he remained inert. Ida Lou stroked his cheek. An alarm on the heart monitor blared. Ida Lou pressed the nurse call button. Richard's breathing grew labored. *Was this the end?*

Staccato footsteps sounded as a nurse emerged from a nearby room. The nurse adjusted a dial, then checked Richard's pulse. The machine's shrill noise stopped, and Ida Lou expelled a deep breath.

"I'm going to call the doctor to see about adjusting his medicines," the nurse said. "I'll be back in a few minutes."

For almost two days, Richard had shown no response to the tests. How long could she hold onto hope? Ida Lou smoothed the sheet around her husband's torso.

The nurse returned. "Mrs. Besco, it's midnight. You've got to get some rest."

Ida Lou stared at the nurse, too exhausted to agree or argue.

"We'll take good care of your husband tonight. Don't worry."

She should follow the woman's advice. Sweetie was probably about to burst and must be frantic, wondering where she was.

Ida Lou removed Betty's red cardigan and tucked it on Richard's chest. Maybe that warmth would comfort him while she was gone. She would get the sweater back tomorrow when she brought his fleece. Betty wouldn't mind.

"Good night, dear. I love you." She kissed him on the forehead, then shuffled through the ICU like a traveler deplaning from a red-eye flight.

In the concrete parking garage, her fingers fumbled as she pulled the key fob from her purse. Like a robot, she unlocked the door and started the engine. Her car seemed to navigate the route home on autopilot. Turn right at the first traffic light, go two blocks, then left at the stop sign.

Nearing home, she noticed exterior lights shining over the garage. Odd. She didn't remember turning them on. At the touch of the remote, the garage door lifted. She pulled inside and parked. After exiting the car, she opened the door and stumbled over the threshold into the house.

Ceiling lights brightened the hallway. Hmm. Hadn't used those in years. Richard hated their harsh rays and preferred using lamps. Extreme fatigue made one do strange things.

Sweetie lay on a couch cushion in the family room. She lifted her sleepy head and cocked it to one side, as though wondering where Richard was. Ida Lou stifled a sob, stumbled to the couch, and scooped up her precious Yorkie in a tender hug.

Topknot hair tickled Ida Lou's nose as she buried her face in the soft fur with a hint of the oatmeal shampoo. Then she let out the flood of tears that had amassed all day. Without Richard, nothing mattered. He was the rock in her life, and he wasn't there. Sweetie snuggled into Ida Lou's chest, as if she understood the pain, and accepted the tears that soaked her fur.

After weeping for an hour, Ida Lou felt drained. Wadded-up tissues covered the couch. She pushed strands of limp, blonde hair behind her ear, straightened her shirt, and stroked the little dog's frame. The soothing motion helped create a measure of composure.

As Ida Lou gathered the used tissues, she realized someone had picked up the couch cushions and righted the end table that had gone flying when EMTs moved furniture to administer an AED to Richard. His pipe, which had fallen to the floor, now rested on newspapers stacked on the footstool. Fresh vacuum tracks ridged the carpet. Someone had cleaned. But who?

Carrying Sweetie and the handful of tissues, she tiptoed into the kitchen. The sink and countertops sparkled. A fresh arrangement of purple flowers brightened the table. Near the vase, she saw a handwritten note:

Dear Ida Lou,

Sweetie got a long walk this afternoon, and she protected the neighborhood from a peanut butter-stealing raccoon. Then, she helped me pick up the house and ate all her vegetables at dinner. She likes kohlrabi!

If you're hungry, there's homemade lasagna in the fridge. Not sure if you count calories, so I used low-fat cottage cheese instead of ricotta.

Betty said she'll stop by the hospital after church tomorrow. I'll come over then to walk Sweetie.

We're praying for you.

Letitia Larrimore

She didn't know anyone named Letitia. But Betty had mentioned a friend who was good with dogs. How sweet of her to clean the house and watch out for Sweetie.

After dumping the tissues in the wastebasket, Ida Lou leaned over to inhale the fragrant pansies. Wouldn't Richard be happy to see them when he got home?

Feeling hungry, she set Sweetie down, then pulled the casserole out of the fridge. After microwaving a small plateful, she sank into the chair at the table. Sweetie jumped into her lap, an eager look on her adorable face.

Savoring a bite of cheesy tomato heaven, Ida Lou dabbed a bit of meat onto her fingertip and held out the treat for Sweetie. "Thanks for being such a good girl today."

The dog licked off the morsel and wagged her tail. Would Letitia share the recipe? Richard loved Italian food. He was going to be delighted to meet the new friends they had.

After rinsing the plate in the sink, Ida Lou walked to the bedroom. A bedside lamp shed a gentle glow on the turned-down coverlet and fluffed pillows. Letitia was thorough.

Ida Lou slipped off her shoes and slid onto the linens. She stared at the framed picture on the bedside table of her smiling daughter in a college cap and gown. "Darling, I wish you were here. Daddy's sick, and I need you."

Ida Lou blew a kiss at the photo, then turned off the light. After tossing on the bed a few moments, she rolled to Richard's side. Grabbing his pillow, she savored his musky scent. Sleep transported her to a place of happy dreams, with Richard splashing her at the beach and handing her sandy shells.

Ida Lou awoke to Sweetie licking her cheek. Rays of a cantaloupe-orange sunrise peeked through the blinds as she squinted at the clock. Six a.m. She kissed Sweetie, who sat on her pillow, then stood. The dog ran in happy circles as Ida Lou went to the bathroom. After splashing her face with cold water and brushing her hair, Ida Lou cleaned her teeth and placed her toothbrush beside Richard's in the stand.

Sweetie's topknot featured a new tie-dyed bow with Easter eggs. More of Letitia's thoughtful handiwork, no doubt—but Ida Lou had been too ravaged with grief last night to notice. A sudden thought put a smile on her face. Today's Easter! Surely, God would work a miracle for Richard on this special day.

She showered and dressed hurriedly, eager to see her husband rise from that horrible bed and walk home, holding her hand as he used to in high school.

CHAPTER TWELVE

STAND FIRM

Betty walked with Letitia to church, keeping a companionable silence as they strolled down the concrete sidewalk. Blooming flowers perfumed the tree-lined avenue. Easter had a way of making even dismal circumstances seem bearable.

They waved when they saw Juan Rivas sharpening a set of pruning shears near a shed at the edge of the villas. He tipped his hat, which made Letitia giggle.

Letitia broached the subject Betty had been trying not to dwell on. "How is Ida Lou?"

"Not good. Her husband hasn't responded to any of the cardiologist's tests. There's no sign of brain-wave activity." Betty rubbed at the burn of tears forming.

Letitia slowed. "Oh, Betty, this must be extra difficult for you, what with the anniversary of Donovan's death."

Betty shrugged. "Who better to understand what losing a loved one feels like?"

Letitia took her hand. "I can go to the hospital this afternoon instead of you."

"And leave me to walk that dog? No, ma'am." Betty squeezed her friend's hand. "I appreciate your offer, but this is something I want to do. We can activate the WUFHs for extra shifts if I get too tired."

"That's true. Our Women United for Him support group is always there for anyone in need."

They approached the crowded church parking lot, which resembled the Indianapolis 500 as cars jockeyed for the few remaining spaces. Once inside, they scanned the packed sanctuary for seats.

"Psst! Betty. Letitia. Over here." Elizabeth Robinson waved them over. She wore a sky-blue dress that complemented her beautiful, golden-brown complexion.

Lovely and dignified, Elizabeth served as Prosper's mayor. Her friend's savvy social skills made Betty proud. Sitting with her was an honor.

Murmuring their thanks, Betty and Letitia squirmed into the tight space. Betty compared her scuffed brogans with Elizabeth's leather pumps and Letitia's dainty, pink sandals with seashells on top. She'd never been one to dwell on outside appearances. What was on the inside counted most.

Elizabeth leaned forward. "Are you ladies going to the Easter egg hunt this afternoon at the women's shelter? I can drive."

"I'd like to." Betty smoothed out her faded, striped skirt. "But I need to go to the hospital today. I'm helping someone whose husband is in the ICU."

"Oh my! Is it anyone I know?"

"It's Ida Lou Besco, the woman who visited our Bible study last week. She's new to Prosper and doesn't have any family—"

Letitia interrupted. "I'm taking care of Ida Lou's dog after church. You could pick me up afterward to go see the children."

"I'd be happy to." Elizabeth smiled.

"I can't wait for the little ones to see my newest outfit." Letitia fiddled with a ruffle on her pink sleeve. Then she flipped open the hymnal to find the first song. Betty groaned inside. No telling what costume Letitia had come up with.

Pastor James walked to the podium. He was tall and wore a black robe. "We gather today to celebrate a special occasion, one that symbolizes the end of sorrow and proves God can use even devastating circumstances to bring good."

Betty sent up a silent prayer for Ida Lou and Richard Besco, wondering how God would use their situation for something positive.

"Death has no hold over those God calls to life. That is what we celebrate on Easter. Because of Jesus' loving sacrifice, hope is not lost, no matter where we've fallen short or what losses we've sustained."

Letitia reached across her pink chiffon to pat Betty's arthritic hand. Betty's life hadn't been the same without Donovan. Would she find joy again?

"If we trust God with our greatest sorrows, He will transform our suffering and pain with love and mercy."

Tears pricked Betty's lids. She rustled in her handbag for a tissue. How embarrassing to cry in front of everyone. People expected her to be strong.

"But death does sting those left on earth after a loved one goes. We feel agony when cancer eats flesh. We experience pain when an automobile collision wrecks limbs and lives." The minister looked compassionately at his congregation. "Sometimes, life stinks."

Some in the congregation chuckled in appreciation of his candor.

The pastor looked toward the image of Christ on the north wall's colorful window. "Many times, we cry to God, asking Him, 'Why?' But God rarely answers that question. In dark times, when nothing seems to make sense, we need to hold on to His promises."

Easier said than done.

"Jesus," Betty prayed, "please spare Ida Lou's husband and send him home strong and healthy."

"Brothers and sisters, as Paul told the Thessalonian believers in 1 Thessalonians 4, I do not want you to be 'uninformed about those who sleep in death so that you do not grieve like the rest of mankind, who have no hope.' God resurrected His Son to demonstrate victory over circumstances—even physical death. Jesus didn't stay in the grave, and because of that, we have hope."

Pastor James stepped away from the podium and moved down a riser to be closer to the congregation. Then he opened his arms in an inclusive gesture. "You do not have to face your battles alone. Jesus is with you because you are His beloved. So, no matter the challenges ahead, stand firm and see the deliverance the Lord will give you."

Flanked on either side by Elizabeth and Letitia, Betty felt strengthened by their presence. They looked after her. She must have zoned out because the pastor offered the closing prayer.

"Oh, God, many here today hurt and need reassurance that You're real and love us. Please comfort them with Your presence and help them understand the mystery of Your ways. Amen."

People opened their eyes and shifted in the pews.

Pastor James motioned for the choir to stand. "Let's sing our closing hymn, 'It Is Well With My Soul.'"

Betty turned to her friends. "I'm going out the side entrance. I want to get to the hospital as soon as I can." She also didn't want to deal with the commiserations of members who would ask her how she was doing on this anniversary of losing Donovan.

Elizabeth scooted to one side so Betty could get by.

Behind her, Letitia called out, "Give me a call when you get home, so I can bring Sweetie over to see you."

That Letitia, always teasing her. But she felt grateful for the distraction. Letitia knew she hated to cry in public.

CHAPTER THIRTEEN

DAWNING REALIZATION

When Charles McAdams woke up Sunday morning, his head thundered, and his mouth tasted as though a dentist had crammed it full of gauze. Where was Sarah? She should have his coffee ready.

The pounding in his brain made it difficult to think. He fell off the couch when he rolled over to tell her to bring aspirin and a cold soda. He sat up on the floor and let the disorientation subside. Weaving a bit, he took deliberate steps to their bedroom. But Sarah wasn't there. And she had made the bed. Where on earth was she?

In the bathroom, he pulled a bottle of aspirin out of the medicine cabinet. He threw back five tablets and drained a cup of tap water.

He went to Ricky's room, figuring Sarah must be there. But she wasn't. And neither was his son. Thoughts tried to surface, but they got hammered by the pain roaring inside his head.

The last thing he remembered was pulling into the driveway well past two a.m., after a long night partying at Doug's house, then turning on the television and crashing on the couch.

Heading to the kitchen, he was surprised no smell of frying bacon greeted him. The clock on the wall told him the time was nearly noon. Long past breakfast. But where could his family be?

A note rested beside the empty phone charger on the kitchen counter. He picked it up and read. Sarah must have taken the kid outside to the park so he could sleep in. Thoughtful of her.

He opened the pantry, hoping to find coffee, but saw nothing except a few cans of soup. He slammed the door in anger. The noise made him wince.

He found a can of dark roast on the shelf over the stove. He pulled it down and set it beside the coffee maker. When he opened the lid of the appliance, there was no filter.

He ripped a paper towel off the roll and stuffed it into the corrugated plastic basket. Then he dumped in a wad of grounds, added water, and flipped on the switch. Could Sarah have gotten mad that he hadn't called her yesterday? Maybe he should have called her from Doug's.

The stimulating aroma of coffee wafted through the room. Charles grabbed a mug and poured some of the steaming liquid into it. Grounds flecked the surface. He swept out the black dots as best he could with his finger and wiped them on his trousers. If Sarah had made his coffee as she was supposed to, he wouldn't have had this problem. He sipped from the mug, then spat the mouthful into the sink. A bitter taste assailed his tongue.

Charles looked out the window, hoping to see his wife coming back from the park so she could fix a fresh pot. But Sarah was nowhere in sight. He grabbed his phone from his pocket. She'd answer right away if she knew what was good for her. But after three rings, he got her voicemail. His hand squeezed the phone. Hadn't he made it clear yesterday how much he hated voicemail?

He texted her to return home immediately. Then he stared at the screen for several seconds, waiting for her reply. None came.

Swearing, he tossed his phone onto the countertop. How stupid could that woman be? He grabbed the coffee mug and launched it at the refrigerator. It crashed and cracked, sending black coffee oozing down the freezer door and ceramic shards across the white linoleum.

He yanked the coffee pot from the machine and chucked it across the room. The glass carafe sailed through the doorway, ricocheted off one end of the couch, and bounced to the other side, spraying grounds and dark liquid all over the cream upholstery. When Sarah came home, she'd regret the damage and mess she'd caused. That ought to teach her not to neglect him.

Charles stormed to the bedroom to change out of his crumpled uniform. He'd drag her back from the park if she didn't show up soon.

CHAPTER FOURTEEN

CROSSING THE RIVER JORDAN

Ida Lou drowned in the silence of the bleak hospital room. While most people enjoyed a fun afternoon watching children search for hidden Easter eggs, she huddled in a hard chair and leaned on the cold, metal railing of Richard's bed. She almost missed the cacophony of machine noises because that steady hum at least meant there'd been hope. She pressed her hands together in her lap, positioning them for prayer, yet no words came.

Brisk footsteps announced the day nurse's arrival. "Hello, Janelle."

The brunette nodded and neared the bed to study Richard with a practiced eye. After touching the purple bracelet that circled his wrist with "DNR" in large white letters, she looked at Ida Lou, compassion brimming in her light blue eyes.

"Do you think I did the r-right thing?" Ida Lou stammered.

Janelle sat beside her. "You made a courageous decision because you don't want your husband to suffer. I admire that."

Ida Lou tucked a wisp of hair behind her ear and sighed. She and Richard had discussed this when they had updated their wills last year. He'd said he wouldn't want to go on as a vegetable. But she never thought she'd have to make the call.

"I thought when they removed all the machines, he'd go right away. But he's hanging on." A sob racked her.

Janelle took Ida Lou's hand. "We haven't detected brain-wave activity since he got here. But in ICU, anything can happen at any moment."

Ida Lou leaned close to her husband's face. "Darling," she whispered, "are you there? I wish you could tell me what to do."

The nurse took a deep breath. "Have you thought about telling him you'll be all right if he chooses to go?"

Ida Lou stared at her. Could he really hear her? If so, did that mean he might rally?

"Some patients have difficulty saying goodbye to their loved ones, especially if they're not sure what will happen after they've gone."

Was it possible Richard hung on to ensure she was okay before allowing himself to go?

"What do you think happens when people . . ." Ida Lou couldn't bear to say the rest.

"I believe there's a Power higher than ourselves, Who loves us and calls us from this dimension to live with Him in all eternity. What we see here isn't all there is. I'm certain of that." Janelle stood near her, as though to comfort her.

Ida Lou wanted to believe in Heaven. Since she was a little girl, she'd heard loved ones go there and sing with angels. "How can you be sure?"

Janelle smoothed the sheet around Richard's chest and tucked it around his shoulders. "When I was a young nurse, a woman who'd injured her hand while gardening came into the ICU. Sepsis set in, and we couldn't stop the infection." Janelle's jaw tightened. "Her husband sat with her for hours. We knew she wasn't going to make it.

But we kept everything going, hoping she'd last long enough for her daughter to arrive from out of state."

Ida Lou drew back a bit from Janelle. Was Richard waiting for their daughter?

"Severe weather delayed the girl's travel, and the interim was agonizing."

Ida Lou glanced at Richard's still face. She brushed her hand along the mussed and unwashed hair on his forehead. They had waited three years for their daughter. She wouldn't let him suffer anymore if she could help it.

"What did you do for that man while he waited for his daughter to come?"

Janelle gave a small smile. "On an impulse, I asked him if he wanted me to open a window, so his wife's spirit could go free. He hesitated but finally agreed to try and see what happened. As soon as I did, I felt something stir by the bed. I looked back and saw a feathery cloud rise from the woman's body and fly toward the window. I thought maybe I'd imagined it. But the husband sat bolt upright in his chair and said, 'Did you see that?'" Janelle swallowed. "We both knew she'd left—and that she was finally free."

Ida Lou pushed herself out of the chair and walked toward the third-story window. She gazed at wispy clouds coasting by on a robin-egg-colored sky. Birds soared on invisible currents, dipping and wheeling with effortless abandon. "I want to believe there's a Heaven—and a God Who loves us. But how can I when there's so much suffering in the world?"

Janelle joined her at the window. "Mrs. Besco, have you ever watched a butterfly emerge from its chrysalis?"

Ida Lou blinked at this unexpected question. "I did once when my daughter had a science project for middle school." She and her third-grader had set up a butterfly kit and waited day after day for a caterpillar to hatch. Each morning before school—and every day after school—the two of them had eagerly looked for signs of life in the little bundle suspended from a twig.

"A caterpillar has to struggle to free itself from the cocoon's tight bindings before it can fly."

In the third week of her daughter's experiment, just when they'd both given up hope, the cocoon had split open, and dark wings with colorful splotches had emerged. The butterfly had begun an agonizing journey to free itself from the sack, clinging with wobbly feet to the empty shell.

"You don't need to be afraid, Mrs. Besco. Your husband is getting ready to leave his earthly bonds and become something beautiful and eternal."

Ida Lou put her palms on the windowsill and pressed her forehead against the cold glass. "But how can I say goodbye to the love of my life? He's only fifty-three."

Janelle reached out to hug her, but Ida Lou stepped back. "He took an early retirement. We were going to buy a motorhome and travel around the country." Without him, what did her future hold?

Janelle put a warm hand on Ida Lou's shoulder. "When it's my time to go, I hope someone loves me as much as you love your husband."

Ida Lou checked Janelle's hand and noticed no ring. She glanced at her sparkly wedding set. "Thank you for reminding me of my blessings."

"Your devotion is obvious. Some people go their whole lives and never have that. I don't blame you for holding on as long as possible."

She wrapped her arms around herself. "I need to sit here and think a while."

"I understand." Janelle lifted Richard's closed eyelids, lowered them gently, then inclined her head to listen to the ragged breaths coming from his chest. "I need to check on my other patients. But I'll be back soon. Push the call button if you need anything."

"I will. Thanks."

After Janelle left, Ida Lou moved to her husband's side. His face, chest, and arms that so often held her tenderly were part of a body that no longer functioned as it should. But inside this disintegrating shell, the person she loved still lived. Would Richard's soul sprout shimmery wings that unfolded in glory? Then he could launch into the unknown, his wings whispering forward.

"Dear Jesus, Richard never was one to hold back from adventure. If it's time for him to move on to Heaven, I release him to You."

She leaned close to her husband's ear. "I don't want you to suffer anymore, darling. Don't worry about me. I'm going to be all right. I love you."

CHAPTER FIFTEEN

PLAY BUNNY

As soon as the Easter service ended, Letitia went to Ida Lou's house to walk Sweetie. The second the door opened, Sweetie zoomed up to her feet, dragging a leash. "Ooh, you're so cute!" Letitia scratched behind one of Sweetie's ears, and the dog leaned into her with appreciation. Then, they were off for a quick romp around the block.

Along the way, Sweetie nuzzled admirers of all ages and excitedly wagged her nub of a tail at each new fan who found her irresistible. That Yorkie sure knew how to work a crowd. Perhaps Elizabeth should feature the canine celebrity in her campaign literature. That darling, little face could sway many votes in the next mayoral election.

When they returned to the house, Sweetie slinked under the dining table and covered her face with her paws. Letitia crouched and gave the poor, little animal soothing strokes. "I'm sorry, baby. I wish I didn't have to leave. But I have ten Easter baskets lined up on my kitchen table needing last-minute items." Before guilt could consume her, Letitia fled the pitiful sight and hurried home.

Fake, green grass spewed out of colorful containers that held chocolate bunnies, speckled malted candy eggs, and bright yellow marshmallow chicks. Letitia nestled a child-size toothbrush and a tube of strawberry-flavored toothpaste inside each basket.

She loved being around children and watching their abandon. She regretted that she hadn't overruled her husband Bernard when he hadn't wanted to adopt after discovering they couldn't have children. Instead, he had wanted them to be free to travel with his business ventures. Now, she had all the freedom in the world and no one to share it with except her friends.

Finished in the kitchen, she went to the huge walk-in bedroom closet and pulled out the costume she'd rented for the afternoon. She'd managed to squirm into furry, white legs and tug up the cotton-tailed rear when the doorbell rang. She drew the drawstring at her waist and shuffled to the front door, the huge, fuzzy feet flopping on the hardwood floor.

Elizabeth stepped back to take in the complete picture. "You never cease to amaze me, Letitia Larrimore!" The stylish woman wore a tailored pantsuit with Nine West heels. Not a single wrinkle dared show itself on her slacks, and her hair was swept up neatly in a bun, without a single strand breaking rank—quite a contrast to Letitia's half-rabbit, half-human appearance.

"I'm glad you're here, Elizabeth. Could you follow me to the bedroom so you can zip up the back?"

Letitia shuffled to her room with Elizabeth close behind. Together they wrestled the tunic into place. Then Letitia put on the plastic mask with long pink-and-gray ears.

Letitia twirled her whiskers. "How do I look?" The mask muffled her voice.

"Like a Bugs Bunny who grew up too close to a nuclear reactor."

"Ha-ha." Letitia maneuvered with care down the hallway toward the kitchen.

Behind her, Elizabeth said, "Those kids at the shelter are going to love your get-up."

"I sure hope so. It stinks like a locker room in here and feels as hot as Hades."

Her friend chuckled. "Lucky for you, my Mercedes has great air-conditioning."

Letitia approached the table with the Easter baskets and lifted her furry paws, which were too big and bulky to grasp the handles.

"Don't worry. I'll get these to the car." Elizabeth hooked five baskets over each arm and followed Letitia toward the front door. Letitia bumped the side table in the narrow foyer and stumbled into the doorframe.

Elizabeth snickered. "You look like you've been at a wine tasting again."

Letitia whirled around. "I swear, if you tease me about that little faux pas one more time, I'm defecting to your opponent during your reelection campaign."

Elizabeth's remark tugged at the old wound of feeling inferior. Letitia practiced a moment of meditation as Elizabeth rounded her to open the front door.

"Yeah, right." Elizabeth closed the front door behind them, making sure it locked, but she must have realized her comment hurt. "Sorry, I didn't mean to embarrass you. I know you are careful now not to overdo." As they walked toward the driveway, she pushed a button on her car remote, which made a cheery beep.

Letitia tried to shake off Elizabeth's criticism. Her friends worried. Truth be told, she regretted the whole incident. But why did everyone remember her getting tipsy rather than how much money had been raised for Elizabeth's war chest? Letitia had worked for months to stage everything from the caterer to the venue decorations.

Juan, who had been trimming a holly tree near the corner, came up and offloaded the baskets into the backseat. Letitia stood by the front passenger door, unable to get her furry paw around the handle. When Juan noticed her predicament, he grinned.

Then he hurried to open the door, sweeping out his left hand in a broad stroke and bowing. "Ma'am." After she'd seated herself, he shut the door with a gentle click.

The V8 engine barely whispered as the Mercedes warmed up.

"Oh, goodie, I finally get to ride in this marvelous car." Letitia admired the white leather seats, gray granite console, and black trim on the door panels. "Girl, is that real wood on your steering wheel?"

"Same stuff they use to make the keys on Steinway grand pianos."

"No way! Did you convince the town council to give you a raise?" Letitia lifted one shoulder. The tart remark slipped out before she could filter it. Maybe she wanted to get back, too, for the judgment about drinking.

Elizabeth put the car in gear. "No one gets rich working in local public service. The Mercedes dealer had to unload this, and he made an offer I couldn't resist. So, I tapped into some savings from when I was a real estate investor."

Letitia sighed. "I can't even stand to think how much we have compared with those poor kids who end up at the shelter. Having to flee from their homes just to be safe. It's horrible!"

Elizabeth levered the turn signal. "Yesterday, I had to make an emergency transport for a mother and her son. She was trying to escape her husband, who's in law enforcement. Wilma asked me to bring them across state lines from North Carolina."

"Did you take them to the shelter? When I called Mindy to ask how many baskets to make, she told me Solutions was at capacity." She could shift items and make a couple extra goodie bags if needed.

"It is, but Mindy managed to squeeze them in." Elizabeth sighed. "I wish there were more places to house all the victims. I've tried convincing the town council to subsidize Solutions, but our tax base has shrunk with the economy dipping."

Letitia admired Elizabeth's financial savvy. She could build consensus and get things done. That's why Letitia worked hard in her campaign. "Can't they get into some cheap housing? That apartment complex downtown has For Rent signs."

"Many of these women can't get jobs. Most don't have cars, so they couldn't drive to a job if they found one."

"Elizabeth, I have a confession to make." She watched her friend sit straighter as though preparing for a blow. Maybe the costume hid her inadequacies, but Letitia wanted her friend to see beyond antics to realize the fears below the surface.

"I never went to college. Bernard was a few years older, and we married as soon as I graduated from high school. After that, I was a housewife. I admire all that you have achieved in the business world."

The sedan slowed at a yellow traffic light beside a station wagon full of children. Peals of laughter erupted as the little ones pointed at Letitia's rabbit face.

Elizabeth waved back. "They love you, and I do, too. You are my friend."

"The worst part is my butt itches, and I can't do a thing about it." Letitia couldn't resist saying something outrageous to try and get a reaction and lighten the moment.

Elizabeth turned and smiled. "Girl, you are crazy. And that brings lots of joy into the world."

"I want to live fully with the time I have left. No sense looking back at the what-might-have-beens." Letitia tried to cross her legs but gave up.

"There's wisdom in that. Did I ever tell you I was married?" The light turned green, and Elizabeth eased the car forward.

"What! You never said anything about that." Letitia put a furry paw on Elizabeth's shoulder. "Do you want to tell me what happened?"

"Not much to say. He didn't stick around long. Decided I wasn't for him and that he loved someone at his office." Elizabeth glanced at her. "I have a real hard time trusting. Too many people have let me down along the way. That's why I stay as independent as possible."

Amazing how she could know someone for years and not see the deep hurt until now. Elizabeth thought Letitia must trust her a lot to share such intimate history.

After another mile, Elizabeth slowed to look for the shelter's driveway. A wall of mature evergreens hid Solutions from passersby. If a person didn't know it was there, they would never notice the slim line of gravel winding between the trees. Elizabeth followed the path a half mile and parked next to an old two-story house.

Letitia waited for her friend to open the door and unlatch the seatbelt for her. Then they walked to the front stoop, where Elizabeth pushed the intercom button.

"Who is it?" asked a voice behind the solid metal door.

"The Easter Bunny and her friend."

A deadbolt clicked, and the door swung open to reveal the resident manager, Mindy, whose smiling mouth gleamed with braces. "Thanks for coming. The kids are in the backyard, hunting for eggs."

As soon as Letitia stepped onto the lawn, a crowd of giggling children surrounded her. She hugged them with furry arms and pointed a paw toward Elizabeth, who dangled the baskets.

A girl about six years old, with braided pigtails, a shirt that was too small, and shorts that were too large squealed with joy as she rifled through the plastic nest to score a package of malted eggs.

Nearby, two boys around ten years old yelled in unison, "It's mine!" They tugged on either side of one basket, which broke the fragile handle, spilling the contents like a ruptured piñata. A distressed-looking mother charged toward the contentious pair and yanked the rascals apart while another woman picked up the goodies.

As the children munched on their sweets, Letitia noticed an untouched basket on the lawn. She looked around and saw an empty-handed young boy with red hair, clinging to his mom's leg. They sat apart from the group under the shade of a large oak. Silky dark tresses shielded the mother's face.

Letitia scooped up the last basket between her paws and hopped toward the little boy. Sensitive to his fear, she placed the gift close enough so he could reach it when ready.

The young mom waved a shy thank you, and the movement of her arm shifted her hair to reveal a purplish-blue outline on her cheek. Bruise marks also showed on either side of her throat. Grateful the mask hid her dismay, Letitia offered a little twitch of her bunny tail and bounced toward the porch, where Elizabeth visited with other residents.

She sidled beside her friend and whispered, "I've gotta go to the bathroom. Can you help me get out of this costume?"

With a broad smile, Elizabeth nodded and moved toward the back door. Letitia followed, navigating around patio furniture and little children as best she could.

The two friends crowded into the tiny bathroom and bumped into each other, trying to close the door.

"Hurry up," Letitia pleaded as she yanked off the mask. "This is an emergency."

Elizabeth unzipped the costume. "Next time you do this, I'll get you diapers."

"Ha ha. Next time, *you're* going to be the bunny." Letitia dropped the mask onto the counter, then pushed her friend out and slammed the bathroom door.

A few minutes later, Letitia emerged wearing the shorts and t-shirt she had on under the costume. Her hair hung in damp tendrils, and she carried the rabbit get-up folded over one arm. She found Elizabeth at the kitchen table, pouring pink lemonade into plastic cups.

"What happened to the Easter bunny?"

"She got a heat rash. I must sneak out and put this in your trunk before the kids see it."

Elizabeth handed her the keys. Letitia accomplished her mission with great stealth. When she returned to the house, she and Elizabeth read stories to the children for an hour.

All too soon, it was time to say goodbye. Mindy walked the two volunteers down the narrow hallway lined with old floral wallpaper peeling off in a few places. "Mayor, do you think you could stop by tomorrow?"

"What do you need?" Elizabeth asked.

"I'm concerned about that new gal and her son. I'd like to discuss how to protect her from her abusive police-officer husband."

Elizabeth took the cell phone out of her purse and brought up a calendar on the screen. "If I get out of my meeting at city hall on time, I can be here around eleven o'clock. Will that work?"

"That would be great. Thanks so much."

Once inside the Mercedes, Letitia said, "So far, the shelter's location has remained a secret from the general public. But what if the new woman's husband manages to track her here? If he shows his badge to one of our local officers and claims he's conducting official business, they would be sure to help."

"That's the kind of scenario that keeps me up at night." Elizabeth shuddered.

CHAPTER SIXTEEN

CLOSETED KNOWLEDGE

Charles combed every inch of the park around their Shady Oaks neighborhood, searching for his wife and son. Several mothers with strollers caught his attention, but none of the women were Sarah. With each passing minute, he grew more frantic—and furious. The headache from partying at Doug's house the previous night pounded even more in the bright sunshine.

At the house, Charles looked up the phone number for the one friend he allowed his wife to keep: Doug's girl. But Gabby didn't know where Charles' family was. Her surprise at his question let him know she wasn't hiding anything.

What was going on? Sarah had only eight dollars and change. She couldn't have gone far. Had she taken Ricky to the convenience store down the block for ice cream? But that didn't explain why she wasn't answering his calls. Something chewed at the back of his mind like a rodent raiding garbage in a back alley. The lingering headache made concentrating impossible.

Sarah's only jobs were to take care of their kid, have a good meal on the table when he came home from work, make his lunches, keep the house tidy, and answer his phone calls promptly. Apparently, she was getting lazy. He'd correct that.

Slamming his fist against his palm, he stormed down the hallway and out the front door to check outside. Their nosy neighbor, Mrs. Connell, was pulling into her driveway.

He wanted to duck inside so she couldn't ask him to do more handyman work. But she might know something about Sarah. Fortunate that he'd cultivated goodwill with the old woman so that he could pump her for information. She kept tabs on Sarah's comings and goings. He waved and smiled, though the sunlight sent splintering shards into his brain.

"Happy Easter, Charles." She gave him a toothy grin. "Will you take Ricky for an Easter egg hunt this afternoon?"

"Oh, we have all kinds of fun things planned. But I can't find Sarah. Do you have any idea where she might be?"

Mrs. Connell rubbed her hands together and frowned. "I'm afraid not. I haven't seen her since yesterday when she and Ricky went to try out the new carousel at the park."

Charles fought to keep his face composed. Had Sarah's note been on the kitchen counter since *Saturday* after he had left for work? No. That couldn't be. *Maybe they went back there today. Sarah was keeping Ricky quiet this morning so that I could sleep in.* He had pulled another late shift last night.

"You are the hardest working man I know. That wife of yours is one lucky woman."

Charles gave her what he hoped passed as a humble smile, thanked her, then went back into the house. He grabbed his cell phone and checked for any unread text messages. Nothing.

Sarah knew to inform him of her whereabouts at all times. Since he hadn't told Sarah he was coming home late, she should've prepared a meal for him, but he'd been too wasted to eat. Maybe he should go to the kitchen and look for leftovers. He yanked open the fridge. Nothing except the leathery pot roast from Friday. Why hadn't she cooked dinner Saturday? He charged into the bedroom to see if the suitcase was gone, but it sat in the usual spot in the closet.

Maybe she'd planned a special surprise for him to apologize for the tuna fiasco. Perhaps she was out somewhere getting her hair done. She might come waltzing in the door any minute, all dolled up.

When she did dress up, she liked wearing the special gifts he'd given her. He grabbed her jewelry box, pleased Sarah had restored the bedroom to order. He pulled out the drawers one by one. Brooches and bracelets twinkled at him as if enjoying a secret joke.

When he yanked open the last drawer, the expensive diamond tennis bracelet he'd given her for their second anniversary was missing. Where was it? Sarah wore that only on special occasions. He returned to the closet. She owned one fancy dress, and it still hung on a hanger.

There had been an alert from work cautioning officers about an armed fugitive on the loose in Summit. Could his wife and child have been kidnapped? Dangers like these from work justified his rule that Sarah use no social media. He explained to her the risks of stalkers trying to get back at him by surfing the web for personal clues about residence, etc.

The house didn't appear vandalized. What if she'd opened the front door, and some creep had overpowered her? He should have trained her on how to react to a hostage situation. Could she have used the valuable bracelet to bargain with an intruder?

Nearly doubled over in fear, Charles phoned the station. "Sergeant, this is Deputy McAdams. Any word on that armed fugitive?"

"No. Why? You got a lead?"

"I don't know. Maybe. My wife and son are missing. I haven't seen them since yesterday morning when I left for work. The next-door neighbor says she saw them twenty-four hours ago."

"So, you think our fugitive might've taken them?"

"It's possible. We jail so many deadbeats that any one of them could be waging a vendetta."

"I'll let the duty officer know. Can you bring in pictures of your family?"

"I'll be there in fifteen minutes."

"Great. Charles, we'll do everything in our power to find them."

Ignoring his splitting headache, Charles shaved, nicking himself in two spots. He pressed small pieces of toilet paper to stop the bleeding, then left for the station.

If someone has harmed Sarah, they will pay.

CHAPTER SEVENTEEN
UNDERGROUND RAILROAD

Elizabeth let the purr of the Mercedes engine soothe her. Visiting the shelter was the right thing to do, but seeing the overwhelming needs tired her. She turned on the radio to a classical music station.

"Wow! I feel like I'm in a concert hall." Letitia swung her arm back and forth like a conductor as she listened to one of Mozart's piano concertos.

Her friend never seemed to run out of energy. "It should. The stereo system in here runs about sixty-five hundred dollars."

Letitia's face scrunched into a frown. "You know, Elizabeth, we are lucky to have all we do. Sometimes, I feel guilty when I look at those poor women at Solutions. I wonder if we should do more for them."

Was her friend implying Elizabeth should donate more? Heat crept into her face. She hadn't paid all that money for the sound system. It came with the car, which she'd gotten at a deep discount.

Still, Letitia was right. What she'd spent on the Mercedes could have helped fund a down payment on a house to shelter battered women. But she couldn't save everyone. Did God expect His children to give up all pleasure to help a few people? Besides, she shouldn't be the only one who had to sacrifice. After all, she wasn't the one who'd been a pampered housewife most of her life.

"And how much have *you* given lately to support Solutions?" Elizabeth regretted the bitterness in her voice, but it was too late to take back the words.

Letitia recoiled. "I didn't realize I had to report my donations to you."

"You don't. But I worked hard to get where I am today. And I don't think enjoying a few luxuries makes me greedy. Besides, I bought this car used."

Letitia raised her hands in surrender. "I didn't say you were. Look, I know how many charities you help fund—most of them anonymously. I just feel sad when I think about how many people are suffering . . . especially when our lives are so good by comparison."

Letitia's quiet answer relieved some of the tension simmering in the car. Elizabeth took a breath to calm herself. Letitia meant well. It's just that her friend didn't have much tact. If Letitia was thinking something, it came right out—often without the benefit of appropriate social filters.

"My life hasn't always been easy. Maybe that's why I enjoy symbols of success like this car so much. They remind me with God's help, I can overcome any obstacle." Elizabeth hoped her friend understood how hard she had worked to get where she was.

"I just hope I can overcome the aches and pains coming on after my stint as an Easter bunny," Letitia said, rubbing her calf muscles and wiggling her toes.

Disappointed Letitia didn't delve deeper, Elizabeth accepted that when people saw her now, they had no idea of her struggles to attend college and overcome prejudices. "I've got Bengay and Advil at home. You want to swing by my place before I take you home?"

"Sure. Thanks." Letitia gazed out the window. "I wonder what that new woman at the shelter is doing for her pain. Did you notice the bruises on her face and throat?"

"I wish some over-the-counter medicine could help Sarah. She seemed to be in shock during the entire ride from the North Carolina border to Prosper. Her teeth kept chattering. Every few seconds, she'd whirl around and look behind us to see if anyone followed."

"How'd she find out about our shelter?"

"A public librarian she met a few months ago told her about the National Domestic Violence Hotline. When she called them, they connected her with Family Matters, the agency where my niece Wilma volunteers. Sarah's been talking with Wilma for weeks about escaping her abusive marriage."

"I can't imagine living with constant fear." Letitia shifted on the leather seat.

"During my volunteer training for Solutions, Mindy told me most women try to leave an abuser at least seven times before they're successful."

Elizabeth approached a railroad crossing with lights flashing and bells clanging. She braked before the tracks. A large dog paced by the fence near the train tracks. Had Sarah's husband activated an official search party using his special connections?

Letitia clucked her tongue. "I don't understand why good women get involved with bad men. Don't they know better?"

As freight cars barreled through the intersection, Elizabeth struggled with a flash of anger and sadness. Sarah hadn't asked for the situation in which she found herself.

"Letitia, haven't you ever done something that led you into a situation you never expected?" She knew the discussion about alcohol was fresh in both their minds.

"Of course. But God gives us free will to make wise choices." Letitia pursed her lips. "So, we don't have to stay in a bad circumstance."

Letitia's self-righteous attitude was getting on her nerves. More train cars whistled by as Elizabeth tried to figure out how to explain that trapped people needed help, not condemnation.

"Do you remember learning in history class about how Harriet Tubman risked her life to guide slaves north to freedom?"

Letitia looked at her leather sandals. "Kinda."

Elizabeth faced Letitia. "My great-great-grandmother escaped slavery when she was seventeen. She would have been trapped if it weren't for the people who helped her. I want to repay that family debt by helping other women."

Letitia gripped the door's armrest. "I'm sorry. I didn't know."

"How could you not know?" Elizabeth swept her left hand along the golden-brown skin of her right forearm.

Letitia gulped. "I guess I never really thought about it."

Privileged blindness infuriated Elizabeth. Yet was it fair to hold her friend responsible for understanding something her family had never endured?

Letitia broke into her thoughts. "What else do you know about your great-great-grandmother?"

Childhood stories of resilience came to mind. "Grandma Lizzie grew up in Fredericksburg, Virginia. She belonged to a family of merchants. In 1862, when the Union Army marched on the city, she and thousands of other enslaved people took advantage of the chaos to make a break from their owners. They crossed the Rappahannock River to freedom in the North."

"I don't remember hearing about that in school."

Elizabeth grimaced. "It's not the kind of history promoted by communities that count on tourism dollars from Civil War buffs."

The red-and-white-striped bars lifted above the cleared train track, and cars took off.

"I'd like to hear more."

"We'll be at my house in a minute. I can show you a photograph of Lizzie that my mom found in a church archive in Fredericksburg." The picture always made Elizabeth smile. "Her grandmother was seated like a queen on a wooden cart piled high with bundles, pulled by oxen across that river on her way to liberty."

Letitia splayed her fingers on the car's leather seat. "Sarah made her escape in style, too."

"They both needed a lot of courage to make a getaway because they had no guarantee of being successful. Just like Lizzie, Sarah lives in constant terror of being found."

Elizabeth pictured slaves wrapped in rags with bruised and weary feet, tramping through muddy fields, hiding in freezing forests, and wading through murky swamps. Hungry, foraging for wild berries along the trail, reaching with gratitude toward a few slices of cold cornbread extended over fences by kindhearted farmers' wives.

"Was Lizzie ever captured?"

"No. She made it to Ohio, where she later married."

"I hope Sarah can find a happy ending to her story, too." Letitia wrapped her arms around herself.

Elizabeth visualized old-fashioned lanterns glowing in wooden-frame windows, signaling refuge for runaway slaves needing shelter. She wanted to show others how to brighten their lives and navigate beyond dark bitterness.

"During the Civil War, a slave could sell for a thousand dollars—about the price of a middle-class home at the time. These days, a thousand dollars doesn't cover the retainer most lawyers charge to help an abused woman file for divorce."

"Is that why many victims stay in dangerous relationships?"

Elizabeth shrugged. "Without the means to support oneself and afford food and shelter, freedom is an elusive dream."

As Elizabeth pulled into the driveway, Letitia asked, "What do you think will happen to Sarah?"

"I don't know, but I'm going to do whatever I can to help her stay strong, so she won't give up and go back."

CHAPTER EIGHTEEN
CONTRABAND

After church on Sunday, Betty sat across from Ida Lou in the hospital room. Ida Lou passed over the folded red sweater and made an impossible request. Betty gulped.

"You can't be serious," Betty sputtered. "Dogs aren't allowed in hospitals."

Tears coursed down Ida Lou's face like streams of water on a shower curtain. "Sweetie needs to see Richard. It's the only way she'll understand that he . . . isn't coming home." Ida Lou wept so hard that Betty considered pressing the nurse's call button. Maybe crying was what she should be doing. People pressured Betty to be strong instead of letting her mourn.

When sobs dwindled to sniffles, Ida Lou asked, "Will you get her for me?"

"I'm sure there are regulations against animals—"

"Please, Betty, I'm begging you. I can't go through that again—watching her wait by the door and perk up her ears at every footstep, scanning faces in crowds but never seeing the one she pines for. I can't stand to think of her moping around the house and sniffing in every corner, looking for someone she'll never see again."

Hospital rules existed for good reasons. But none of them outweighed the anguish on Ida Lou's face.

Thirty minutes later, Betty returned to the hospital. Over her right arm dangled a brightly colored cloth bag big enough to hold a Yorkie.

As she entered the double glass front doors, Betty noticed Kara at the front desk, dressed in her usual bright pink hospital jacket. She dodged into the little gift shop and peeked through the bouquets in the front window, hoping someone would come along to occupy the girl's attention so she could slip past unnoticed. How was it in movies that criminals created diversions so they could get away with their dastardly deeds?

With a sigh, she rejected the idea of pulling the fire alarm or asking the man in the waiting room to stop reading and fake a seizure. Instead, she walked to the desk as casually as her shaky legs could manage.

"Hello again, Mrs. Herndale. That's a beautiful designer bag. Did you get it in the gift shop?"

Betty's knees nearly buckled. "No, no. I've had this old thing for so long, I don't remember where I got it."

Sweetie sneezed inside the bag. Betty nearly had a seizure herself.

"What was that?" Kara cocked her head.

Betty coughed and rubbed her nose. "That oak pollen is getting to me." *Lord, forgive that lie.* "Honey, could you phone ICU again to let them know I'm here to visit a patient?"

"I'd be happy to."

Clutching the bag, Betty hurried down the corridor and waited for the elevator. When it arrived, she hustled inside and breathed a sigh of relief. Before the metal doors closed, a tattooed arm thrust through the narrow sliver of space and wedged them open.

A bearded man jumped inside. "Sorry, ma'am, but my wife's in labor!" He jabbed the third-floor button.

Sweetie squirmed in the bag, making the fabric sides heave like bellows. Betty scooted to the back corner of the tiny metal box, noticing the intruder's upturned collar, the haphazardly tucked work shirt, and his manly sweat. During their short ride together, he paced and cracked his knuckles. Good thing she only had to ride to the second floor.

Sweetie poked out her head and licked Betty's wrist. She pushed the dog inside the bag, then glanced at the man, who didn't seem to detect anything unusual.

When the elevator door opened, Betty eased out and squeezed the bag to her side. She hoped the little dog wouldn't suffocate. "Good luck to you," she called out to the distracted father-to-be.

On the way to the ICU, Sweetie lifted her head every few seconds to see what was happening. Betty kept pushing her down like a jack-in-the-box. Would Letitia have enough money to post bail if she got caught? If all else failed, maybe Mayor Elizabeth could put in a good word for her with the judge.

Near the ICU entrance, a couple came through the door. What luck! If she hurried, she could sneak through without standing in the hall, risking exposure while pressing the intercom button and waiting for someone in ICU to let her in. As the door started to close, she scurried through. So far, so good. She scuttled to Room 1202 and ducked inside. After glancing over her shoulder, she closed the curtain and handed Ida Lou the bag.

The smile on the woman's face as she pulled Sweetie into her arms almost made the perilous venture worthwhile. The dog smothered her owner's face with unsanitary kisses. Betty tried not to gag.

Ida Lou carried Sweetie to the bed and set her in the crook of Richard's motionless arm. The dog sniffed him, whimpered, and burrowed under the covers by his chest. Ida Lou stood by the rail, keeping her hand nearby to reassure her pet.

Betty tore her gaze from the heart-rending scene . . . partly to give the little family privacy, but also to avoid being overcome with emotion. Besides, she needed to watch the door in case a nurse came by. A nurse might discover her crime if she wasn't careful. But, then, how would she explain to Pastor James that the prayer chain leader was in jail?

After a while, Sweetie emerged from Richard's arm and placed her feet gingerly on the hospital mattress. Her topknot tilted to one side, and she whined.

Worried the sound would give them away to a nurse, Betty whispered, "Do you want me to take her back to the house?"

Ida Lou cuddled Sweetie and kissed her nose. "If you wouldn't mind. I don't want to leave Richard."

Before Ida Lou could change her mind, Betty picked up the designer bag and held it open for the dog. Sweetie backed up and whined. Ida Lou scooped her up and set her inside. Two pointy ears poked up by the handle.

Once Betty secured the animal, she crept toward the curtain, hoping she could make it out of the hospital with her contraband as successfully as she'd come in. She prayed Sweetie wouldn't whimper or bark.

"I'll take her for a quick walk. Then I'll come right back to check on you. Letitia would be happy to take her out later."

Ida Lou covered her mouth with clasped fists. "You are such a dear!"

She didn't feel like a dear. Deer in the headlights, maybe.

Betty stuck her head outside the curtain and scoped the hallway. A nurse looked up from computer monitors. "Do you need something?"

"No, thank you. Just headed home for a quick snack." Betty moved the bag to the opposite side.

"The cafeteria has fresh-baked macadamia nut cookies today."

"Sounds delicious." Betty fled down the hall, hoping the nurse didn't notice the bag wiggling.

Betty tiptoed around other medical staff, milling in the area. She'd almost made it to the ICU exit when a man behind her hollered, "Ma'am, wait a moment."

Pretending she didn't hear, Betty kept moving. A large hand landed on her shoulder as she reached out to push the metal bar and open the door. Clutching the designer bag under her elbow, Betty whirled around and saw the barrel chest of a hefty security guard. She looked up with indignation. "I'd appreciate it if you would unhand me, sir."

The guard blinked. He took a step back and pointed to her foot. "Sorry, ma'am. Didn't mean to scare you. But I noticed your shoe's untied, and I didn't want you to trip."

She looked down, swallowed, and then smiled apologetically. "I appreciate your kindness. I'll fix that lace as soon as I can find a place to sit." She edged toward the double doors.

The guard reached into a nearby room and pulled out a chair for her.

What would that pup do if she released the death grip on the satchel? "That's very sweet. But I can't sit on that hard chair." She cupped her hand over her mouth and whispered, "Hemorrhoids."

Noting his shocked expression, she pushed through the doors and made a beeline to the stairs. She wasn't about to take a chance on encountering someone in the elevator.

CHAPTER NINETEEN
DOUBLE CROSS

Charles leaned against the desk at the police station, holding a foam cup of steaming black coffee.

"Might wanna take that tissue off your face," First Sergeant Wilson said in a raspy voice. He chain-smoked cigarettes outside the back of the building.

"Oh, yeah. Sorry, boss." He brushed away the little wads, then continued answering the questions necessary to fill out a Missing Person's Report.

"When was the last time you saw her?"

"Eight o'clock yesterday morning, when I left for my shift." Charles paced like a caged animal around the stark, gunship-gray room.

"Don't you usually go home for lunch?"

Charles broke eye contact. "Yeah, but Doug owed on a bet and took me to Sissy's Diner for the meatloaf special yesterday." He hoped his fake smile looked genuine.

Sarge looked up from his notebook. "Did you talk with her during the day?"

"No. Several 911 calls kept me hopping." Charles glanced toward the hallway where staff walked by.

The old man shifted his weight in the worn office chair with cracked upholstery. "Was she there when you got home?"

"I don't know." Charles lowered his eyes. "Hung out with Doug for a while after work. We watched the baseball game at his house and had a couple of beers. Gotta relieve the stress sometimes, you know?"

Sarge's face remained impassive. "What time did you leave Doug's?"

What was Sarge's deal? This interrogation made Charles feel like a perp. "I crashed on Doug's couch in the fifth inning. Didn't wake up till the wee hours, then drove home." That was close enough to the truth. Doug had gone to bed earlier and slept like a log. He would back him up.

The sergeant shook his bulldog jowls. "You sure she's not out with friends or shopping?"

Charles gave him a withering look. "The car wasn't working. And I already talked to her friend."

"Okay, okay, don't get huffy." Wilson raised one dark eyebrow. "You sure she didn't take off because she was mad at you for something?"

Saturday morning haunted him. "Sarah never goes anywhere without telling me." Sarge was wily. Did he know more than he was letting on?

The sergeant glanced at his wristwatch. "So, it's been more than twenty-four hours since you've had contact with her or your son?"

"Yeah." He crushed the empty coffee cup in his fist. A trickle of dark liquid ran over his knuckles. Charles clenched his jaw, tossed the mess into a waste basket, and then grabbed a napkin off the counter to wipe his hand. "I'm worried sick about my family."

"I understand. Sarah is a beautiful lady. Visited with her at the Christmas party." Sarge stared him in the eye. "This is personal. We're going to do everything we can to find them."

Wilson jotted down a few more details for the report, then looked up. "Anything out of order at the house?"

What should he say? The kitchen was a wreck from his coffee fiasco. But that had only his fingerprints. "No, sir. No sign of forced entry." He'd better clean up the broken mug and spilled coffee when he got home. "Just the ordinary mess of a toddler spilling stuff. I gotta find my son!"

The sergeant tapped his pen on the desk in a staccato beat and gazed at the ceiling.

Charles took the cell phone out of his trouser pocket and texted his wife for the fiftieth time in the last twenty minutes. After their discussion yesterday morning, she wouldn't intentionally fail to respond. Could she be tied up or unconscious? And where was Ricky?

He wished Wilson would hurry. His family's lives could be at stake.

An idea struck. He'd been fuzzy-headed not to think of it before. He pushed his phone's Family Locator app. The icon showed his wife at an intersection just outside the city limits. A small dot indicated she was traveling west on the main parkway. The blue circle on his screen showed her within three hundred yards of a major crossroad.

"Sarge! I've got something."

The grizzled old man leaned over the desk. "What?"

Charles showed him the screen. "My GPS tracker spotted Sarah's signal a few miles from here." He hoped her phone had enough battery charge to sustain transmission until he could get to her. The charger had been in the kitchen.

The sergeant reached for the radio. "Dispatch, this is Wilson. Send a patrol car to the west side of the parkway for a routine traffic stop."

"Yes, sir," crackled a female voice.

"Once the patrol car is under way, let me know, and I'll provide more details. Over."

"Ten-four."

Charles slid into a chair across from his boss' desk. "Thank you, sir."

Wilson drummed his nicotine-stained fingers on the armrest. "Let's hope that vehicle doesn't pass the city limits before our guy gets there. If it goes out of our jurisdiction, we have to juggle coordination with other agencies."

Dispatch put through a callback from the officer in the area. Charles stared at his cell phone's screen almost without blinking, calling out updates, which Wilson repeated into the radio. "Left on Truman. Right on Sandhaven Road."

The sergeant sat up abruptly, and his chair nearly toppled over. "Hold on. Sandhaven is the old service entrance to the landfill. No one travels there on Sunday."

"That's right." Charles' stomach cramped as if someone had sucker-punched him. "And there's no way my wife would go there . . . not of her own free will."

"George," the sergeant barked into the radio, "what do you see?"

"Only thing out here is a front-end loader hauling garbage."

"Pull it over and see who's in the cab."

For tense moments, only the hum of the computer interrupted the silence pervading the room. Had Sarah and Ricky been murdered and their bodies dumped?

The radio crackled again. "The old guy driving the truck says he came from picking up trash behind the shops around Shady Oaks."

Charles swallowed hard. His neighborhood!

"All right. Run the tags, then get back with me."

"Yes, sir."

Charles tried not to panic. Didn't law enforcement teach him to be cool-headed in emergencies? But his throat constricted.

The sergeant narrowed his gaze at Charles. "We can't check the contents of that truck without a search warrant unless the owner gives consent. Not sure we could provide probable cause."

Charles gripped his cell phone like an anaconda squeezing its prey. "This isn't good enough?"

"Even if it was, those trucks crush their contents as soon as they take on a load."

Visions of someone smothering his wife and son in a trash truck tortured him.

Wilson scratched the back of his head. "Look, go home and make sure your wife hasn't returned. Meanwhile, I'll call the lieutenant and ask how he wants to handle this."

"Yes sir." Charles rose stiffly.

Crime scenes replayed in his mind with horrific possibilities. Would he ever see his wife and son alive again?

CHAPTER TWENTY

THE TREASURE OF TOOTHPASTE

Sarah cuddled next to Ricky on the lumpy twin bed at the Prosper's shelter.

"Mommy, where's Daddy?" Ricky held his favorite, old stuffed bear from home.

Sarah dreaded this question. What could she say to a two-year-old that he'd understand?

"Daddy can't come here, honey."

With his free hand, he stroked the bruised side of her face with whisper-soft fingertips. "Daddy bad."

Sarah sucked in a quick intake of air. He knew! How much of her late-night terrors had he heard?

He released the teddy bear and held her face in both of his tiny hands. "Mommy sad?"

"Yes, honey. I am sad. But don't worry. We've got lots of new friends here." Anxious to change the subject, she asked, "Did you like the present the Easter bunny gave you today?" His face dimpled.

Sarah reached for the basket of goodies and drew out a colorfully wrapped chocolate egg. The tinfoil crinkled as she tore it off. She handed it to him, got one for herself, and savored the melting chocolate's sweetness.

Noticing a toothbrush and toothpaste in the basket made her realize all the things left behind: shoes, books, potted plants, and Ricky's toys. This place was safe, but it wasn't home.

What about her framed family photos and other mementos from childhood? Charles might destroy them while she was gone. All those memories of good times with him she'd desperately tried to preserve . . . or was it create?

She looked for a cloth in the carryall to clean Ricky's hands. Maybe she should also wipe the slate clean of the illusion she and Charles could have a fairytale ending of happily ever after.

A light knock sounded on the bedroom door.

"Come in." Sarah tensed and tightened her hold on Ricky.

Mindy entered. "How are you guys doing?"

"We're okay." Sarah expelled a deep breath. "Thanks for the candy."

"Letitia brought those. She's one of our volunteers." Mindy giggled at Ricky's messy face and extended her hand toward a chocolate egg on top of the basket. "May I?"

"Sure. They're delicious."

"Have you had dinner?" Mindy unwrapped the candy and popped it in her mouth.

Sarah slumped. The carryall hadn't had much room, and they'd eaten the crackers and cheese. "Do you offer meals here?"

"We don't have a cafeteria, but there's a kitchen where you can cook." Mindy crumpled the wrapper in her hand.

"I have only a couple of apples with me."

"Don't worry. There's food in the pantry." Mindy ruffled Ricky's hair as he looked up and grinned.

"I have almost six dollars. Will that be enough?"

"Your first meal's free. Later today, I can help you apply for food stamps. And we can connect you with some local churches with food pantries to tide you over while your paperwork gets processed."

Sarah sagged onto the limp pillow. "I never thought I'd be on welfare."

Mindy patted Sarah's shoulder. "Don't think of it as charity. Consider it a short-term loan. When you get a job, you can contribute back."

"I haven't had a job since Ricky was born." Sarah plucked at a loose thread on the frayed edge of the pillow.

"No problem. We have many good contacts with local companies and placement agencies, and we'll walk you through every step." Mindy extended her arms to Ricky, who leaned into her embrace without hesitation.

Sarah trusted these strangers who had risked much to whisk them away from danger. But she didn't want to be a freeloader. She reached into the carryall and took out the small plastic bag with the opal ring and diamond bracelet. "Do you think you could help sell these?"

Mindy looked startled. "If you're sure that's what you want. But we can talk about that later. For now, let's start putting together a spaghetti dinner. After that, you can get a good night's sleep. Tomorrow, we'll come up with a plan."

What kind of plan could they possibly devise? The obstacles seemed overwhelming. She had no money, no car, and no job prospects. And pursuing any of those crucial things meant taking the risk Charles could find her.

Minimum wage barely covered day care. She didn't know who could give her a reference. She'd lost contact with everyone in her past as Charles consumed her world. Her parents wouldn't have anything to do with her. After the graduation fight, she'd tried to make up with them, but they had ignored all overtures.

"Relax, Sarah. You're safe here." Mindy settled Ricky on her hip and turned toward the doorway. Sarah followed.

Mindy had a point. At least, she was safe. But for how long?

CHAPTER TWENTY-ONE
READY OR NOT

Betty walked to Ida Lou's villa with Sweetie on the leash moping behind. As soon as the dog saw Juan resting in the shade of a large maple, she barked an excited greeting and vaulted forward. Betty almost lost her grip on the nylon cord.

Juan smiled and clapped his hands. Betty released the lead. Juan crouched down to pet Sweetie, picked her up, and then crooned to her.

Betty took a moment to exchange pleasantries. She used a few Spanish phrases she remembered from her mission work. The young man seemed grateful—and a little amused.

Trying to converse with her rusty Spanish and his limited English made talking a chore, and Betty didn't have enough energy to make an effort. Besides, she wanted to settle down the dog and return it to Ida Lou. So, she cut their interchange as short as politely possible.

Once inside Ida Lou's house, Betty set out a fresh bowl of water and dry dog food. Then she texted Letitia to stop by later, in case the night was another late one for Ida Lou. She left Sweetie crunching on kibbles.

Betty hurried back to the hospital. Once inside the ICU, Janelle waved her over. She cringed, concerned a reprimand for breaking sanitation regulations was forthcoming. But Janelle's expression was sad, not stern.

"I'm sorry to have to tell you this, Mrs. Herndale. Mr. Besco passed away while you were gone."

She squared her shoulders. "How's Ida Lou taking it?"

"As well as can be expected," Janelle said, straightening the collar on her uniform.

Should she leave Ida Lou alone to grieve privately or peek in and see if she could do anything? One of the few comforts she'd had when Donovan was dying was sitting by his side and holding his hand as he released his last breath. He had the reassurance of her presence by his side until the very end.

Janelle touched her shoulder. "No matter how often we've seen death, it's never easy."

"No, it's not." And challenging times were harder when faced alone.

Betty forced her feet toward room 1202. With timidity, she pulled open the curtain, wondering what she could say or do to offer solace for an unbearable loss.

Ida Lou sat next to Richard, as though waiting for him to wake up and ask her what time it was. Betty sat down quietly. Deep grief needed time to settle, and she didn't want to interrupt Ida Lou's mourning with inane words.

Ida Lou turned pain-clouded eyes toward Betty. "How am I going to live without him?"

Betty looked down at her left hand, where she still wore Donovan's wedding band. "His memories will always be with you."

After Donovan passed, people told Betty the yearning would lessen in time—that eventually she'd get over his death, as one got over a cold or the flu. But she knew the longing didn't stop.

"Who's going to laugh at my dumb jokes?" Ida Lou's face scrunched in pain. "I don't know how to pay our bills."

Undercurrents of anger and panic trying to figure out how to do the things Donovan had taken care of troubled Betty, too.

Ida Lou's cheeks bloomed a bright pink. "Can you imagine losing the man you've loved since eighth grade—the one who taught you how to drive his truck and took you to the ocean when you skipped school your senior year?"

Of course. Betty lived it. But she understood Ida Lou's frustration. "It sounds like you two had a wonderful relationship."

The soft answer took the angry wind out of Ida Lou's sails. She took a big breath and leaned back in the chair. "We really did."

"Tell me more about your lives together," Betty invited, hoping good memories might lessen the loss at the moment.

Ida Lou crossed her legs tightly at the ankles. "Richard played football in high school. He used to salute me in the stands whenever he made a touchdown. In his junior year, when he made the winning play and won most valuable player in the regional playoffs, he gave me the game ball. We still have that old thing on a shelf in our den."

"I'd like to see it sometime." Betty noted the use of "we." Changing pronouns from a team to solo hurt. Donovan had loved football, too. He'd lived for fall when the season began. Since he'd passed, she hadn't watched a single game because those powerful memories threatened to tear her apart.

"How'd you two meet?"

Ida Lou's shoulders relaxed, and her face wore a winsome expression. "His locker was beside mine in eighth grade. My lock stayed stuck most of the time. Richard wrenched the metal loop free so that I wouldn't be late for class. After a while, he started slipping love notes through the metal grate between periods. I couldn't wait to see what he'd write next."

Donovan used to write Betty "roses are red" poems with silly twists like, "Roses are pink, but my feet stink." She bit her lower lip and focused on Ida Lou.

A smile glimmered on the woman's lips. "The day before Christmas break, he wrote, 'Will you go steady with me? Check yes or no.'" She chuckled. "I didn't write back for two whole class periods. Then I scribbled 'Maybe' and slid the note inside his locker."

"How did he respond?" As long as Ida Lou kept talking, Betty would listen, even if it hurt her to hear stories that dredged up her own longings.

"I was afraid he'd be mad or ignore me. But at the end of the day, he waited for me by the lockers, holding something behind his back. As I approached him, he held out a bouquet of eight wilted flowers and said, 'Since we're *maybe* going together, I wanted you to have this. I picked them during P.E.'"

That Richard must have been some charmer. It was a shame he and Donovan would never meet. They would have liked each other.

Ida Lou touched her husband's limp hand. "He's always pulled through for me. I was sure he'd do it this time." She brushed at the tears streaming down her cheeks.

God, please give me the right words to comfort Ida Lou.

"He's always been my rock. Even when we lost our daughter, he gave me the strength to keep going. I don't understand why God would take him, too." Bitterness filled Ida Lou's voice.

What had happened to the daughter? For now, curiosity had to take a backseat to comforting this woman who'd experienced much tragedy. She needed to say something. Lapsing into self-pity might cripple Ida Lou at this critical juncture.

"I honestly don't understand why some things happen. I only can trust God will help me get through it."

Ida Lou bolted upright, her face suddenly hard. "If God is so good and loving, why would He take the only people I care about and leave me alone?"

What in the world could she say? She had wondered the same thing. "I do understand your pain—"

"You have no idea what I'm feeling!"

Janelle poked her head inside the curtain, looking concerned. Betty waved her away.

"Actually, I do," Betty said in a low, gentle tone. "My husband died of cancer a year ago, right in this hospital."

Ida Lou gasped, covering her mouth with her hand. "Betty, I'm so sorry."

"It's okay. You didn't know. But I do understand. Losing your husband is like removing half your body and soul. Going on without him seems impossible."

Ida Lou stared at the ceiling. "What's going to happen to me?"

Ida Lou needed hope, but Betty had to be honest. "You'll replay a thousand memories every day. The touch of his hand. The sound of his laughter. The scent of his clothes. Those memories will help you cope. Eventually, you'll find a way to go on."

"I'm not sure I can do this. Will you help me?"

"I'll be right by your side every step of the way. I promise."

How strange that Betty's anguish might serve to console someone else. Only those who grieve could understand navigating sorrow. Others, even those well-intentioned, tended to get bored with the mourning process and expected survivors to "move on" after a few weeks. Maybe she and Ida Lou could honor God and their husbands by sharing their losses.

Ida Lou leaned closer to her husband's face. "I love you, darling," she whispered. "You're the best husband in the world, and I'm going to miss you terribly." She brushed his cheek with her lips in a tender goodbye.

A quiet knock startled the women. Janelle came through the curtain, a look of distress on her face. "I apologize for interrupting. We just got notified of a nine-vehicle pile-up on the interstate causing numerous casualties. We're going to need this room soon. I am so sorry."

Ida Lou's fingernails scraped the armrest of her chair. "But . . . but I'm not ready."

"As soon as the physician finalizes your husband's paperwork, an orderly will come by to move him. Is there a minister or someone you'd like us to call for you?"

Ida Lou doubled over in agony, clutching her stomach. She uttered a high, keening wail. Betty scooted beside her, wrapping her arm around her shoulder.

When the heaving subsided, Ida Lou looked up, panic in her watery eyes. "We just moved here. I don't know anyone well enough to ask."

Finally, something tangible she could help with. "I will let Pastor James know, if that is all right. I can also call Terrence Carter. He owns and operates the local funeral home. He's the man who took care of my Donovan. He goes to First Church, and he's sensitive and reliable."

Ida Lou nodded, too overcome to fully process the decisions she needed to make.

Janelle looked at Ida Lou. "Remember what I told you about open windows. Your husband's soul is free."

CHAPTER TWENTY-TWO

MAKING PAYMENTS

Juan Rivas didn't mind working weekends at Horizon Vista. Being outside on a Sunday afternoon was better than being stuck in the cramped room his hourly pay purchased, though the square footage of the place equaled the home his family of six shared in Mexico. Four hundred a month paid for nice drywall and air-conditioning, but those amenities seemed hollow without the comfort of his loving family. He'd trade the rental in a heartbeat for the shack of his childhood, if only he could have his parents and siblings with him.

They sheltered miles away under a simple roof of woven palm fronds with wooden slat sidings. His parents sacrificed their dream of a concrete block home to finance his future. Would he be able to repay them? Back home, they thought the United States was a gold mine. They had no idea how much things cost here.

While hurrying down the sidewalk, Juan scrolled through a mental checklist of what he wanted to accomplish. Sunlight spotlighted emerald grass, and birds trilled greetings. Picturing his father praying, Juan silently conversed with his Heavenly Father, as he often did throughout the day.

Señor, thank You for this job and the chance You have given me to help my family. Please keep them safe.

Since he didn't have a key to unlock the shop for the lawn mower, he watered the purple pansies he'd planted the day before by the white house on Begonia Lane.

He missed seeing the friendly wave of the man with the pipe who walked the little dog there each morning. Noticing a few newspapers on the driveway, Juan picked them up and stacked them in a neat pile by the front door. The couple must have gone out of town for a few days.

Juan looked out for everyone as best he could. He adopted the retirees in this subdivision as his new village, but they seemed unaware.

As he rinsed the pansies' faces, two gray-haired men trundled by, toting leather golf bags behind them. They gave Juan an imperious nod.

"Hi!" He waved with his free hand, hoping he pronounced that simple English word correctly.

The men kept walking, clubs clacking as their bags bumped over the sidewalk cracks. One golfer mumbled to the other, "Good thing we have plenty of manual labor for the immigrants to do—they don't know anything else."

Just because he didn't fluently speak their language yet didn't mean he couldn't hear or understand. Didn't they realize that? Or was their jab intentional? He concentrated on the stream of water cooling the new transplants near his worn boots. Why did people look down on him? Didn't they know the risks he'd taken to come here?

The second golfer humphed in agreement. "I just wish they spoke English. Yesterday, I told my gardener to spread sixteen bags of potting soil around my azalea bushes to cover the bare spots. He smoothed over the existing mulch with a rake but didn't add any more."

Juan winced as the men's rubber cleats trampled his joy. When at the apartment, he surfed YouTube to prepare for the GED. But textbooks didn't have exercises on communicating with men who dismissed him as a fool simply because he had a strong accent. So, why work hard for people who only pampered themselves?

In his teens, Juan had started learning English from an American archaeologist who had visited his village one winter. The professor had hired him as a local guide of Cobá. They explored the jungles and impressive ruins of his ancestors. The Mayans' ability to construct massive temples centuries before Columbus sailed from Europe to "discover" America made Juan proud.

When the archaeologist had returned to the States, he had connected Juan with his uncle Greg, who owned a landscape company. Full of hope for an economic opportunity, Juan and his family scrimped for a year, setting aside a few pesos at a time. Finally, they had saved enough to pay for the expensive paperwork the embassies required to apply for a work visa. He remembered the many trips and hours spent waiting in long lines with hordes of others who wanted a chance to work. Wasn't the American dream all about finding a better life?

The water dried up from the hose's end, and Juan turned to find the kink. He backtracked to loosen the coils.

Thanks to the professor's recommendation and connections, Juan managed to get a work visa and traveled to the United States before his twentieth birthday. However, pursuing dreams of a better life came at a high cost.

The archaeologist assured Juan before leaving Mexico that his uncle would treat him like family. But Greg paid little attention to him. Juan often went for several days without talking to a soul. The archaeologist lived several states away. Travel there seemed impossible.

During lonely times, Juan held imaginary conversations with his family, telling them about huge grocery stores with aisle after aisle of colorful packages. He'd tell funny stories about how the label on a can seemed to say one thing, but when he opened the container, he got something else. He made it a point to get something new each time to expand his vocabulary. And he'd gotten good at doing math in his head, converting currency. Multiplying a peso times twenty almost equaled a U.S. dollar.

Juan sighed. Sure was a lot simpler raising hens for fresh eggs and trading produce with neighbors. He grinned, remembering feeding the pair of whitish-pink pigs he'd named Chulo and Chula. Every morning, the animals rubbed against his leg in anticipation of their meals and grunted in satisfaction when he fed them. Their ears drooped over like tent flaps. But he couldn't imagine the people in Prosper living like that.

A tan Taurus cruised by. A man wearing glasses stared at him from the driver's seat. Juan tensed. Was the man inspecting his work? Residents sitting in their air-conditioned homes monitored his labor. These people were quick to point out their dissatisfactions but slow to realize how much he did to groom their beautiful lawns.

The stranger parked the car, exited, and approached him. He had a crew cut and military bearing, though he wore no uniform. Juan's heart raced. He'd heard horror stories from people waiting in lines at the embassy about U.S. officials harassing immigrants.

His documents were back at the apartment so that they wouldn't get lost or soiled. The boss had a copy of his work visa, but Greg didn't work on Sundays. What if this man in glasses requested proof of citizenship? Could he be taken away?

"Hello," the man said, extending his hand to shake Juan's. "I'm Detective Smythe."

"My name is Juan." What did *detective* mean?

"You sure keep things looking nice around here. As I drive to work at the police station, I've been admiring your plantings."

Police? Sweat beaded on Juan's upper lip.

Smythe leaned over to finger a deep plum flower head. "How do you keep these looking so good?"

Juan struggled to find the right words. He held up his forefinger to signal he'd be back in a minute, then hustled to the storage shed. After turning off the water, he lifted a bag of fertilizer from behind the building and brought it for Smythe to read the label.

The detective jiggled his glasses and peered at the bag in Juan's arms. "Ten-ten-ten, huh? Guess I haven't been using enough potassium."

Juan shifted his weight, wondering if this man wanted anything else. He considered asking if he might have a garden that needed work but feared saying the wrong thing, particularly to someone who worked at a police station.

"You been here long?" Smythe studied him with penetrating brown eyes.

"No, sir. Just a few weeks." Was the man trying to trap him into saying something incriminating?

"Keep up the good work, kid." Smythe turned toward his car, waving as he drove off.

What was that all about? Was the man really being friendly, or did he have ulterior motives? Navigating every nuance exhausted him.

CHAPTER TWENTY-THREE

PROCESSIONAL

Betty's throat tightened in the hospital corridor as Janelle handed a clear, plastic bag with Richard's personal belongings to Ida Lou, who shivered. Betty wrapped a steadying arm around her slender waist. She also kept a firm hold on Ida Lou's elbow in case she collapsed.

Janelle walked over and wrapped them both in a tender, tearful embrace. Ida Lou's raw sorrow compounded Betty's last memories of Donovan. Shouldn't there be a limit on how much pain a person has to bear?

Their slow steps reverberated off the white tile as they approached the elevator. Ida Lou stopped twice to look back. Each time, Betty turned her toward the exit. They could do nothing else.

On the ride down, Ida Lou used her sleeve to wipe her cheeks. Betty had no words to comfort, so she stayed close as they returned to Ida Lou's house.

They could see the little dog through the bay window from the sidewalk. She sat on top of the couch, staring at them. As soon as Ida Lou unlocked the front door, Sweetie jumped on Ida Lou's legs. She picked up the wiggly little body and held her close to her chin. Sweetie's long, pink tongue swiped her cheek.

Betty tried not to wince. At least that little dog offered lots of affection and gave Ida Lou something to hug.

Ida Lou kicked off her shoes and slumped into the sofa cushions. "This feels surreal. How can I plan a funeral when I keep thinking Richard's going to walk in that door any moment, whistling his favorite Broadway tune?"

Sweetie perked up her ears at the mention of Richard's name and swiveled her head toward the garage entry. The dog sailed off the couch and ran toward the door by the laundry room, barking like crazy.

"She feels the same way I do." Ida Lou got up, shuffled toward the little dog, and picked her up. "Daddy's not coming home," she said, petting the quivering fur as the dog struggled to free herself.

Ida Lou loosened her arms, and Sweetie took off toward the master bedroom. Ida Lou looked at Betty and shrugged, then ambled back to the sofa.

Witnessing Ida Lou's devastation was hard and threatened to undo Betty's facade of composure. Raw pain opened her own loss all over again.

Growls and sounds of something ripping carried from the bedroom into the living area. "What's that noise?"

Ida Lou shrugged. "Whenever she's upset, Sweetie steals newspapers from the recycling stack and shreds them under our bed."

Why would Ida Lou let such destructive behavior go unchecked? Didn't she mind having to clean up the mess? If Sweetie got swatted on the rear with a rolled-up newspaper even once, she'd probably think twice about tearing up any more papers. "Are you going to stop her?"

"Not right this minute. Actually, I envy her. At least she has an outlet for the pain."

That made sense in an odd sort of way. "Want me to get a newspaper for you?" Betty stifled a chuckle. "I saw a couple stacked by your front door."

Ida Lou grinned. "I don't think Sweetie would share her special spot. Besides, I can't fit under the bed."

"Good one!" Betty smacked her leg in delight. "Ida Lou, you have been brave throughout this whole ordeal. Somehow, you've managed to keep going. I admire your courage."

"Thank you, but I don't have much choice. I wish I understood why things like this happen."

"When you figure that out, please let me know. I'm wrestling with God about it myself."

CHAPTER TWENTY-FOUR

THE VARIABLE

Juan watched Betty help the blonde inside her villa. What had happened? The man with the pipe was nowhere to be seen. The ladies looked sad. He hated not knowing what was going on. Back in the village, he knew everything.

At the sound of voices, he turned and saw three attractive young women in fancy heels sashay along the sidewalk. Their floral perfume wafted across the breeze. Hoping to make new friends, he waved. One girl tossed a lock of her long, auburn mane over her shoulder while the other two giggled. None slowed her pace.

He looked down at his ripped denim and dirt-crusted boots. Guess they wouldn't give him the time of day. How strange they judged his work clothes when they wore slashed slacks as a fashion statement. He toted the fertilizer bag back to the shed and set it on the ground. As he stood, he heard fabric rip.

Denim threads covering his left knee gaped even more. Perhaps he should buy new jeans. But his little sister, Maria, had grown a lot the past few months and no doubt needed bigger clothes. He would send money home instead. She could get several dresses in Mexico for the cost of one pair of trousers here.

He turned the spigot on and dragged the hose to a bed of blue hyacinths and orange-faced daffodils. Juan calculated how to send an extra twenty-nine dollars to his family this month. He would walk to work two days a week instead of taking the bus. New jeans would have to wait.

Juan patted the shirt pocket with his free hand. This touch assured him the tiny clay bird Maria had made him was secure. She gave him the figurine the day he left and told him to keep it with him always. That way, no matter where he was, he would remember her love. He wished the token macaw, with its tomato-red plumage and blue tail feathers, could make a loud, throaty squawk and carry a message of love across the miles to his family.

Would he ever be able to afford an immigration lawyer to navigate the mountain of paperwork required? Residency and bringing his family members over would take decades. Could he persevere that long? Maybe he should stop fooling himself and go back to Mexico.

Then he imagined the delighted surprise of his brothers visiting Prosper's bowling alley. He'd treat them to pizza and ice-cold sodas until their bellies bulged. He pictured the astonishment of his parents as he gave them the key to a beautiful brick home he'd buy for them. If only. His ambition wilted at the enormity of the hurdles. Maybe his dreams would erode like an ancient stele with elaborate hieroglyphs battered and erased by the elements over time.

The music from the hose's cascading stream took him back to childhood when his grandfather showed him a waterfall in the tropical forest near their village. Juan pretended the nearby live oak was a forty-nine-feet-tall sapodilla tree from his home, bending toward him and whispering wisdom in the old language. In his mind's eye, dappled light filtered through branches onto swaying ferns while lime-green lichen and moss spotted the ground around gnarled roots.

But burning rays of sunshine brought Juan back to the scorching reality of being exposed in a strange land. The stab of homesickness passed. He concentrated on the work at hand. Each hour toiled earned essentials his family needed.

Juan slurped a drink from the hose, letting the cool liquid soak his shirt. Then he turned off the spigot and coiled the hose in a tight circle. He rolled up his sleeves and mopped his forehead with a rag from his back pocket.

Yellow canna lilies lined the development's fence. Each stem grew six feet high with broad leaves raised like hands in prayer. The plant resembled corn—a crop his ancestors cultivated hundreds of years ago, and one his dad still struggled to harvest. Working with the steadfast rhythm his father had taught, Juan moved along the canna lilies and pulled weeds.

Without electricity or heavy-duty equipment, his industrious forefathers had terraced stone steps into temples and engineered miles of roadways. Their faith kept them full of hope and gratitude. He would persevere, too.

Father in Heaven, I thank You for a strong back to labor with.

The Mayan temples would dwarf the one-story American villas around him. Ancient artisans in his nation had designed pyramids to rival those of Egypt and constructed buildings with such care that some stood hundreds of years later. How many of these homes would exist in two hundred years?

Royal blood raced through Juan's veins—kings who'd commanded legions to build massive structures. Yet here he was, invisible—unless someone wanted a hole dug.

A brown-skinned lady in a fancy blue car backed out of her driveway. Juan admired the sleek metal and purring motor. Would he ever be able to afford something that nice? Get real. He had no vehicle to practice with for the driving test to get his license.

A blue jay screeched from a nearby tree. The bird dared a bright red cardinal to approach a feeder full of sunflower seeds. Wouldn't it be fun if his brothers were here to imitate the calls with him?

Juan stood to stretch his back, then gathered several stacks of pulled weeds into a pile. Priests in his ancestry created glyphs to record messages about the dynasties. There was much of his story to share . . . if only he knew how to pronounce the English words—and could find someone willing to listen.

Maybe that white-haired lady would help. He would ask her— if he could catch her when she left her friend. He studied the rose garden near one house. Roses held special meaning.

His mom used to tell him how she picked his name. She said in her soft, musical voice, "My son, you have a special destiny. Just as your namesake, Juan Diego, was an ordinary man chosen for a Divine task. In 1531, the Virgin Mary appeared to Juan Diego near Mexico City and showed him where roses bloomed, despite winter. He was to take these as proof of a miracle to the occupying Spanish archbishop."

His mother always smiled at the next part. "Juan Diego placed the precious flowers under his cape. When he appeared before the bishop, Juan Diego's cape revealed not only the beautiful roses but also a permanent image imprinted on the coarse fabric of Our Lady. You, too, my son, will be a messenger of hope and Divine revelation if you keep your heart pure."

He wanted to be used for a good purpose, even if he couldn't see it yet. He would maintain a pure outlook and not allow rude people to blacken his heart with jealousy and anger.

In their last conversation, his mother, with her dark braid falling over her shoulder, had studied his face. Then, with great conviction, she said the Lady would protect him if he acted in faith and always did the right thing.

"Let the rose be a symbol of hope," she said. "Miracles will happen when you find the courage to obey whatever the Lady calls you to do, no matter how impossible it might seem at the time."

Juan needed a miracle.

"*Confías en Dios para entregar*," his mother whispered.

"Trust God to deliver," Juan said out loud. He squared his shoulders and moved toward the next task. He'd bring back fertilizer to spread on the white-haired lady's rose bushes.

CHAPTER TWENTY-FIVE

INCONVENIENT QUESTIONS

Charles paced from one end of the house to the other for hours, staring at the flickering light of the GPS on Sarah's phone. It remained at the landfill address. He ached to drive there and find out why, but the boss had told him he had everything covered.

Around eight p.m., the screen went dark. Dead battery? Charles snapped his phone shut and sank onto the couch.

An hour or so later, Sergeant Wilson called. "The waste management company permitted us to search the refuse. But they don't want their truck tied up, so they agreed to dump the load a few yards away from the landfill."

"Let's go see what we can find," Charles said as he leaped off the couch.

"Calm down, son. You aren't going anywhere. I'll send the officers on duty to investigate."

Not more hours of uncertainty! How could he stand it? Why wouldn't his boss let him help? Did the sergeant distrust what Charles told him? No sense arguing with his boss. "Okay. What time should I plan on meeting them there?"

"Oh, no. I'm not going to let you muck this up. An emotional cop with personal issues can make things harder for everybody else. You take some time off."

"But—"

"That's an order."

Charles slammed down the phone.

Doug came over shortly after he hung up, no doubt sent by the sergeant. He stayed until about one a.m., offering mostly silent compassion with a few platitudes of assurance tossed in for good measure. After Doug found himself nodding off on the couch, he went home to rest before his next shift.

Alone again, Charles paced and catnapped. He watched the sun rise on Monday. He itched to go in and access the databases at the office, but the sergeant would find out. Who said he wasn't in shape to focus at work? No one was more motivated than he to find answers.

A silent emptiness filled the house. What would he do without his wife and son? Exhausted, he flopped onto the couch in the den and surfed news channels. None of them said anything about the missing wife of a local police officer. He didn't know whether to be angry or relieved.

His stomach growled, so he went to the kitchen to scrounge up breakfast. He couldn't stand the fish odor and hauled out the garbage with the destroyed coffeemaker and mug. Then he hunted around in the cabinets for a skillet. He pulled a carton of eggs from the refrigerator. It'd been years since he had cooked. He stared at the pan, wishing Sarah were here to make his favorite omelet with bacon and Swiss cheese.

Shoving the skillet across the range top, he abandoned the kitchen to put on a shirt and shoes. The convenience store had ready-made food. And maybe he'd turn up another clue there.

No messages on his phone. He scrolled through the gallery with fleeting images of Sarah holding Ricky in a Superman costume for Halloween, the pair smiling at him in front of the Christmas tree. He tapped on that to enlarge it. These would be good to show around. He pocketed the phone and strode the few blocks to the store.

At the busy intersection, six cars fueled up at the pumps. A steady stream of commuters and day laborers ducked into the store and came out with cups of coffee, donuts, and snacks.

Charles canvassed the parking lot, looking for anything suspicious. Had his wife been here in the last forty-eight hours? He'd never been apart from her this long in their three years of marriage. It was like having his right arm amputated. Sarah had always been at his side, doing his bidding and making life easier. He shouldn't have lost his temper and yelled at her the way he had Saturday. *What a jerk.* He'd apologize as soon as he found her. He'd get her a dozen red roses, like the night Ricky was born.

Charles skirted the area where motorists pumped gas and approached the building, eager to ask the clerk if he knew anything about Sarah. At the entrance, he opened the door for a young woman wearing bright blue eyeshadow and a sundress and carrying a paper sack of purchases. The scent of her strawberry shampoo collided with the odor of old cigarette butts in the trash can at the front. He longed to bury his nose in Sarah's freshly washed and dried hair.

The woman smiled and thanked him as she passed. Then he entered the store and walked the perimeter aisle. He pretended to study drinks in the cooler while examining shoppers through the reflection in the glass. Could any of them be serial killers who haunted this busy place to locate unsuspecting prey? An old lady shuffled to the counter with a loaf of bread. A pimple-faced teenager eyed smokes behind the register. Neither looked dangerous.

Chocolate-frosted donuts in the bakery display caught his attention. He grabbed the plastic tongs hanging on the case to pull out one donut and an apple fritter. After placing the treats in a cardboard box, he moved toward the coffee dispenser. He took his time adding cream to the cup, waiting for the checkout line at the register to thin.

As the dark-skinned cashier rang up Charles' purchases, he asked in an Indian accent, "Will there be anything else, officer?"

Even without a uniform, the guy recognized Charles from his regular morning coffee stops. That could come in handy. "As a matter of fact, there is." He pulled out his phone and showed the cashier the close-up Christmas picture of Sarah holding Ricky. "Have you seen this woman and child?"

The man studied it. "I do not think so. Is she in trouble?"

"We believe she might be in danger."

"I wish I could help." He placed Charles' donut box in a brown paper sack.

"Could you add a banana to my bill?" Charles stalled for time as a man in a business suit rushed into line behind him.

The cashier pulled the piece of fruit from a basket on the counter, punched buttons on the register, then muttered, "Could be this lady came by. I'm trying to remember. She does look familiar."

"When?" Charles leaned forward and handed the cashier a twenty-dollar bill.

"Early Saturday. Wore sunglasses. I think maybe she had a stroller. Not sure." The register dinged, and the man pulled coins from the drawer.

"Keep the change." Charles pocketed the photo and slid a business card over the counter. "Here's my number if you can think of anything else."

The cashier dropped the change into a tip jar and smiled. "Thank you, sir."

Charles picked up his coffee and bag of food, then stepped outside. A Frito Lay truck pulled up, and a woman with wavy black hair and huge, gold earrings got out, toting a clipboard. If she delivered every day, maybe she'd know something.

Blocking the doorway, he nodded at her. "Good morning."

She gave him a funny look. Did she think he was hitting on her? Most women appreciated his rugged good looks, and some, on occasion, mistook his interest as being more than professional.

"Would you mind if I asked you a question . . ." He glanced at the silver-embroidered name on her uniform. "Wilma?"

The woman stepped back, a wary look in her eyes. "Sorry. I'm running late." She headed around him.

He scurried after her and grabbed the metal bar on the glass door but didn't open it. "Please?" he asked in a soft tone.

She took a deep breath. Charles set his coffee and bag on top of the trash container, then pulled out the picture of his family.

Clutching the clipboard like a barrier, Wilma gave a cursory glance to the photograph, blew a large, pink bubble with her chewing gum, and then popped it. "Pretty lady."

"I need to find her. I'm concerned she's been a victim of foul play."

"A whole lot of foul play goes on around here." She looked him up and down, smacking her gum.

Charles couldn't identify the source of her obvious disgust. "Have you seen her?"

"Dunno. I see a lot of people in my workday driving around."

He handed her a business card. "If you think of anything, could you please call me?"

She cocked her head and peered at him. "Any reward?"

"Depends on how good the information is."

She popped another bubble. "You got any flyers with the photo?"

Charles hesitated, then realized the merit of her suggestion. The more people looking, the greater the chances of finding Sarah. He would print leaflets on the home computer and bring them back. "Not yet. I'll bring some to put by the register later today."

"Can I go now? I'm running late and don't want to get in trouble with my boss."

Charles opened the door and let the woman pass. No luck so far. But he would keep trying. Somebody had to know something.

CHAPTER TWENTY-SIX

ADDRESS UNKNOWN

Betty wondered what secret Ida Lou wanted to share this morning. Still wearing pajamas, Ida Lou returned to the bedroom to retrieve something. While waiting in the living room, Betty gazed out Ida Lou's bay window. Juan mowed grass, and sweat soaked his shirt. A black-masked cardinal flew to the sunflower feeder, the sunlight making its brilliant red feathers shimmer like a polished garnet.

The sight transported Betty to when she and Donovan watched birds and lazed away afternoons leafing through the *Peterson Field Guide*. That worn guidebook served as a tangible link to her husband. She often held it, imagining his rough hand brushing hers to flip well-thumbed pages and point out a photograph. What object would help Ida Lou connect to fond memories? What was so important Ida Lou had to show it to her within hours of Richard's death?

Ida Lou emerged from the bedroom, baby-talking to Sweetie in a soft voice as she cradled the dog in her left arm with another item partially obscured. After plopping onto the couch, Ida Lou motioned for Betty to sit beside her. Sweetie sprawled on Ida Lou's lap, her pointy ears alert. Betty repositioned herself to move as far from the dog's drippy tongue as possible.

Ida Lou held out a framed portrait of a young woman wearing a black cap and gown. "This is our daughter at her college graduation three years ago."

"She's beautiful." Betty recalled Ida Lou's comments in the hospital about losing her daughter. "You must have been very proud of her." Was it safe to ask what had happened to the daughter or wait and let Ida Lou lead the conversation?

Ida Lou stared out the window, lost in memories. "Richard and I wanted children immediately, but I had trouble conceiving. We waited two-and-a-half years before we finally got a baby. Richard started a savings account for her college tuition when she was three months old."

How could she comfort this woman? "Tell me more about her."

Ida Lou ran her fingertips along the outline of the face in the photo, as though pushing back strands of her daughter's windblown hair. "I haven't seen her since this picture was taken. We planned to meet for lunch after the graduation ceremony, but she never showed up."

Something terrible must have happened to prevent a daughter from meeting her parents on such a festive day. Betty gulped, imagining possible scenarios.

"For forty-eight hours, we searched everywhere, checking with police and hospitals. On the third day, we got a postcard stamped from a beach resort in Florida that said she had eloped, and everything was fine."

How could a daughter do something so irresponsible and inconsiderate? Betty restrained herself from making the indignant remark out loud.

Ida Lou's brow furrowed. "We called and texted her, but she never answered."

Betty would have been beside herself with fear. "Couldn't the police help?"

"Richard reported our concerns to authorities. They told us she was an adult and under no obligation to us. Since no one had broken any laws, they couldn't do anything."

Ida Lou used the hem of her pajama top to wipe a smudge off the corner of the glass. "Within a week, her voicemail stopped working. We guessed she'd closed her account. Next, we tried mailing a letter to the beach resort, but there was no response."

"Why would your daughter cut you off like that?" Betty regretted her outburst when she saw a pained expression cross Ida Lou's weary countenance.

She tapped fingernails with chipped polish along the picture frame. "We didn't get along with her boyfriend."

Betty's son had dated one young woman she hadn't cared for. It was difficult to be a parent and allow young adults to make their own decisions. "Why didn't you like him?"

"At first, everything seemed okay. They started dating during her sophomore year of college. He was a few years older than her. He always dressed nicely and carried himself well. Even opened doors for me and brought Richard his favorite brand of pipe tobacco."

"Sounds like a nice young man."

"Yes, well, I thought so, too. But Richard never liked him. Said there was something shifty in his eyes. But our little girl saw only Prince Charming. She stopped coming home from college because she said her boyfriend wanted her with him, and she didn't want to upset him."

Betty bristled. "What about upsetting you?"

Ida Lou dropped her chin and shook her head.

Betty regrouped. "Sounds like she was captivated. Was there anything else that worried you?"

Ida Lou crossed her legs. "She asked her dad for a large increase in her allowance. She didn't say why, but we suspected she was helping support her boyfriend."

"If he was older than she and not working, I can see why you would be concerned." Betty wiggled on the couch to get more comfortable.

Ida Lou lolled her head against the back of the sofa. "Shortly before the graduation ceremony, Richard met the young man privately and told him to leave our daughter alone."

"How did he respond?"

"He told Richard that Sarah was a grown woman, and we'd better not interfere—or else." Ida Lou wrapped her arms around herself as if suddenly chilled.

"That sounds like a threat."

"Things went downhill. Sarah was angry and told us to let her live her life." Ida Lou scooted to the edge of the couch and stood. "The worst part is I already had pulled her aside on graduation morning while Richard parked the car at the breakfast diner and told her to stop being foolish and selfish. I said she needed to focus on finding a job and using the degree her dad had paid for."

Sweetie tiptoed onto the glass of the picture frame, blocking the smiling face. Betty was glad for the interruption. She had no idea what to say.

"You miss her, too, don't you?" Ida Lou crooned, scratching behind the dog's ears. "That conversation was the last I had with her."

Betty arose from the couch with difficulty as her legs had become stiff. She patted Ida Lou's arm. "I am so sorry."

Ida Lou paced around the living room. "As the months went by, I kept hoping she'd show up one day. Christmas after Christmas, we put presents under the tree, all wrapped in her favorite color, yellow. Every Mother's Day and Father's Day, we held our breath, wondering if this would be the time we'd get to see her walk in the front door with her arms open—"

"Weren't you able to track her through her friends or social media?"

"That was the crazy part. It was as though Sarah had dropped off the face of the earth. We asked her high school and college friends if they knew anything, but they said they hadn't heard from her either. We managed to get a forwarding address from the college since we were on her billing account. We sent letters, but they came back 'Return to Sender.'"

Betty heard from Ben weekly. She couldn't fathom not knowing how her son was for years. Had the Good Friday vigil been only a couple of days ago? If she'd known then what she knew now, she wouldn't have batted an eye at Ida Lou bringing Sweetie to the sanctuary. Anyone who'd gone through what Ida Lou had and still came to church to talk with God must be a saint.

"After three years, I told Richard I would lose my mind if I kept looking in the backyard at Sarah's old swing set and tree house, imagining her playing with her dolls but never getting to see a grandbaby. He suggested we move to get away from all the painful memories. At first, I refused. How could she find us if we left? But after several months, he finally convinced me she didn't want to find us—and that if she ever did, she could track us down."

Ida Lou seemed like such a nice person. How could a daughter be so insensitive?

Ida Lou scooted Sweetie off the picture and set the frame on the coffee table. "I wish there was a way for me to let Sarah know what happened to her dad."

Betty puzzled over the problem. If they could locate the daughter, would she change her ways and care for Ida Lou now that she was alone? Or would she and that rat-fink husband cause more problems?

Perhaps the girl should at least be given a chance. "If you put an obituary announcement in the newspaper, Terrence also posts the information online. Maybe your daughter will see it and contact you."

Ida Lou sat up straight. "It's worth a try." A tiny spark of hope lit her eyes. "Could you call him for me?"

"Of course."

Betty hoped that was good advice. No one should have to deal with an estranged daughter while having to bury her husband. Betty would regret getting involved if the girl and her spouse showed up and made waves. But abandoning Ida Lou when she'd lost so much wasn't right. Betty would do what she could and accept responsibility for any fallout. She needed to get a hold of Pastor James. He was the one who put her in this mess to begin with. High time he showed up to help. She was in over her head.

CHAPTER TWENTY-SEVEN

PRAYER CHAIN PITFALL

Fascinated, Letitia observed Melissa Stout preen in the reflection of the grocery store's glass doors before entering mid-morning on Monday. That Melissa always was good entertainment. Her Miss-High-and-Mighty demeanor irked everyone. Melissa's husband was an elder at First Church, but she acted as though that position elevated *her* to royalty. She never let anyone forget her status. As though anyone cared. No one could figure out how poor Stan put up with her for twenty-eight years.

Letitia trailed behind Melissa inside the store, noting how her form-fitting jacket accentuated straight shoulders and elongated her imposing five-feet-eight height. Letitia looked down at her flip-flops and bright blue toenails. More comparison didn't bode well. Melissa's cream pumps matched her handbag. She looked as though she were headed to a Fortune 500 board meeting instead of the produce aisle. Good grief.

Letitia schlepped up beside Melissa as she inspected apples. "Hi, Melissa. How are you?" She prayed to avoid the temptation of baiting Melissa, although that often proved fun. Melissa got horrified when Letitia did a zany stunt like sampling fruit from a display, even though Letitia made sure to tell cashiers to charge her for the produce.

"Hello, Letitia." Melissa angled her slender left hand toward a higher row of fruit to show off her huge diamond anniversary ring. Then she made a pointed glance down to Letitia's feet. "Been cleaning house today?"

Letitia struggled to come up with an appropriate retort, but someone called out their names before she could.

AnnMarie Higgins approached in faded blue jeans and a curly ponytail. The young woman walked to Melissa and placed a gentle hand on her forearm.

"Melissa, I'm so sorry to hear about your husband."

Letitia gulped. Uh oh. She had been too embarrassed to tell anyone of her mistake. She hoped to dodge culpability.

Melissa stared at the young woman and blinked a few times. She stepped back. "Why, whatever are you talking about, dear?"

AnnMarie's arm dropped, and her forehead puckered into wrinkles. "I've been out of town a couple of days. George and I took the family to our lake cabin for Easter break. We got back late last night."

"I'm confused. What does my husband have to do with your vacation?" Melissa's lips thinned into a line.

Letitia's stomach tightened. Was there a way to derail this conversation? "You know, I can't believe what people wear for swimsuits these days."

Melissa sniffed. "It's true that many social conventions have lapsed." She eyed Letitia's tank top.

AnnMarie shook her head, and the ponytail swished. "I saw girls in tiny bikinis that made me wish for younger days."

"Stan went fishing last Saturday but didn't say anything about a bunch of bikini bimbos." Melissa drew herself up tall.

That self-centeredness drove Letitia crazy. She couldn't resist egging her on. "I heard your Stan goes fishing a lot at the lake."

Melissa raised a perfectly plucked eyebrow. "Oh?"

AnnMarie played peacemaker. "But enough about my trip. Is everything okay with you and Stan?"

Melissa's back went rigid. "I assure you, Mr. Stout and I have never been better."

Unaware of Melissa's frosty tone, AnnMarie beamed. "Prayer can accomplish miracles."

The devil must have made Letitia say what she did next. "Many mighty men of God have fallen prey to temptation, you know. We studied that with King David and Bathsheba."

AnnMarie's mouth opened and closed like a fish flopping in a boat.

Melissa cut to the chase and jutted out her hip. "Did something happen at the lake I should be aware of?"

An awkward pause ensued as AnnMarie looked back and forth from Letitia to Melissa, trying to figure out what was happening. Letitia juggled how to extricate herself from the innuendoes. She hated when her wacky sense of humor took a prank too far.

Melissa pinned AnnMarie with a gaze. "There's no need to be shy, dear. You can tell me. Whatever it is, I can handle it—with the Lord's help, of course."

"Umm, Letitia," AnnMarie ventured.

Letitia signaled silence with her forefinger to her lips but dropped her hand as Melissa turned on her.

"Oh, dear. Look at the time. I must fly to finish these few purchases for Ida Lou since *her husband* is the one we prayed about." Letitia hoped AnnMarie would pick up on the hint for a graceful out.

Melissa put both hands on her hips. "There's something you two aren't telling me. What is it?"

AnnMarie picked up a head of lettuce, her hand trembling. "Umm . . ." She dropped the cellophane-wrapped green ball into her basket. "When I played the messages on my phone this morning after we got cell service again, there was a prayer request about Stan. I—"

"Excuse me?" Heat flushed up Melissa's neck and scorched her cheeks.

Enough was enough. Letitia had to get out of the store before Melissa's fury flambéed the oranges on display, not to mention poor AnnMarie.

"Goodness, those prayer chain messages can get garbled," Letitia crooned. "Someone must have gotten confused. That can happen sometimes. Melissa, Stan loves you dearly, and the many anniversaries you two have celebrated testify to that."

AnnMarie scratched the back of her head.

Letitia lifted her eyebrows and shoulders in a silent plea. Would AnnMarie tell on her to Betty? Letitia had already been put on prayer chain probation once.

"Beg your pardon, but I need to finish my shopping." Melissa whipped her grocery cart around and stalked toward the canned goods.

"Gotta run." Letitia yanked a banana off the shelf and rushed toward the register before AnnMarie could get in another word. Betty wouldn't speak to her for a year if everyone realized how she'd messed up again. She'd stop by AnnMarie's floral shop later to make amends and buy Ida Lou a fresh arrangement. Maybe even Melissa, too.

CHAPTER TWENTY-EIGHT

CONFESSION

Sarah sat on the bench by the shelter's picnic table in the fenced backyard. Nearby, Ricky played with a dump truck in the sandbox. No car. No home. No prospects. She was hungry and had to depend on others for lunch. Had she made the right decision to leave Charles?

"Could you give me a hand?" Elizabeth Robinson approached, jostling a bag of carryout food and drinks. The mayor moved with poise, and her neat bun accentuated high cheekbones.

Sarah stood and reached for a bag, savoring the aroma of fried chicken. "What a feast! Thank you."

Elizabeth settled on the bench. "I'm delighted you can share it."

Sarah called Ricky to join them. He drove the dump truck across the sand, over the wooden railing, and along the grass, making motor sounds with his puckered lips. A slight whiff of wild onion mingled with the mowed lawn.

When he was seated beside her, Elizabeth asked, "Would you mind if I pray?"

"Go ahead if you want." Sarah had given up the habit long ago, but she didn't want to offend Elizabeth.

Elizabeth bowed her head. "Dear Lord, thank You for this food and all that You do for us. Amen."

Sarah hadn't talked to God in a long time. Maybe that was part of the problem. How could He forgive her when she couldn't forgive herself? She nibbled on a piece of crunchy coating and let the sunshine warm her.

Ricky wolfed down his nuggets and half a cupcake, then wiped his mouth on his shirt sleeve. "I go work now." He trotted back to the sandbox with his truck.

When he was occupied and out of earshot, Elizabeth asked, "How are you doing, Sarah?"

She smoothed one side of her dark hair and looked at a split end. "Okay, I guess. I didn't sleep well last night. Kept waking up at the slightest sound."

"I had to live in a cheap hotel at one point in my life," Elizabeth confided. "Money was hard to come by. Listening to strangers outside your room makes relaxing hard. It's difficult getting used to a new place."

If only Sarah had somewhere else to go. She had left one fear only to find another.

"Do you have family you'd like me to contact?" Elizabeth asked as she reached for a piece of chicken.

Sarah stirred soggy green beans with her fork. "The only family I have are my parents. But they haven't talked to me in years." Her shoulders slumped. "They didn't even come to Ricky's first birthday party."

"Do you mind if I ask what happened?" Elizabeth set down her food.

Sarah wanted to share her sorrow. She tired of carrying that burden alone. "Actually, it'd be a relief to be able to talk about it."

Elizabeth smiled but didn't press for details. Sarah spooned out potato salad from a tub. "The last time I saw them was at my college graduation. They gave me a beautiful pearl necklace, and we took pictures."

Elizabeth leaned forward. "Did they move away after you graduated?"

"Actually, I'm the one who took off. My college sweetheart got upset with my dad at the ceremony. He wanted us to elope."

"And you agreed?" Elizabeth sipped her soda with a straw.

"I didn't want to lose Charles." Sarah bit one of her jagged fingernails. "And I had just found out I was pregnant with Ricky. I was embarrassed. I thought my folks would be disappointed in me."

"Oh, honey. Things happen. Didn't you let your momma know what was going on?"

Sarah crumpled her napkin into a tiny ball. "I tried to tell her before breakfast when we were alone; but before I could say anything, she started lecturing me about how Charles was a deadbeat, and I needed to start a new life and step out on my own with my college degree."

Would Elizabeth think less of her, too? Though pregnancy outside marriage didn't have the same stigma it had years ago, Sarah knew the church frowned on that.

Elizabeth folded her hands in her lap. "But what about after Ricky was born? Didn't you want your parents to see him?"

"Of course, I did! I didn't know how to say everything over the phone, so I wrote them and begged them to come to see us and work things out. I even sent pictures of Ricky."

Elizabeth leaned closer. "Didn't they respond?"

Sarah glanced to where Ricky jumped over toys in the sandbox. "No. Not a word. I guess they wrote me off."

"But what if they didn't receive the letters? Could there be some mistake?" Elizabeth pushed aside her empty plate.

"No. Charles mailed a certified letter for me with the invitation to Ricky's first birthday that required a signed receipt. He told me the post office said the recipient refused delivery."

At the sound of his name, Ricky turned toward them. He ran over and kissed Sarah on the cheek. Hugging him, she said, "Can you find Mommy a pretty flower in the yard over there?"

"I will find the most beautifulest flowers ever." He skipped off toward yellow dandelions that beckoned by the fence.

"But, Sarah, what if Charles never mailed that letter?" Elizabeth steepled her fingers. "When I took the training to become an advocate for survivors of domestic violence, I learned abusers often isolate victims from their support network. That's a classic maneuver abusers use to gain control."

This was news. There was a *pattern* to what Charles did? Sarah thought about girlfriends from college he hadn't liked, so she'd let the relationships lapse to devote more time to him. Anger and doubt roiled inside her. "I have a hard time believing Charles could be so deceitful."

Then again, maybe she had missed crucial details all along. Charles said having a post office box was safer than curb delivery, and he kept the key. He picked up the mail since the post office was near the station. She thought he'd been considerate to take care of that chore, so she didn't have to. But what if he'd had ulterior motives?

Elizabeth kept her voice neutral. "Mindy has a great graphic developed by women in Duluth, Minnesota, based on their experiences with domestic violence. It's a picture of a wheel and shows patterns of manipulation."

If Charles could wound her body and destroy her things, maybe he lied, too. She didn't know what to believe anymore. "Maybe I should take a look at that."

Ricky ran toward her with weeds in his little hand. What was her son learning about how to treat loved ones? She could shield him only so long. And she hadn't done a good job of that. What if he started hitting others?

"Do you think it might be a good time to reach out to your parents again?" Elizabeth reached for a cupcake with chocolate frosting.

Sarah scrunched her face. "I would if I knew how to contact them. My husband went out of town a few weeks ago for a two-day training. While he was gone, one of the volunteers from the agency in North Carolina drove Ricky and me to the house where my folks used to live. But the place had sold and was empty. None of the neighbors knew where my parents had moved. I figured they had washed their hands of me for good."

"Mindy has a computer in the office if you want to search your parents' names and see if we can get an address for them." She dabbed her mouth with a napkin.

Ricky approached and offered her the simple bouquet. She accepted his gift. "Thank you, Ricky. What a nice thing to do."

He skipped off toward the playset. "I wish my folks could see Ricky. They'd love being able to play with him." Tears welled up.

"We'll figure something out, honey; don't you worry."

Sarah kept her eyes on her son. "I have to keep Ricky safe—that's the main thing. But I don't have money or a job, and we can't live here forever."

"My church has a special emergency fund for people in need. I'm sure they'd be happy to help until you can get on your feet."

Sarah looked down. "That is kind. I do have some things I can sell to tide me over—a diamond bracelet and an opal ring. Could you help me find a buyer?"

"Are you sure?" Elizabeth shifted with discomfort. "I respect your decisions, but once sold, you can't get those precious items back."

Sarah touched the sore spot on her face. "Whatever Charles gave me isn't precious anymore."

Elizabeth stacked empty containers to clear the table. "Okay. If you need a ride, I could drive you to the pawn shop in town."

Her face blanched. "No! My husband has a way of finding out things. It's better if I stay hidden."

"I do business with the owner of a local pawn shop occasionally. I could take your jewelry to him for a quote. I warn you, though, he won't pay much. You'll be lucky to get a hundred dollars for both pieces."

"That's a hundred more than I have now," Sarah said, fiddling with her diamond wedding band. "This doesn't mean what it used to. Might as well throw it in, too."

"Are you sure?"

"Yes." No more second guessing. She had left Charles, and she wasn't going back. Neither was Ricky. She took off the ring and placed it in Elizabeth's palm.

Elizabeth tipped up Sarah's chin with her right hand. "When did your husband strangle you?"

Sarah leaned away, fluttering her hand up to cover her neck. "How did you know?"

"Large thumbs can cause round bruises like that on either side of your windpipe. I'm surprised you're alive—most victims don't survive strangling."

"It wasn't like that. My husband just lost his temper. He didn't mean to hurt me."

"Honey, what your husband did was not an accident. He chose to show you he had power by cutting off your oxygen flow."

"Maybe you are overreacting." Sarah felt naked. She didn't want to see her husband as a monster.

"The last woman I saw with marks like that didn't survive the next attack. I was a witness at her murderer's trial. I suggest you see a doctor, at the very least, so if you need evidence in court later, you have it."

Sarah recoiled. Her predicament kept getting worse. She just wanted a safe place where she and Ricky could live. Seeing a doctor and attorney seemed as impossible as financing a home of her own.

"But the insurance company would report that to my husband!"

"Not if you went to Prosper Memorial. Solutions has a special grant with the hospital for assisting survivors of domestic violence. No insurance is required."

Sarah wrung her hands. "I don't know. I'm afraid he'll find me if I go anywhere."

How could she have been so blind? She ignored warning signs in Charles for too long. Or had she chosen to see only what she could live with?

Elizabeth nodded toward the slide where Ricky played, and sunlight spotlighted wisps of his red hair. "Your son needs you. And you won't be able to take care of him if you don't take care of yourself."

Sarah expelled a long breath. "You're right." She sat up straighter. "Okay. I'll get checked out."

"If we call now, we can probably get you in this afternoon." Elizabeth put the trash into the plastic bag.

"What will I do with Ricky? I couldn't take him to the exam with me."

"Do you remember yesterday's Easter bunny?"

"I sure do." The corners of Sarah's mouth gave a slight upturn.

"That was my friend Letitia. She loves kids. She'll probably have Ricky eating veggies and practicing yoga by the time you get back, but besides that, she's harmless."

The last thing she wanted to do was leave Ricky with someone else. But it wouldn't do to take him to the hospital. That probably would scare him more. A little one-on-one attention in a pleasant setting might be just what he needed. "Thank you, Elizabeth. I appreciate all you are doing for us."

"Great. Then it's settled." Elizabeth edged away from the bench and stood. "I'll go call her. If she's free, you can make that appointment."

Elizabeth stuffed the garbage into a waste bin beside the shelter's side wall. Sarah walked to where Ricky landed at the bottom of the slide. She knelt beside him and kissed his sweaty forehead.

CHAPTER TWENTY-NINE
FERRETING OUT A DEAL

Letitia slumped in the passenger seat of Elizabeth's plush car Monday afternoon as they parked in front of a rundown strip mall outside Prosper's city limits. "Are we safe?"

"C'mon. You're my bodyguard." Elizabeth turned off the engine and released her seatbelt.

Wedged between a seedy gym and a tattoo parlor was a tiny store. Fred's Pawn Shop, in garish red letters, lighted the window, although a few bulbs were missing.

Waves of heat bounced off the asphalt as Letitia exited the air-conditioned vehicle. "Remind me why we must sell jewelry here, of all places. This area looks rough."

Elizabeth adjusted her sunglasses. "Sarah needs cash, and I don't want to draw attention to her or any of the other shelter women in town."

"Instead of inviting a mugging, why don't we all chip in and give her what she needs?" Letitia sidestepped a broken bottle on the pavement.

A beat-up motorcycle, a rusty generator, and a pile of tires cluttered the sidewalk outside the pawn shop. Elizabeth almost tripped on an orange extension cord lying across the entry mat. She adjusted the lapel of her blouse and tugged down the blazer that fit firmly around her waist.

"Girl, you know we can't become the Solutions ATM." Elizabeth reached for the grimy glass door. "Besides, we want to empower those women to be resourceful and stand independently."

Musty air greeted Letitia inside the shop, and country music piped through the stereo system. The back wall displayed a row of guns locked in a cabinet. Elizabeth marched toward the jewelry, and Letitia followed. White plastic trays in glass cases held dozens of rings organized by gemstone—emeralds, rubies, pearls, sapphires, blue topaz, and small diamonds. Of course, none wore a price tag. The ferret-like shopkeeper emerged from the back room, wiping his pointy chin with the back of his hand. The aroma of Chinese food drifted out with him.

"Hi, Fred." Elizabeth set her designer bag on the countertop.

"Welcome back, Ms. Robinson. What can I do for you today?" He stroked the wispy, black hair on his chin.

Elizabeth studied the selection of rings and found one with a stone about the same size and color as Sarah's. "I'd like to see that opal with the green fire in it."

"Sure." He unlocked the case and pulled out a tray.

Letitia drifted along the exhibit and noted attractive pieces. How sad that beautiful jewelry ended up here. She couldn't imagine being desperate enough to sell a cherished gift.

For the next several minutes, Elizabeth asked Fred to show her various rings like the one inside her purse, taking note of the prices he provided for each. Many were engagement and wedding rings. Letitia's heart ached over the discarded dreams they represented.

Fred shifted his slight weight from one foot to the other, displeased at Elizabeth's leisurely examination. He directed his attention to Letitia. "Is there something you'd like? That diamond necklace just came in."

"Thanks, but I am just keeping her company."

Fred slicked back his thinning greasy hair.

"Let's look at your diamond bracelets." Elizabeth took a few steps down the counter. But before she reached her destination, something caught her eye. "Look at this, Letitia. This pocket watch has a gold-plated cover etched with a steam train."

Fred perked up and moved closer at the excitement in her voice.

"What in the world would you do with that old thing?" Elizabeth usually had much better taste. Why would she want to buy a clunky, old watch?

"This makes me think of train conductors rumbling north, offering help to weary folks fleeing bondage from the South during the Civil War."

"Oh." Sometimes, Elizabeth waxed philosophical. Given their current circumstances, though, Letitia understood her friend's interest in that piece. Timing made all the difference between freedom and danger for many like Sarah.

Fred removed the timepiece from the locked space and dangled it from a silver chain in his hand. "Would you like to hold it?"

"How much?" Elizabeth's charm bracelet jingled as she moved her purse to make room.

The shopkeeper peered at the small paper tag. "Fifty-nine ninety-five. Quite a bargain."

"Does it work?"

"Sure, it does." Fred flipped open the top lid, revealing a clean, white clock face with Roman numerals. Elizabeth stretched out her hand to hold the timepiece. Letitia peeked over her shoulder and imagined hearing a whistle blow, seeing smoke rise from the stack, and feeling the ground shake.

With a sigh, Elizabeth handed the watch back to Fred. "Sorry."

Now, why wouldn't Elizabeth buy herself such an inexpensive trinket? She didn't mind tootling around in the Mercedes. Maybe she shouldn't have said anything to her earlier about expenses. Elizabeth did work hard for others. She deserved a few pleasures.

He rolled his eyes. "You got anything for me today?"

Elizabeth opened her purse and pulled out the plastic bag. "Some very nice things."

Fred's eyes grew wide as he took the fiery opal ring, the tennis bracelet bristling with diamonds, and the gold wedding band. "I gotta take these to the back and look at 'em under the glass."

After he disappeared through the doorway, Letitia corralled Elizabeth. "Why don't you buy that watch? It has special significance to you. It's not a sin to enjoy things on occasion. So why don't you go ahead and treat yourself?"

They heard an unseen woman's voice behind the employee section. "Fifty-one round diamonds, total of five carats, I-J color . . ."

Fred muttered something unintelligible, then let out a whistle.

"How much do you think we can get for Sarah?" Letitia leaned forward to eavesdrop on Fred and the woman in the back.

"Shh." Elizabeth elbowed her.

"SI2 clarity, bead-set, polished finish." The unseen woman sounded impressed.

Fred emerged from the back room and shuffled toward the counter with a frown. "Lots of charcoal and flaws in these." He scratched his belly. "I can give you ninety for the lot."

"Those pieces have to be worth more than that!" Letitia turned to stalk out the door. She wasn't going to let that guy bamboozle them. Enough was enough.

Elizabeth pointed at the business license posted on the wall behind the register. "I can't quite make out the date printed there, but it looks to me like that expired two years ago."

Fred strained his neck to see where she pointed. "Must have the new one in the office."

She patted her hair. "You do know there's a substantial fine for operating without a license, right?"

Letitia stared at her friend. This was a side she hadn't seen before, but Elizabeth played a dangerous game. The shopkeeper didn't seem trustworthy.

Fred bared yellow teeth like a cornered animal, then examined the jewelry again. "Seeing how you're a regular customer, I reckon I can give you two hundred."

"Six." Elizabeth didn't bat an eye.

"Four." Fred chewed his bottom lip.

Letitia tracked their haggling like a professional tennis match.

"Make it five, or I go elsewhere."

Fred grumbled, walking to the cash register. He pulled the usual form out of a drawer behind the counter and shoved it toward Elizabeth. While she wrote down her name and address, he opened the cash drawer. "Hundred-dollar bills okay?"

"No. I'd like eight fifties and five twenties."

"Yes, ma'am." He glowered as he counted bills from the till.

Way to go, Elizabeth. Letitia refrained from cheering out loud. Her friend sure was a savvy negotiator. Hopefully, this money would buy Sarah enough time to see if she could take care of herself and Ricky. That way, she wouldn't go running back to a man who supported her financially but beat her. Cute, little Ricky deserved a peaceful home.

Elizabeth and Fred exchanged paperwork and the stack of bills. "It's been a pleasure doing business with you," she said, stuffing the money into her leather purse. "Be sure to update that license soon." Elizabeth waltzed out the door with Letitia in her wake.

Once inside the Mercedes, Letitia said, "Elizabeth! You sure showed him."

"He made me so mad," Elizabeth said, looking behind her to back out of the parking space. "Sarah has suffered enough. She deserves better."

"Totally agree. But I hope he doesn't try to get back at you for the whole business license thing."

CHAPTER THIRTY

THE DISCOVERY

Letitia helped Ricky climb to her kitchen counter and handed him a cherry Popsicle. Before she had the wrapper off one for herself, the phone rang.

"*Buenas noches,*" she chirped.

"I hope you had a good night, too," Betty said, "but it's only afternoon."

Letitia giggled. She had much to learn about speaking Spanish.

"I'm going to take Ida Lou to the funeral home to meet Terrence. Not sure how long we're going to be. Think you could walk Sweetie in a little while?"

"Sure. You know I love that dog." Letitia watched Ricky slurp his frozen treat. "And I've got company here who'll like her, too." A piece of Popsicle fell from the child's mouth. She couldn't catch it without losing the receiver. The bright red chunk avalanched down Ricky's lime-green t-shirt.

"Who's there with you?" Betty asked.

"A handsome, young man." Letitia couldn't resist baiting her friend as she flicked the fallen icy chunk straight into the sink.

"Is this another guy you met at Friday night bingo?"

"Nope. Met him on Sunday after church, so I know the Lord sent him to me." Letitia drawled *Lord* for good effect.

"And you let this stranger into your house?"

Letitia nearly chuckled out loud at Betty's agitation. "Uh huh. He's in the kitchen with me."

Betty gasped. "When the Lord gave out good sense, you must have gotten in line behind a goose! Don't you know how vulnerable lonely widows are?"

"I'm touched you're worried about me." She truly was. "But I know what I'm doing."

"I hope so because I don't have time to take care of you today. You'd better make sure you don't get distracted by this man and forget to walk the dog."

"I'll remember." Letitia's Popsicle dripped down the wooden stick onto her hand. She turned on the faucet, held Ricky's hands with hers under the water, then set the rinsed wooden sticks on the sink's edge. "We'll go over as soon as we finish setting up the ranch."

"What ranch?" Betty's voice squeaked.

"Our new one." Letitia hummed her favorite Ella Fitzgerald tune, "Ain't Misbehavin'," as she dabbed Ricky's t-shirt with a damp kitchen rag in a futile attempt to remove the red stain. Hopefully, Sarah wouldn't be mad about the shirt.

"You barely know this guy, and you've already bought property together?"

Ricky cocked his head at the loud voice coming through the phone. She handed him the washed Popsicle stick and did mock swordplay with him.

"Yeah. We've got farm animals fenced in near the barn, and we need to get hay for their dinner." Letitia couldn't hold back a peal of laughter.

"You'd better explain what on earth you're talking about before I lose my mind."

"I met Ricky at the Easter egg hunt yesterday. Elizabeth wanted to take his mom on an errand, so I offered to bring him home with me for the afternoon."

Betty heaved a deep sigh. "So, you're babysitting a child from the shelter."

"Yup."

"Well, why didn't you tell me that up front?"

"And miss the fun of teasing you? Not on your life." Letitia could practically see Betty shaking her head. The image made her want to laugh all over again.

"Look, I've got to go. Ida Lou's standing by the front door with her purse over her arm. I'll call you when we get back."

"*Adios*." Letitia hung up, then helped Ricky off the counter. "C'mon, buddy, let's finish corralling those cows."

Ricky reached for her with a red-stained hand, pulled her toward the barn made from a tissue box, and pointed to an empty spot in the carpet pasture. "We need more moos."

Letitia settled on an ottoman, opened the bag of plastic animals, and put out three more brown horses with black manes to graze on Berber loops. Squatting beside her, Ricky found spots for twelve sheep, six cows, four goats, and two pink pigs. He surveyed his ranch with satisfaction.

"Neigh! Neigh!" Letitia grabbed one horse and propelled it across the couch. Ricky jumped up and galloped in pursuit.

Collapsing in a hug at the end of the sofa, they giggled. Ricky untangled himself to reach into the bag and remove an orange-and-white collie. "Woof, woof."

"Hey, that reminds me. You want to see a real doggie?"

Big, blue eyes sparkled at her. "Let's go!"

"C'mon. We'll go for a walk. Do you need to go potty first?"

Ricky nodded, and Letitia took him to the bathroom. After he finished, she helped him pull his shorts up. "Good boy! Do you want to flush?"

He stood on tiptoe and strained to reach the silver lever. As he pulled, he sang out, "Bye-bye."

Letitia's lips twitched in amusement. It had been a long time since flushing a toilet entertained her. She lifted the little boy to reach the sink and turned on the faucet so he could wash his hands. "You're heavy, kiddo."

"I am a big boy now," he said.

She set him down and held out her hand. "You ready to go see somebody special?"

Ricky dodged her outstretched arm and ran into the living room, where he grabbed a pig. "Hurry up! I'll beat you to the door."

Outside, hot sunshine greeted them. The AC units on nearby villas groaned as they tried to keep the homes cool.

As Letitia led Ricky across the lawn toward Ida Lou's place, she breathed deeply, appreciating the fragrance of sweet almond bush flowers. Juan trimmed a boxwood hedge. "How are you this afternoon?" she asked and gave him a big smile.

His broad shoulders turned toward her. "Fine, thank you," he said, dangling the pruning shears.

Noticing dirt rings crusted on the man's neck and half-moon sweat stains under his armpits, she asked, *"Muy caliente?"*

"Yes, it is very hot." His words sounded stilted.

How did he endure the heat outside hour after hour?

Ricky put his hands over Juan's on the shears and tried to close them, mimicking the movement Juan had been making. However, instead of taking away the tool, Juan added his strength to the boy's and controlled the blades as they opened and closed on several green sprigs at Ricky's height.

"Is this your son?"

Letitia gave Juan an impish grin at the gallant remark reversing her birthday a few decades. "No, this is my new friend. We're going to walk a dog for a neighbor. Would you like us to bring you something to drink?"

"Oh, yes, please." Juan set down the shears, then pulled a rag from his back pocket to wipe the sweat off his forehead.

"We've got an errand to run first, but after that, we'll bring iced tea." Letitia held out her hand, but Ricky didn't budge from the man's side.

"No. I work." His small lips pursed.

"No. You go," Juan gently instructed. The boy poked out his bottom lip, but he obeyed.

Letitia hustled to Ida Lou's garage and keyed in the code. Ricky stood beside her with longing glances toward Juan, who resumed clipping branches. They heard yips from inside the house as soon as the garage door rattled open. Ricky charged ahead.

When Letitia opened the interior door, Sweetie's whiskered face peered up at the child. She stopped barking and sniffed Ricky, then rubbed against his legs with her tongue hanging out. Then, after a quick pat on the head, she shot off down the hallway. The little boy hesitated only a second before he raced after the dog.

"Hey, you two, wait for me!" What in the world were those two up to?

Letitia followed, hoping the dog and boy wouldn't break anything as they careened toward the back of the house. When she made it to the master bedroom, she saw a little denim-clad bottom sticking up in the air like an inchworm, with the boy's head and half of his torso concealed under the bed. The dust ruffle moved in a ghostlike wave.

"Ricky, come here." She couldn't have the child playing around under Ida Lou's bed.

The boy withdrew from under the coverlet, his red hair mussed and poking up in all directions. Then Sweetie's head popped out from behind the bedspread, a plastic banana in her mouth.

The toy squeaked when the dog chomped down. Ricky reached for the toy, but the dog took off before he could grab it. Sweetie dodged to the other side of the mattress. Not to be outdone, the freckled child scrambled to follow.

The impromptu circus might have gone on for hours, but Letitia hurled a pillow to barricade Sweetie by the bedside table in the corner. The feather missile halted Ricky in his tracks, blockaded Sweetie's maneuvers, and narrowly missed the lamp. Letitia panted. "Yoga's not doing enough for my cardio."

Ricky pointed a chubby finger at a framed photograph on Ida Lou's bedside table. "Mommy!"

Letitia picked up the picture of a smiling young woman in graduation attire. Though the hair and eye colors differed from Ricky's, the heart-shaped face and perky nose were identical. As she looked from the photo to Ricky, the resemblance was unmistakable. "Wow, this lady sure does look like her, doesn't she?"

She set the picture back on the table. The child put his little pink pig next to the frame and kissed the glass.

Sweetie climbed from under the pillow, shook herself, and rattled metal tags.

"Let's take the doggie for a walk and get Juan a drink."

"Okay, but I hold the doggie."

Letitia led her merry troop outside. She couldn't wait to tell Betty and Elizabeth about the picture in Ida Lou's bedroom.

CHAPTER THIRTY-ONE

CONNECTING THE DOTS

Charles' stomach growled as dinnertime approached, but he didn't have the energy to do anything. He slumped in his leather chair, elbows on knees and chin in hands. Stains on the couch from the coffee still showed, although he'd done his best to remove them.

All day long, memories of arrests and court testimonies tortured him. Criminals leered at him and crowed about getting even for ruining their lives. Collages of newspaper headlines and crime scenes collided, highlighting the real chance harm had come to his wife and son.

No one had seen Sarah except the old neighbor Connell, who'd talked with her and Ricky before they had left for the playground Saturday. No follow-up reports had been filed on the armed fugitive reported loose in their jurisdiction. The whole force had been on the lookout, but not a single lead had turned up.

He wished Sarah were snuggling and watching his favorite, old war movie with him. Instead, the silence of the empty house terrified him. He couldn't stand the absence of her clattering pots and pans in the kitchen, fixing good meals, and his boy saying *beep beep* while zooming toy cars under foot.

Another memory flashed. Sarah cowered by the closet as he punched a hole in the drywall because she hadn't ironed his shirt right. He shook his head to clear the image. He needed to tell her how much he loved her—if he got another chance.

Frantic calls to the sarge resulted in nothing but grunts of irritation. Not wanting to wear out his welcome, he picked up his cell and phoned Doug. "You hear anything?"

"Not yet."

Charles let loose a string of curse words.

"Hang in there, buddy. Something's gonna turn up."

Charles ran a hand through spiky hair. "Sarge should let me come in and stay on top of the databases."

"We've got Sarah and Ricky's faces, dates of birth, and descriptions everywhere. We'll find them."

"But will we find them in time?" Without waiting for an answer, Charles disconnected.

Too agitated to sit, he stomped barefooted into the kitchen. The coffeemaker mess was gone, and he yanked open the fridge for a beer. The room smelled better, too. Nothing seemed out of order—even the milk wouldn't expire for four more days. *Did Ricky have anything to drink?*

Charles popped the top on his can, remembering his troubled youth. Food had been challenging to come by as Mom had raised him alone. His earliest memory was hiding under the bed when their entire trailer home shook from his dad pounding on the aluminum front door, demanding to be let inside.

He never wanted to be a deadbeat like his dad. Charles worked hard to provide for his family. He surveyed the kitchen with its oak cabinets and stainless-steel appliances. Sarah hadn't wanted for anything. True, she didn't have much spending money, but he gave her a beautiful home and the freedom to raise Ricky without having to work or worry about daycare. They went out to dinner once a month. She had nice clothes. He'd even given her expensive jewelry, something his mother had never had.

He wandered to the bedroom and looked for any clue he might have overlooked earlier. He rifled through the dresser to see if clothes were missing, but everything was arranged in neat stacks, like always. He stormed to the closet. All in rows on hangers. Even the shoes aligned in formation. He yanked open the clothes hamper and pulled out every piece of dirty laundry to see if anything might be hidden at the bottom.

After the frenzy subsided, he sank onto the bed. Staring at the mess of clothes on the floor, he noticed the white eyelet nightgown— with a brownish-orange stain around the front collar. Sarah had worn that the last night they were together. Dried blood stained the neckline where she'd wiped her face after his attack.

He picked up the gown and held the soft material to his cheek, detecting a slight trace of her fruity perfume clinging to the fabric. What if he never got to hold her again?

He must solve the mystery of her disappearance. "Think, Charles!" he said to mute walls. "You've been in law enforcement for years. What's the next angle to investigate?"

He reviewed facts. Sarah didn't have a credit card or vehicle, so law enforcement databases wouldn't pick up anything there. Her only friend was Gabby, Doug's girlfriend. And she wouldn't have loaned

Sarah a car or given her a ride without him hearing about it. Could someone else be involved with her without his knowledge?

He paced the room, clutching the nightgown in his fist. There couldn't be another man. Charles seldom took Sarah to office parties, and she didn't go anywhere she could meet someone—except the grocery store, and she always had Ricky with her. A flicker of fear tightened his stomach. What if she'd reconnected with her parents?

Impossible. He monitored her computer and cell phone use. Checking mileage on the car ensured he knew her travel routes. He controlled the key to their post office box and returned every pathetic letter Sarah's parents sent. Had one managed to slip through? He dropped the gown to the floor.

For several months after they married, Sarah had written letters to her folks, which she asked him to get stamps for and mail. But he'd tossed them into trash receptacles away from home. She'd made a special card inviting her parents to Ricky's first birthday party. But he never sent it.

Charles glanced at a photo on the bookshelf. Blue balloons framed Sarah's smiling face as she sat beside Ricky and his first birthday cake. She had no idea how much trouble he'd spared her by keeping away those nosy parents. They would have micromanaged every decision.

When Sarah received no response from her parents about Ricky's celebration, she finally gave up. Secretly relieved, Charles commiserated with her. He commented how cruel her parents were to ignore their only grandchild. He'd wondered aloud why her parents refused to forgive them for being in love and eloping. Then he held her in his arms while she cried, promising never to leave her.

Sarah's parents stopped sending letters. A few months ago, he had driven by their home and seen a For Sale sign in the yard. He'd sighed with relief. Finally, he had Sarah and Ricky all to himself with no worries about anyone luring them away. But if his wife didn't have friends or family helping her, and there was no proof of foul play, what happened?

As he prowled the room, Charles stepped on something sharp. "Ouch!"

He hopped on one leg, lifted the injured foot, and saw a tiny V carved into the skin of his heel. He rubbed the spot a moment, then eased his foot down. Kneeling, he ran his hand along the carpet until he located a bent piece of metal with a pearl dangling from it. It was part of the necklace Sarah's parents had given her for graduation, the one he had broken during one of his violent episodes. Where was the rest? Maybe he could find the pearls and have the necklace repaired as a way of apology. He could go to a jeweler—

The tennis bracelet! He'd forgotten about that. He yanked out the jewelry box drawers again. He'd given her only one other thing with much monetary value: an opal ring. It wasn't there.

He had a lead. Starting bright and early tomorrow morning, he'd visit pawn brokers and interview them. What if a robber forced Sarah's hand so Ricky wouldn't be harmed? But that didn't make sense with the note in the kitchen. Connell never noticed anyone coming back with Sarah and Ricky to the house. Things didn't add up. Unless . . .

His blood pressure soared. Sarah would never have the guts to strike out on her own. She wouldn't be that daring. Besides, she'd never risk Ricky's well-being.

He hurried to the closet, spun the combination on his safe, and then withdrew receipts and pictures for the diamond bracelet and opal ring. Seeing the receipt for Sarah's wedding ring, he paused. What if she'd gotten fed up with him? Would she hock her wedding ring? His heart pounded. He grabbed the slip of paper and fought not to crush it.

Charles stormed back to the living room. Even if, by a wild stroke of luck, he found a pawn shop owner who recognized the pieces, how far could Sarah have gotten on the money the owner would have paid?

He couldn't think about that now. The first step was finding numbers and addresses for area pawn shops online. At least, he had a plan. As soon as businesses opened tomorrow, he would knock on doors. He would find his wife and son if it was the last thing he did. And somebody was going to pay for the worry caused.

CHAPTER THIRTY-TWO
STUNNING VISION

Betty sank onto the edge of the bed and loosened the brogans over swollen ankles. Helping Ida Lou take care of funeral arrangements had kept her on her feet most of the day.

Hoping to get a quick nap, she rolled onto her side on the soft mattress, snuggled her favorite pillow, and pulled the quilted comforter around her waist. She closed her eyes and felt her legs twitch as they relaxed. The next thing she knew, *Donovan called for her to hurry so they could drive for ice cream. He beeped the car horn impatiently.*

The insistent phone ringing on her bedside table dissipated the pleasant dream. Betty groped to find it and swiped *Accept.*

"*Comma estev, mi amigos!*" chirped an all-too-familiar voice.

How could anyone butcher a language that badly? Betty disconnected the call and rolled over. Two seconds later, the phone dinged again. She picked it up and grunted, "Stop calling me."

"Betty?"

Hearing Elizabeth's cultured voice, Betty stopped in the middle of hanging up and brought the phone close to her ear.

"I need to talk with you right away."

She struggled to sit up. "What's so important?"

"I took that new woman at Solutions to the hospital for her forensic exam. The doctor said she was amazed she survived the strangling."

Betty clutched the bedspread.

"She also told Sarah she'd be in grave danger if she returned to her husband."

Betty pulled the comforter tightly to her chest. What must it be like to be betrayed by someone you loved? In the forty-nine years she and Donovan were together, the worst thing he ever did was bring home stinky gym clothes for her to wash.

"I think this young lady has the fire to make it on her own, but I'm not sure how she'll support herself and her son. Do you think there might be an opening for a day-care worker at church?"

"I could call tomorrow and ask." Betty glanced at the clock, which showed the time at almost six. "Have you eaten dinner?"

"No. Would you like to get something with me?"

"How about seafood at Downtown Grille?" That was one of their favorite places.

"I'll pick you up in half an hour."

"I'll be ready." Betty flung off the bedspread, scooted to the edge of her bed, and stood. Before she could reach for a boot, the phone rang again.

"Hello?" Who could this be? Betty grunted as she used her bare foot to slide the boot closer.

"I've been trying to get a hold of you for hours." Letitia's shrill voice barraged her ear. "Where have you been?"

"Helping Ida Lou at the funeral home." Betty lifted the boot. Letitia had such bad timing. Why couldn't she bother someone else for a while?

"That's why I'm calling. I've got to tell you something about Ida Lou!"

Betty gritted her teeth. She didn't have the patience to listen to Letitia's ramblings. "Whatever it is, it'll have to wait. I'm going out with Elizabeth for dinner, and I—"

"Great! I want to tell her, too. What time can you pick me up?"

That woman had no shame, inviting herself along. Wouldn't do to hurt her feelings, though. Betty peered at the clock. "Thirty-five minutes?"

"See you then."

Elizabeth's Mercedes pulled up outside Betty's house at exactly 6:30. A few moments later, Letitia joined them, wearing a peacock-green petticoat embroidered with tiny mirrors, a cadmium-yellow blouse, and a violet silk sari draped over one shoulder.

Goodness! Letitia looked like she belonged to an exotic region featured on the covers of *National Geographic.* They only were going downtown for a bite to eat.

As Letitia climbed into the car, she widened her eyes, drawing attention to blue contact lenses and theatrical false eyelashes. "I'm promoting multicultural awareness."

Elizabeth and Betty kept their opinions to themselves during the short ride to the restaurant. Once inside the establishment, the maître d' looked at Letitia and escorted the threesome to a secluded table in the back.

Letitia swept her garments out of the way as she sat. After the host left them menus, she whispered, "I bet every woman here is jealous of this fab outfit my husband bought me in India. Isn't it amazing I can still fit into it twenty years later?"

"It's . . . stunning, all right." Elizabeth bumped Betty's knee under the table.

She rolled her eyes. "Hopefully, the candlelight will dim the other diners' views, so they won't be beside themselves with envy."

Their sarcasm seemed lost on Letitia, who whipped the linen napkin out of her empty wine glass. With a flourish, she folded it in her lap, then put her elbows on the table as if she were about to explode with something she couldn't wait to say.

A white-coated waiter glided to their table, preventing Letitia's revelation. "What beverages would you ladies like tonight?"

Elizabeth and Betty ordered water with lemon.

"I would like Pinot Grigio," Letitia requested. "And make sure it's clear, please."

Elizabeth exchanged a worried glance with Betty. Nothing they could do. Letitia definitely was of age. Betty hoped Letitia learned moderation after the embarrassment of her getting too tipsy at the wine-tasting fundraiser for Elizabeth.

"Would anyone like an appetizer?" The waiter pointed to the menu features.

"We'll have the bang-bang shrimp." Letitia turned to her friends. "It's the house specialty."

"Very good, ma'am. I'll place that order for you and be right back with your drinks."

The second the waiter left, Letitia exclaimed, "I've got something incredible to tell you!"

Elizabeth opened her menu. "I think we should decide what we want to eat first, so we'll be ready when the waiter returns."

Betty was hungry and studied the evening's specials. Letitia fidgeted in her seat, but she kept silent.

The waiter arrived with the tray of beverages. He set down the drinks, then took their entrée orders. When he left, Letitia burst out, "I know who Ida Lou's daughter is!"

Elizabeth's sculpted eyebrows knit with confusion. "I thought she didn't have any family."

"Actually," Betty said, "I found out today Ida Lou has a daughter, but they've been estranged for years."

Letitia took a sip of her wine, enjoying her friends' attention. She hoped they weren't gawking at her to monitor how much wine she had. "While I babysat little Ricky today, we went to Ida Lou's house to walk Sweetie. Do you know that dog has the funniest toy? A plastic banana that squeaks."

Elizabeth sighed. "Will you please get to the point?"

"Sweetie ran into the bedroom, and Ricky chased her there. And—"

The waiter returned, bearing a plate of fried shrimp. Letitia dove right in, smacking her lips after the first bite into the golden, crunchy breading.

After putting a few shrimp on her appetizer plate, Betty waved her hand for the sari-clad beauty to resume talking.

Letitia continued, speaking while she chewed. "Ricky noticed a portrait on the bedside table."

Betty took one bite of her shrimp, then ejected it into her napkin. "You should have warned me 'bang-bang' meant lots of cayenne pepper!"

"That's the best part." Letitia grinned. "Lights your mouth up like the Fourth of July."

Betty gulped down water, then used her napkin to dab her perspiring brow. She wondered if a fire hydrant might be nearby. "Those are hot as Hades."

Elizabeth covered her mouth with her napkin, spat into it with discretion, and hid the wadded-up bundle under her appetizer plate.

Letitia relished her mouthful. "Anyway, the photo was of a young woman in a college graduation gown. And Ricky said the girl in the picture was . . . his mommy!"

It was too soon to jump to conclusions. "Letitia, are you sure you heard right? That's a lot to believe based on one random comment by a young child."

Elizabeth touched Betty's arm. "Hold on a minute. There might be something to this."

"What?" Betty could understand Letitia making wild assumptions. Happened all the time. But not stable Elizabeth.

"When I took Sarah to the doctor's office today, she said she hadn't seen her parents since college graduation three years ago."

Betty reconsidered the possibilities as the burning on her tongue subsided. "You know, Ida Lou told me she'd lost touch with her daughter . . . after her college graduation . . . three years ago. And when she and I talked about what to put in her husband's obituary notice, she said her daughter's name was Sarah. She told me today that her daughter eloped right after graduation and never returned." The pieces seemed to fit.

"What a cruel thing to do to your parents!" Letitia straightened her sash.

"Right there with firing up your friends." Betty pointed at the half-eaten shrimp on her plate.

The waiter's arrival staved off any retort Letitia might have offered. Tempting aromas wafted over the table as he served the dishes.

"We're going to need more water," Elizabeth croaked.

"Yes, ma'am. Right away." He grinned slightly as he whisked Betty's plate away with discarded shrimp.

Before Letitia could dive in again, Elizabeth suggested, "Let's pray."

The friends bowed their heads. "Lord, thank You for the many blessings You provide. We're grateful for this food. Please help us to know Your will and do Your work."

All three said, "Amen." The waiter refilled their empty water glasses. Then the women grabbed their forks and began sampling the gourmet dishes.

They spent the next few moments enjoying their meals and chatting about the complex situation surrounding Ida Lou and Sarah.

"Three years is a long time to go without speaking to someone," Elizabeth said as she took a dainty bite of her flaky white flounder.

"I don't think I could forgive my daughter—if I had ever been fortunate enough to have one—for taking off without saying goodbye." Letitia cracked a crab leg, dipped the pink meat in butter, and sucked the morsel from between her fingers.

"Ida Lou may not feel that way," Elizabeth pointed out. "If there's even a remote chance of reconciling an estranged family, we must do everything we can to facilitate that."

Betty squeezed fresh lemon on her grouper fillet. "We can't be sure Ricky's mom really is Ida Lou's daughter. It would be cruel to get her hopes up, only to dash them."

Letitia sprinkled salt on her grilled vegetables. "A two-year-old child has no reason to make something like that up." She sipped her wine. "Besides, I saw Sarah at the shelter during the Easter egg hunt."

"That's right!" Betty slammed down her glass so hard that ice water spilled over the rim. "Did she look like the woman in Ida Lou's picture?"

Letitia dabbed at a drop of butter on her chin. "Even with that bruise on her face, the similarity is remarkable. If Sarah isn't Ida Lou's daughter, she has an identical twin."

Elizabeth set down her fork. "There's one way we can know for sure."

"How?" Betty twisted the napkin in her hand.

"Did you get Ida Lou's daughter's full name for the obituary announcement?"

"Yes!" Betty reached for a cheesy biscuit as she searched her memory. "It's McAdams. Sarah McAdams."

"Then all we need to do is check Solutions' intake records." Letitia speared a stalk of broccoli.

"It's not that simple," Elizabeth said. "They're conscientious not to divulge anyone's identity—for their own protection."

Letitia drained the rest of her wine. "I think we should let this go and not meddle. After all, any daughter who'd walk out on her folks must be awful."

Elizabeth smoothed the tablecloth in front of her. "There are risks to be considered, of course. But if Ida Lou and Sarah can be reunited, they could be a tremendous comfort to each other in this terrible time." She looked up, her eyes moist. "I think this sounds like a worthy project for Women United for Him."

Betty groaned. The last few days with Ida Lou had exhausted her. She didn't want to take on anything else.

Letitia huffed. "I don't know."

"Look at it this way," Elizabeth said. "If these two women don't reconnect, Sarah will probably return to her abusive husband because she needs his financial support, and Ida Lou will become a lonely widow."

Letitia sighed. "Okay, I'm game. But mostly because Ricky is adorable, and I want him protected."

"So, are we all in favor of the WUFHs taking action?"

Elizabeth and Letitia nodded. That put the ball in her court. She could get in trouble for compromising someone's confidentiality. But she'd managed to sneak a dog into the hospital without getting arrested for violating hospital sanitation regulations. Maybe her luck would hold.

Orchestrating a conversation between Ida Lou and Sarah would require the utmost delicacy. And if Letitia were mistaken about Sarah being Ida Lou's daughter, they'd all live to rue the day they'd trusted her judgment.

CHAPTER THIRTY-THREE

PLAY BALL

Ahaze enveloped Ida Lou as dusk came. Numbness set in to protect her from the reality Richard never would come home. She rocked back and forth in Richard's worn armchair with an absentminded hold on the old leather football she'd pulled from the bookshelf. Her fingers traced the dimples in the pigskin, and the rough, white laces scraped her fingers as she clung with desperation to something he'd touched. Ida Lou could almost hear the roar of the high school crowd on the fourth down in the last quarter of the regional championship.

Her favorite wide receiver—wearing a black jersey—flew down the field, dodged a cornerback and then made a smart turn. Richard signaled his quarterback, who launched a brown spiral toward his outstretched arms. But a defensive back on the opposing team saw the opening and tried to bat down the ball. With an Olympic leap, Richard snatched it from the defender's fingertips.

Ida Lou held her breath as he landed on the turf. His legs worked like pistons as he sprinted toward the goal line. She wanted to yell and scream like the other fans as the game clock ticked down the last seven seconds, but she made no sound.

In slow motion, the safety closed in on Richard. He dove headfirst across the goal line, his hands extended with the precious package. The whistle blew; the crowd went nuts; and Ida Lou collapsed with relief as the referee threw his arms up in a V.

Sweetie jumped up to sniff the football. Ida Lou checked her watch. She'd been sitting for more than an hour. "Sorry, baby. Guess you need to go out."

The dog's stubby tail twitched, and Ida Lou stood slowly. Walking barefoot and cradling the football under one arm, she passed Richard's office, pausing to inhale the lingering aroma of pipe tobacco. Once in the kitchen, she opened the back door for Sweetie to scoot out.

As Ida Lou reached for the leash hanging on a nearby hook, another image replayed in her mind.

Richard's teammates surrounded him on the field and lifted him onto their shoulders. From that perch, he sought her face in the stands. When he saw her, he gave a smart salute. Ida Lou smiled as she gave a little wave back and closed the door.

She returned to Richard's chair and curled up with happy memories.

"Aren't you proud of me, babe?" Richard asked as he emerged from the locker room.

"You cut over too far in your pattern. Good thing Bucky corrected with his pass."

He doubled over in laughter, then put his muscular arm around her shoulders. "That's my girl. She knows football!"

"When your dad coaches, it comes with the territory." She put her arm around his waist.

Other images floated by of homecoming with yellow rosebuds on a wrist corsage; ice cream dates where they shared a chocolate-vanilla creamy swirl; and Richard carrying Sarah's dirty diaper at arm's length across the bedroom to the trash receptacle, pinching his nose with his free hand.

Ida Lou launched the football as hard as she could across the room. A lamp crashed on impact. "God," she screamed, "why do You take the people I love?"

The lampshade hung at a crazy angle—damaged and out of balance, like her.

"Is this punishment for the wrongs I've done?" Her voice rang in the open space with no response to her challenge. "Answer me!"

The clock ticking in the silence drew Ida Lou's attention. Six o'clock. When they usually sat down for dinner. No need to set the table for two. Was there anything she could have done to save her husband? Maybe she'd killed him with those big breakfasts of bacon, eggs, and hash browns. Perhaps if she'd insisted he get a physical sooner. Or not play eighteen holes of golf in sweltering heat.

Door chimes brought Ida Lou out of her gloomy reverie. Figuring Betty might be checking on her, she pushed out of the armchair and hobbled to the front door. When she swung it open, she saw the neighborhood gardener wearing grass-stained trousers and cradling Sweetie in his arms like a baby.

"My goodness!" Ida Lou reached for her little dog. Sweetie licked Juan's face before going to her. "I don't know what I was thinking when I let her out alone."

The handsome man smiled. "She okay. I found her there." He pointed to the neighbor's mailbox by the street.

"Thank you so much."

The laborer took off his straw hat and smiled at the dog.

"Can I give you money for rescuing my precious pet?"

Juan looked uncertain. Leaving the front door open, Ida Lou whirled toward the hall table where she'd left her handbag.

When she returned, he was still standing there. After putting Sweetie on the floor, Ida Lou extracted two twenties from her wallet and extended them toward the worker.

A look of surprise crossed Juan's face, and he stepped back without touching the money.

"Please, take these for your trouble." No reward could equal Sweetie's value.

Sweetie peeked around Ida Lou's heels, chomping on a red ball, as though asking him to stay and play.

Juan kneeled to pet the little Yorkie. When he stood, he placed his two work-hardened hands over Ida Lou's soft, white ones and closed her fingers over the gift she offered. Drawing back empty-handed, he said, "Have a nice day." He crossed the sidewalk to where bags of mulch sat by plastic containers of red begonias.

Ida Lou stood in the doorway, wondering at the goodness of people who had cared for her in many ways. The gardener had protected Sweetie. Betty had sat with her in the hospital. Letitia had cleaned her house, fixed dinner, and walked her dog. The warmth from their unexpected kindnesses spread through her heart and removed some of the chilly despair. God hadn't abandoned her. He had sent others to help her in this desperate time.

She stuffed the bills into her wallet and returned the purse to the table. After shutting the front door, she removed the ball from Sweetie's mouth and tossed it toward the kitchen.

Following her pet, Ida Lou poured dry rice-and-lamb mix into Sweetie's bowl. Ida Lou stroked the soft fur as the pup gobbled down the food. "God, I don't understand why You took Richard. But I thank You for sending the good people of Prosper to me."

CHAPTER THIRTY-FOUR

MARITAL STEW AND LAUGHINGSTOCK

The ringing phone interrupted Betty as she reached for flannel pajamas. *What now?* All she wanted to do was go to bed.

"Hello." This better not be Letitia bothering her for more Spanish phrases. She had no patience left after the day's challenges.

"Mrs. Herndale? Pastor James here. Have you got a few moments to talk?"

Uh oh. That phrase signaled a long, involved conversation. Betty plopped on her bed and tried to relax. "Sure, Pastor. What do you need?"

He cleared his throat. "Well, this is a bit delicate."

Letitia must have had another prank go awry. Why did she always have to play clean-up?

"Go ahead. You know I keep information confidential."

"Yes, well, that seems to be the problem. Melissa Stout called a while ago and interrupted my dinner. Something that happened earlier today fired her up."

"Goodness. She can be hotheaded. What set her off this time?" Did the pastor know how Melissa ruled like a dictator at the women's circle?

Pastor James made a strange sound as though coughing. "Melissa said AnnMarie corralled her in the grocery story before lunch and alleged Stan was having an affair."

"What!" Betty couldn't control the shock from that revelation.

"Now, hold on a moment!" Pastor James cautioned. "This whole situation has blown out of control, and I don't want you jumping on the wrong train either."

Betty shook her head. What did the preacher want? She didn't want to listen until midnight.

"Pastor James, today has been long and trying. Could you please tell me what you want me to do?" She refrained from adding "this time."

"I am reaching out because it appears the prayer chain may have had a serious miscommunication that caused great harm to one of our families. Since you are in charge of the prayer chain, I hope you can help me sort everything out."

Betty bristled. She trained her team carefully. How dare he imply otherwise. "Pastor, you need to start at the beginning, so I understand the full scope."

She grabbed another pillow and propped up her head. This was going to take a while. She might as well be comfortable.

"Melissa said her husband had lost his mind and run around at the lake, flirting with other women."

"Pastor, you and I know Stan would never cheat on his wife. He's been a respected elder for two decades."

"That's right, but you know how rumors spread in a small town. Melissa claimed she was humiliated and heard congregation members whispering about her behind barely concealed hands.

She said—and I quote—'Did you hear about poor Melissa? She can't keep her husband home.'"

"That's awful. No one is talking about her. Or her husband. She must have a screw loose." Her reservoir of diplomacy had dried up. Betty pounded the pillow beside her.

Pastor James cleared his throat, and she held the phone away from her ear. "Melissa told me she has made a list of five options."

"And those are?" Betty crossed a foot over the other ankle.

"She said, one, get a divorce; two, shoot Stan as soon as he arrives home tonight from the elder's meeting; three, call his mother and let her deal with him; four, pack her suitcase and visit her sister in Florida; or five, hire a hitman."

Betty smacked her forehead with her palm. "How in the world did you respond?"

"I quoted Scripture from Matthew 5:21 when Jesus said, 'You have heard that it was said to the people long ago, *You shall not murder and any who murders will be subject to judgment.*'"

Betty plumped the pillow under her head. "Bet that went over like a lead balloon." Why did he torment her late at night with this craziness? He was the pastor. Shouldn't he fix the problem?

"Yes, well, then Melissa said she couldn't go to Florida because her younger sister just had a Botox treatment, and Melissa couldn't bear the thought of sitting on a beach and comparing thigh-dimple ratios with her."

At that outrageous comment, Betty cackled. "C'mon, pastor. Are you pulling my leg?"

"Unfortunately, no. I tried to tell Melissa how much her husband loved her. Do you know what she said next?"

He had her on the edge of the bed. No way she could predict where this conversation was going. "Do tell."

"She appeared a bit mollified and relayed that Stan did take out the garbage regularly and kept his sports-watching to a minimum on Sundays."

Betty guffawed, and the pastor joined in. He had a hard job shepherding people with their secret hurts and hang-ups. She had no idea how he kept his composure and continued to love his congregation. Nice that he had a good sense of humor.

"She wants me to give Stan the 'Come to Jesus' discussion. I need you to get to the bottom of this, so I can reassure her there is nothing to fear."

"Wouldn't it be easier if she talked with Stan herself?" Betty didn't have time to offer counseling. Besides, she wasn't a licensed counselor. She had to help Ida Lou at the funeral and possibly reconcile with her daughter. As much as she enjoyed chatting with Pastor James, they had other agenda items to cover.

"She's too upset now to listen to reason. She told me to put the fire of God's justice on the backside of a man flirting with the devil and heading straight toward Hell."

Betty envisioned the flames of Melissa's rage engulfing poor Stan Stout. Such a nice man. He shouldn't get pounded with untruths. "Okay. Okay, Pastor. I get the picture. But how am I supposed to fix this? I'm not about to go talk with Melissa."

She bit her tongue from adding he already had her in up to her eyeballs with Ida Lou.

"Could you please backtrack the prayer requests and find where things got messed up? There must be a simple explanation."

One more thing on her list to do tomorrow. But she would take care of it. She didn't want the integrity of the prayer chain compromised. "Any idea where I should start?"

"Melissa mentioned AnnMarie was the one to tell her about Stan fooling around with Bikini Bambis."

"Excuse me?" AnnMarie had a level head and ran a floral business. She wasn't prone to exaggerations. Somebody else had to be at fault.

"You heard right. Melissa said the indiscretions occurred Saturday at the lake."

"AnnMarie and her family have a cabin there. I'll contact her first thing tomorrow and find out what happened. It's too late tonight." Maybe he'd catch the hint about timing.

"Thank you, Betty. I can always count on you."

She heard gratitude in his voice. Now was the time to bring up Ida Lou. "Pastor, I need to talk with you about something."

"Sure. What is it?"

She wanted to tell him how much she missed Donovan and that nights got lonely. She hadn't cleaned out her husband's clothes from their closet. Sometimes, she'd stand there, wrap one of his coat sleeves around her, and rub her face on the smooth leather.

But this wasn't the time for him to worry about her. "Ida Lou may need to talk with you about funeral details and grief counseling. And it seems that one of the young women at our shelter may be her estranged daughter."

"Whoa. That's a lot going on. Why do you think the young woman is her daughter?"

Betty switched the phone to her other ear. "Elizabeth, Letitia, and I are piecing together facts. We wonder if you would set up a meeting with the daughter and help with counseling? That way, we can confirm the information we have."

"Be happy to. Have to head out in a few moments to pick up my daughter. Choir practice ran late. Could we talk tomorrow to coordinate details?"

"Sure. Maybe I'll have a prayer chain update for you by then." Betty was going to have the hide of whomever messed up this time. She didn't tolerate sloppiness one bit.

"Thanks again, Betty. Have a nice evening."

Indeed. Now, maybe she could go to sleep without anyone bothering her.

CHAPTER THIRTY-FIVE

CALCULATING DISTANCE

When Charles awoke before dawn Tuesday morning, something suffocated him. Lifting his face from the couch, he pushed up with his forearms, and the room began to spin. He waited a moment for the wicked carousel to stop, then gingerly sat upright.

His fingers trembled as they rubbed his prickly chin. He lurched toward the desk and knocked aside empty beer cans to clear space by the computer for his arms. His body smelled sour, and his t-shirt had stains. He didn't have the energy to shower or change.

Why bother? Everything in life was going wrong. There'd been no news about his family, and his boss wouldn't let him come to work. He hadn't found a single clue about Sarah at any of the eight pawn shops he'd visited.

White-hot rage welled up. He slammed his fist down on the computer keyboard so hard that two keys popped out and flew across the room. The lopsided monitor glowed with an idyllic garden desktop background his wife had picked. The image of blooming flowers jeered at him. He missed hearing Sarah's sweet voice.

Where was she? No leads. Staring at the monitor reminded him to check the search history. Maybe that would indicate something about what his wife had done during the couple of days leading up to her disappearance. Mad at himself for not doing that sooner, Charles used the mouse and the undamaged keys to pull up recently viewed websites.

One was a Food Network page with recipes for tuna salad. Charles winced, remembering his tirade against Sarah for ruining his meal. The following site had information about kids' books, giving pointers on how to teach preschoolers to read.

What was Ricky doing? He missed the kid's little arms wrapped around his neck in a cub hug. Sarah was a good mom. He wished his mother had given him half the loving Ricky got. Of course, Sarah didn't have to work. They managed on his salary.

After checking several web pages that showed nothing of substance, Charles got up to relieve himself. The bedroom looked a wreck—linens lay twisted on the mattress; clothes littered the floor; and white toothpaste splattered the bathroom mirror. Charles couldn't wait for Sarah to get back and clean everything. He hated a messy place. But he was not inclined to do anything.

Bloodshot eyes stared back from the mirror as he splashed cold water on his whiskered face. His stomach churned. He wanted another drink to take the edge off but needed to eat. Last night's pizza hadn't settled well.

Returning to the computer, he searched the internet for Sarah's name. With difficulty, he typed "Sarah McAdams" on the busted keyboard. Links to Facebook and Twitter accounts popped up. Had his wife managed to open them without him catching her?

Clicking on those pages revealed strange pictures and odd profiles that proved those were not his Sarah McAdams. LinkedIn showed listings for several people with that name: a consultant in

Texas, a writer/editor in Massachusetts, a middle school band director near Philadelphia, a registered nurse in California, and a banking specialist in New York. More dead ends.

Clenching his teeth, he punched in her maiden name: "Sarah Besco." Still nothing close. With a grunt, he typed, "Richard and Ida Lou Besco." A link popped up at the top of the search page to the *Herald Constellation* online newspaper in Virginia. Hunched forward in concentration, Charles clicked links to get to the announcement in the obituary section.

> BESCO—Richard Steven, 53, of Prosper, died Sunday, April 8, at Memorial Hospital. He was born on March 18 in Atlanta, Georgia. He retired after a thirty-year career in the telecommunications industry. Surviving are his wife, Ida Lou, and his daughter, Sarah McAdams. A memorial service will be held at 4 p.m. April 10 in the Sunset Chapel of The First Church of Prosper. In lieu of flowers, please make donations to the Alexander High School football program in care of Carter Funeral Home.

Charles checked the calendar on his desk. What luck! April 10 was today. If Sarah had gone to see her parents, he could find her.

Heart racing, he printed the obituary and directions to the funeral home and chapel in Prosper. Calculating the distance to be about a two-hour drive, he jumped up to shower, shave, and change. He looked in the closet and grabbed a navy sports coat, a white shirt, and dark trousers. Might need a change of clothes. He lugged those to the car and hung them in the back seat.

He texted Doug to let him know he'd be away a few days, trying to track down his wife's family. He asked him to contact him immediately if headquarters got any updates on the missing-person alert.

CHAPTER THIRTY-SIX
MAKING HEADLINES

Betty thumped outside in her pajamas, housecoat, and brogans to retrieve the local newspaper as the sun's first rays blushed pink. The villas were quiet at this hour. Not even commuters bustled along the street. She marveled over the new red and white begonias planted and mulched around the mailbox area.

Juan's gardening handiwork included a clever herringbone edging created from discarded bricks. Greg, the superintendent, had found a treasure in Juan, who went above and beyond to beautify the grounds.

Wondering if Ida Lou had slept last night, Betty decided to call her later, at a more decent hour.

She headed inside and set the paper on the kitchen table. After preparing her usual breakfast of orange juice and whole wheat toast, she sat at the table and opened the front page. As Betty chewed her first bite, she almost gagged as she read the *Herald Constellation* banner headline: "Mayor Suspected of Stealing Jewelry."

She studied the article in disbelief.

> Prosper—Sheriff Thomas Bottoms III is investigating allegations Mayor Elizabeth Robinson has been selling

stolen jewelry to area pawn shops. Fred Nix, owner of Fred's Pawn Shop, reported the mayor provided him with merchandise valued in the thousands during the last year.

Nix said he got suspicious yesterday when Robinson offered to sell him a diamond bracelet worth three thousand dollars. "I can't really judge whether someone has stolen or not, so I went through with the transaction. But as soon as that woman left my store, I called the sheriff."

"When the citizens of Prosper elected me to keep them safe, I made an oath to uphold the law," Sheriff Bottoms said yesterday in a phone interview. "I intend to keep my promise, even if I have to arrest the mayor. No one, and I mean no one, will break the law and get away with it on my watch."

"If someone has stolen the jewelry, the rightful owners can claim their property if they can provide proof of ownership," Nix said. "We've gotta keep stuff ten days before we can sell it, so family members have a chance to reclaim heirloom pieces."

Nix handed the sheriff's department a stack of receipts documenting payments to Mayor Robinson for twelve jewelry items, including five engagement rings, four solid-gold wedding bands, two watches, and an antique pearl brooch.

"This has become my officers' highest priority," Sheriff Bottoms said. "Why would any woman of integrity have five engagement rings and four wedding bands in one year?"

As of press time, the mayor had not returned reporters' calls. Anyone with information about this case may contact the sheriff's non-emergency line at 555-331-2907.

Betty took a long swig of orange juice. What a sorry example of yellow-bellied journalism. Pictured beside the text column was a serious-looking Sheriff Thomas Bottoms III, wearing a too-large black Stetson. He stood next to Nix in the pawn shop, both men examining jewelry in a glass case.

Impossible!

But doubts arose. What in the world was Elizabeth doing at that slimy place? And why would she be selling jewelry?

Thomas had been a ringleader since his teens, with that weasel Fred Nix as his sidekick. They'd been in some kind of mischief since she'd known them. Once, they stole pies from the auxiliary's fundraiser. Betty caught them red-handed—as cherry juice stained their fingers and faces when she found them hiding behind the fellowship hall, gobbling up the evidence.

She'd complained to Thomas' mom, Candace. However, Mrs. Bottoms refused to see the worms riddling the apple of her eye. Consequently, her son grew up as an opportunist, taking what he could without considering the effect on others.

He hated Elizabeth for initiating a public inquiry last year about why he had authorized funding a beach resort weekend retreat for his officers with tax dollars. Bottoms said the event was for "aquatics training." Yeah, right. The man simply could not be trusted.

Betty phoned Elizabeth—who *could* be trusted.

"Good morning." The mayor's refined pronunciation came across perfectly, even at seven in the morning.

How could she be calm? Elizabeth must not have read the paper yet. "Have you seen today's *Herald*?"

"Unfortunately, yes."

Betty waited for a few beats for Elizabeth to elaborate on the situation. Then, when silence reigned, she prompted, "What are you going to do?"

"Nothing. I refuse to respond to such drivel."

Oh, Elizabeth could be stubborn. Betty shoved aside her plate in agitation, sending the butter knife plummeting to the floor. "You've got to do something! You can't sit there and let them run a smear campaign."

"I appreciate your concern, dear, but there's nothing I can do. If I tell the truth, others might be harmed."

"Who are you protecting?" Betty leaned over with a napkin to dab at the sticky spread by her heel.

"Women at Solutions have been giving me things to sell."

So, that was it. Elizabeth's desire to help others landed her in hot water. That wasn't right. Her misinterpreted actions could destroy her political career.

Betty slumped in her wooden kitchen chair, still holding the sticky napkin. "Why didn't you use the church's emergency fund?"

"I wanted to honor their desire to be independent."

"Yeah, and look where that got you." How was she supposed to protect her friend?

"The sheriff can prove no wrongdoing because I stole nothing."

"But unless you come forward to explain, the public will presume guilt." Betty folded the messy napkin and swiped at another glob.

"People who know me will dismiss this as a cheap shot on a slow news day."

That presumed people looked deeper for answers, which might be expecting too much. Many loved controversies. Pinning the phone to her shoulder, Betty threw the napkin away and went to the sink to wash her hands. "You have a loyal following. But can you afford to alienate swing voters who want to see change? We've all trusted you to break up the good, ol' boys' reign."

"I've made up my mind, Betty, and that's all there is to it."

Fine. No one could knock sense into that woman when she bowed up like that. Elizabeth was resolute when walking out what she believed God expected.

Betty would enlist Letitia's aid to lobby for a fair investigation to prove Elizabeth's innocence. They'd fight for Elizabeth, even if she didn't stand up for herself. Sheriff Bottoms knew about the shelter for victims of domestic violence, though he'd not proven sympathetic to their cause. Still, he wouldn't let a lie remain. Would he?

"Well, I'm going to support you, no matter what. But let the record show, I think you're making a mistake to remain silent and not address these allegations." Betty shut off the faucet. "Anything new on the Sarah/Ida Lou connection?"

Elizabeth heaved a weary sigh. "I called the night manager at Solutions after we got home from the restaurant."

"And?" Betty dried her hands on a dish towel draped over the oven handle.

"Our Sarah with the bruised face has the last name McAdams."

"That doesn't prove she's Ida Lou's daughter." Betty put the butter dish back in the fridge. "But it seems more likely."

"We won't know for sure without asking. When are you going to see Ida Lou?"

Betty refilled her glass. "At the memorial service this afternoon. I don't know whether finding out about Sarah will help her or put her over the edge. Let me think for a while and call you back."

The day posed picklish problems with Ida Lou facing a funeral, Sarah dodging a maniac, and Elizabeth absorbing a career-crushing attack. Could she ride herd on all the goings-on to ensure the folks God had entrusted to her care remained safe?

Betty recited a part of Psalm 61 for comfort as she raised her eyes heavenward. "'You have been my refuge, a strong tower against the foe.'" She sighed, feeling better. Then she recalled a Bible teaching about King David praying this passage while fleeing for his life from a conspiracy. If only the brogans could carry her swiftly ahead of evil plots.

CHAPTER THIRTY-SEVEN

BE DEVOTED TO ONE ANOTHER

Was it too early to call Letitia? Betty wanted her to get the sheriff off Elizabeth's back. Letitia acted goofy, but she could be a formidable ally. Letitia was close to Bottoms' mom and knew the family well.

Opting to let her friend sleep in a little longer, Betty opened the bedside table's drawer, removed her Bible, and took it to the white rocker on the porch. Sitting there with God's Word and the cool morning breeze helped her face a problem.

She opened to a dog-eared page and studied Romans 12:9-11. "Love must be sincere. Hate what is evil; cling to what is good. Be devoted to one another in love. Honor one another above yourselves. Never be lacking in zeal, but keep your spiritual fervor, serving the Lord."

Her fingertips traced along the lacy fern fronds dangling from the pot beside her chair. She looked heavenward. "Lord, You gave us the idea of Women United for Him a year ago. Since then, Elizabeth, Letitia, and I have done our best to help those in need, as Jesus asks us to do."

She squeezed her eyes shut. "Since I know You hate what is evil, I ask You to protect Elizabeth from the lies flying around about her. You know what she's doing for those women at the shelter."

Betty opened her eyes to see the sun's rays casting a spectacular show of sherbet colors in pink, peach, and orange. "And, Lord, I sure would appreciate it if You could ask Letitia to take care of Sweetie instead of me. You know about my allergies and how antihistamines make my heart race. I'd like to be on this earth a while longer to do Your work. And I'll have a bunch more spiritual fervor if I'm not distracted by sneezing, coughing, and trying to breathe."

She rocked back and forth, then read verses twelve and thirteen. "Be joyful in hope, patient in affliction, faithful in prayer. Share with the Lord's people who are in need. Practice hospitality."

Why did the Lord allow His children to suffer? Being faithful wasn't easy. She'd almost fainted when they'd closed the casket lid over Donovan. How could she make it through another funeral? Although she tried to bear up for everyone, including their son, Ben, she often felt as fragile as a soap bubble floating above a warm bath. Did anyone see beyond her outward show of competence to the inner vulnerability?

Juan lugged a hose to water new flowers by the mailboxes.

"Hey!" She waved. He had a good work ethic.

What did he do for lunch? She'd never seen him drive a car. Maybe she should invite him to have a sandwich and picnic on the porch with her. Then she could get to know him better. He'd fertilized her rose bush without her asking. What a thoughtful thing for him to do. How could she return the favor? But first, she had to take care of Elizabeth and Ida Lou.

She had household chores to tend to and hurried to the laundry room to start a load of clothes. Then, moving to the den, she spritzed lemon-scented furniture polish onto the coffee table and swiped it with a dust rag. Too bad removing the blot on Elizabeth's name couldn't be that simple.

She made the bed, then showered. Betty dressed in a button-down navy blouse and yellow skirt and rolled her hair. Since the funeral wasn't until four that afternoon, she might as well be comfortable. If she went to check on Ida Lou this morning, there was no sense getting dog hair on her lovely, black dress.

She could wait no longer to dial Letitia. A groggy voice responded with a grunt.

"Wake up, woman. Daylight is burning." Betty trilled her voice extra, knowing it annoyed Letitia, who was not an early bird.

"It can burn without me. That's why I have tinfoil covering my bedroom windows."

"But there's lots going on you need to know about." Betty tapped her toe.

"At this unearthly hour?"

"Elizabeth's in trouble." Betty balanced the receiver against her shoulder so she could open the dryer door. "The sheriff's after her."

Letitia groaned. "You can't be serious."

"It's the truth! Sheriff Bottoms is investigating Elizabeth for stealing jewelry and selling it at a pawn shop." Betty pulled out warm, meadow-scented clothes and hugged the bundle against her chest, trying not to drop the phone.

"She would never do anything like that!"

"You and I know that. But others may not think so." Betty headed to the bedroom. "You know how small-minded people can be."

"I was with her at that dumb pawn shop this weekend. I warned her Fred Nix was a weasel."

"What else do you know?" Betty dropped the laundry on the bed to fold.

"The stuff she's been selling belonged to women sheltered at Solutions."

"She told me that a little while ago. Why isn't she going to do anything in her own defense?" Betty asked as she untangled the clothing.

"Somebody has to stop the lies." Letitia huffed on the other end of the line.

Betty separated one sock from the pile, set it aside, and then looked for the match. "I agree, we can't let this rumor continue. Now, you might be implicated, too. This could hurt you and ruin any chance Elizabeth might have for reelection." Betty shook out a dress to eliminate wrinkles.

"I'm going to take care of this," Letitia said in a matter-of-fact tone.

"How?" Betty reached for the iron on the top shelf of the closet.

"You'll see."

As Betty plugged in the iron, her mouth lifted into a smile, remembering an image from elementary school. Lanky nine-year-old Letitia, hair in pigtails, had jumped on the back of a boy who'd taunted Betty and called her "fatty." Letitia had knocked him to the ground and pummeled him with her fists. After that, the kids never troubled Betty again.

"I have a feeling Sheriff Thomas Bottoms the Third is about to have a bad day."

"By the time I'm through with him, he's gonna wish he'd never opened his big mouth."

The phone clicked. *Dear Lord, we need Your intervention for the truth to be told and justice to be had.*

With Letitia dealing with Bottoms, Betty could focus on Ida Lou. *Father, You give us hope in dark times, and Your Word teaches us that You work in unexpected ways. Please help me know how to comfort Ida Lou. And bring up the topic of her daughter this morning—but only if You know it will help.*

Betty's jaw relaxed, and the butterflies in her stomach disappeared. She called Ida Lou. "Hi, this is Betty. Would it be okay if I came to see you in a few minutes?"

"Absolutely. I'd love the company. Would you like breakfast?"

Since a slice of toast hardly seemed adequate nourishment for a busy day, Betty accepted the invitation.

"Great. Give me about fifteen minutes, then come on over."

Never good at waiting when something important was on the line, Betty fought anxiety by turning on the radio. She hummed along to the gospel song, "Be Still My Soul."

The peaceful music washed over her. Then the tempo segued to a rousing version of "Joyful, Joyful, We Adore Thee." Betty's feet kept time to the beat as her achy fingers waved. She put away the rest of the clean clothes and finished listening to "Great Is Thy Faithfulness" before heading outside.

CHAPTER THIRTY-EIGHT

FACING UNKNOWNS

When Ida Lou opened her door, Sweetie jumped on Betty's legs, the excited little dog's toenails catching on the brogan laces.

Ida Lou scooped up her pet, murmuring apologies. "Please come in. Do you like blueberry bagels?"

"Love them, especially if you've got cream cheese." Betty followed, giving a wide berth to Sweetie, who leaned over her owner's shoulder with a drooling, pink tongue.

Seated in the kitchenette, Ida Lou passed a container of honey-nut cream cheese. "I'm so glad you came over. I'm upset about a stupid thing I did last night."

Betty swallowed a bite of bagel. "What happened?"

"I let Sweetie out alone. She got down to the road. I don't know what might've happened if the gardener hadn't rescued her. She might have been out all night by herself."

Betty looked at the fuzzy, little face by her feet. "Juan is wonderful. Last week, he rescued a raccoon with a peanut butter jar stuck on its head."

Ida Lou chuckled. "Sorry I missed that." Her smile faded, and she fiddled with the napkin by her plate. "I've never been careless with Sweetie. Do you think I'm losing it?"

Betty put down her bagel and studied her companion. Her eyes were clear, and her bearing erect. She wore jeans with a crisply ironed, striped, blue shirt.

"No, honey, you're not losing it. You're just in a tunnel of grief, which makes doing even simple things difficult. Shock has a way of protecting us from dealing with too many feelings at once."

Ida Lou's shoulders relaxed. "That's good to hear. I'm not sure how I'll handle the funeral this afternoon."

"Under the circumstances, I think you're holding up admirably. When I lost Donovan, I didn't get out of bed for two days."

Ida Lou stared at her glass of tomato juice. "I couldn't wait to get up. I hated lying in that huge space without him."

Betty gazed into the backyard. "Donovan used to give the most wonderful foot massages. He'd hold my leg in his lap on the couch and rub lotion onto the balls of my feet to help circulation."

Sweetie stopped patrolling below the table for crumbs and leaped into Betty's lap.

"Ooh!" Betty froze in panic as Sweetie licked a morsel of cream cheese off the plate.

"Bad dog!" Ida Lou jumped up and swept the animal into her arms. "I'll be back in a minute." She marched toward the bedroom with an unrepentant Sweetie looking back from under her arm.

Brushing fur off her skirt, Betty tried to slow her breathing. Although Noah had allowed critters on the ark, that involved special circumstances. Dogs belonged outside, not in a person's lap! At least, she'd had the foresight not to wear her good black dress.

Ida Lou returned without her pet. "I'm sorry about that. I don't know what got into her. She's normally well behaved."

Eager to get her mind off the dog's attack of friendliness, Betty launched into the discussion she needed to have. "Ida Lou, I found out information last night that I think you'd want to know. But I'm not sure how to tell you."

Ida Lou's light brown eyebrows shot up. "Betty, if there's something I should hear, just say it."

Betty pushed away the plate containing the contaminated bagel. "It's about your daughter."

Ida Lou bolted upright. "You know something about Sarah?"

"Maybe. I'm not positive, but—"

"Please tell me. Not knowing anything for three years is worse than whatever you might reveal."

Betty looked at her boots, praying for the right words. "My friends and I volunteer at a local shelter. A new woman came in Saturday from out of state. Her name is Sarah."

"What kind of shelter?"

Betty swallowed hard. "A home for . . . battered women."

Ida Lou gasped. "Do you think she could be my daughter?"

"Only you two would know for sure. But the pieces I've been able to put together indicate it's possible."

Ida Lou stood up so quickly that she knocked her plate off the table. "I want to go to her right now."

Betty retrieved pieces of bagel from the floor—which had, fortunately, landed cream-cheese-side-up. "It's not that simple." Sarah's right to privacy had to be respected. Betty hadn't heard from Elizabeth yet if Sarah wanted to see anyone outside the shelter.

"Why not?" Ida Lou folded her arms across her chest.

Betty motioned for Ida Lou to sit. "Solutions has confidentiality rules. I can't take you there . . . or even tell you her last name—"

"So, you're just going to bring it up and leave me hanging?" Ida Lou trembled from head to toe.

Betty whisked bagel crumbs into the trash bin. "I could deliver a message. If you'd like to write a note, I'll have someone take it to her straight away."

Ida Lou brought her hands to her chest in prayer. "Yes! I'll do that. I have to know if this young woman is my baby." She ransacked a kitchen drawer and pulled out paper and a pen. Then she gave Betty a pleading look. "Can you at least tell me if she's all right?"

Betty hesitated. "She looks like she's had a rough time. But she's safe where she is."

"Then there's not a moment to lose." Ida Lou gripped the pen and started writing.

Betty watched the furious scribbling, wishing she hadn't let Elizabeth and Letitia talk her into doing this. What if they'd made the wrong decision? "Ida Lou . . ."

The woman kept writing.

"Honey, even if this is your daughter, what if she doesn't want to see you?"

Ida Lou looked up, tears shimmering in her determined eyes. "I can at least tell her how much I love and miss her."

Should she mention the little boy? No. Hoping for a reunion with her daughter presented enough challenge without adding the potential for a grandson. "There's something else to consider."

"What?" The pen paused mid-air.

"The husband of the woman at the shelter is in law enforcement. He's been violent."

Ida Lou's eyes took on a cold, hard look. "Richard knew something was wrong with that Charles."

"Whether this is your daughter or not, you could be putting yourself in danger by contacting her. I'm not sure that's wise, especially with everything you face today."

Ida Lou straightened her back. "We Bescos stick together. I will not abandon my daughter in her time of need." After folding the note, Ida Lou handed it to Betty. "Wait here a minute. There's something else I'd like you to take to her."

Betty held the precious paper. Such a flimsy object, yet the words penned on it could alter lives. *Lord, may each of these women show a sincere love that brings them joy.*

Ida Lou returned and handed Betty a stack of letters bound with navy blue ribbon.

"What's this?" The top postmark was dated three years ago with a red *Return to Sender* stamped over the address.

"This is proof to my daughter of our attempts to find her and let her know we loved her, no matter what."

Betty cradled the package in her arms. "I'll do my best to deliver this. But you need to understand the woman at the shelter may choose not to respond."

Ida Lou dropped her head. "I understand. But we won't know unless we try."

Betty walked home as quickly as her weary old legs would go. She needed to talk to Elizabeth. She prayed they hadn't raised Ida Lou's hopes needlessly.

CHAPTER THIRTY-NINE

COMING UP SHORT

Sarah tossed and turned on the twin bed at Solutions. She peeked over the side at Ricky, asleep on the floor nearby. He curled in a fetal position on two folded towels with a teddy bear tucked under his chin. She reached down to caress his back and pulled a sheet around his little shoulder.

As she stared at the ceiling, her resolve to be free flickered. Obstacles to starting a new life clustered faster than flies at a picnic. She tugged down the t-shirt she'd worn for two days straight, noticing a food stain on the fabric.

How long could she make the money last that Elizabeth had gotten from the pawn shop? At her request, Mindy had placed the cash in the shelter's office safe. Unfortunately, Sarah couldn't open a checking account without giving the bank her social security number, which her husband could track. They also required a local address, and if she listed Solutions as her residence, it wouldn't be long before Charles found her.

Five hundred dollars wouldn't cover much. She needed clothes, transportation, a job, and a place to live. Although grateful for her temporary haven, she couldn't remain here forever. But without proper clothes, she couldn't go on a work interview. And even if she landed a job, how would she get there?

How could she care for Ricky and still earn money? It wouldn't be fair to take her son away from everything familiar, then abandon him to strangers for daycare. Besides, babysitters cost a lot of money. Hadn't Charles reminded her of that time and time again?

Her challenges seemed insurmountable. And overcoming them appeared less likely than her husband having a change of heart, particularly once he realized she would no longer tolerate his violence. Maybe he missed her.

She longed to talk to Charles, to find out what he was thinking. Had he forgiven her for taking off? Or was he enraged? Too bad she'd thrown away the cell phone he'd given her. Maybe she should go to the resident manager's office downstairs and ask to use theirs. But no. Charles could trace her caller ID.

Then again, maybe calling him was a bad idea. First, she'd depended on her parents, and then she'd relied on Charles' strength. Did she have any of her own? Maybe he was right about her inability to manage money or keep a decent job. She had to find out who she was.

Sarah wadded up the thin pillow beneath her head, then studied a watermark on the ceiling. *What a failure.* She couldn't find her way in life, much less do right by her child. At least in Summit, Ricky had a comfortable place to grow up.

Then again, the doctor at Prosper's hospital had confirmed from the exam that she could have died from the strangulation. What would have happened to Ricky then? She had to find a way to protect him. Leaving Charles was the only way to be safe. Time to get out of the crazy lifestyle she had with him. No more lame excuses.

She could hear Ricky's gentle breathing in the quiet. He hadn't been near adult scuffles for the past few days. He seemed to be adjusting fine to the other ladies' attention and played well with the shelter's children. He never once asked to go home. What kind of a man would Ricky grow up to be if he saw violence as routine?

At a gentle knock on the door, Sarah left the bed and opened it so as to not disturb Ricky. Outside stood Mindy, her braces reflecting light in her warm smile.

"Sorry to disturb you, but you just got a phone call from Elizabeth Robinson. She needs to talk with you about something. She'll be here in half an hour to see you."

"Oh." Sarah's hand flew to her mussed hair. Elizabeth was the one who had driven her to Prosper after leaving Wilma. Had Charles tracked her here? Was she going to have to go somewhere else? Sarah's heart beat so fast, she thought her rib cage might explode. "What will I do with Ricky?"

"I can stay here with him while you talk with Elizabeth."

"Thank you." Sarah glanced at her son on the floor and frowned at the wet spot on the empty single bed across from hers. "I'm afraid he had another accident last night." He'd been potty trained a while, but he hadn't had a dry night since they got to the shelter.

"Don't worry. That happens to many children who come here. They get frightened by all the changes. That's why we have plastic mattress covers. I'll get clean sheets, and we can wash the laundry later."

The manager's matter-of-fact approach took everything in stride. That Mindy sure was a gem. Maybe someday, she could repay the kindness.

Ricky rolled over on the floor.

"Do you need a change of clothes or diapers for him?"

"Clothes, yes; diapers, no. He's fine in the daytime. But I changed him into his last pair of clean underwear and shorts before bed last night. Maybe we can wash the dirty ones with the sheets."

"Of course. You can come with me to the storage room." Mindy started down the narrow hall. "It's two doors down on the right."

Sarah followed, leaving the door open in case Ricky called out for her. "I appreciate this so much."

"No problem." Mindy unlocked the storage closet and pointed to full shelves. "We've got almost everything you could need."

Sarah gazed wide-eyed at the neat rows of personal care items and clothing choices. "Where did it come from?"

"Donations. From local church groups, mostly. Help yourself."

Sarah spotted clothes labeled 3T—about Ricky's size.

"If you see anything else you would like, just grab it."

Sarah bit her lip. "Do you think I could have some shampoo?"

"Of course." Mindy hesitated with her hand on the doorknob. "Listen, I know it's hard to ask. I felt the same way a few years ago. But there's no need to be shy. One day soon, you'll be able to give back and help someone else."

Mindy looked young and innocent. How could she have known the terror of fleeing for her life? She also seemed peaceful. Would Sarah ever know that feeling again?

On their way back to the room, Mindy asked, "Does Ricky like pancakes?"

"He loves them."

"Good. While you get ready, I'll start a batch of my famous pumpkin pancakes."

There was a time when Sarah would've turned her nose up at the idea of unusual flavors. Now, they sounded heavenly.

At the bedroom door, Mindy winked. "If you hurry, you can be first in line for the bathroom. Once the other seventeen guests get up, it'll be a stampede."

"You're right." On her first morning at Solutions, Sarah wound up at the end of the line and had cold water for her shower. The second day, she'd gotten up earlier, only to exchange harsh words with another resident who tried to butt in line ahead of her for the toilet.

Sarah glanced at Ricky, who curled close to the metal bed frame. Although she didn't fear Charles while here, could she trust her child with strangers? One of the other kids had coughed a lot last night and had green goo in her nose. Sarah didn't want Ricky to get sick. No way she could afford medicine. The small shelter had little privacy, and sound carried through the halls. This was no place to keep Ricky for long. If only she had somewhere else she could go.

CHAPTER FORTY

SHADOW PROJECT

A little before nine, Elizabeth set the stack of ribbon-tied letters on the floorboard behind the driver's seat and got into her Mercedes with no idea how the day would turn out. Would Ida Lou and Sarah reconcile as long-lost family? She hoped so. Both women had suffered much loss. If only they could find a way to support each other. She backed out of the garage and headed toward Solutions.

A tan Taurus pulled out from the curb after her. Must be someone heading for work. She turned to the road ahead. How was she going to tell Sarah about Ida Lou?

She toyed with options. Should she blurt out the truth, then add, "By the way, sorry your dad's dead"? Maybe she could tell the story of Betty helping someone at ICU, then add details about Ida Lou and Richard if Sarah expressed interest.

The young woman was already under much stress. How would she handle finding out her parents hadn't given up on her? Maybe seeing another of her sorry husband's betrayals would strengthen her determination to be independent.

And what if Ida Lou wasn't her mother? What a fiasco that would be! Elizabeth needed the wisdom to handle this delicate situation. She activated the car's Bluetooth to dial Pastor James' cell.

"Good morning, Pastor. Sorry to intrude on your day off, but I need your expertise. Are you busy?"

"I was about to head to the gym, but that can wait if this is an emergency. How can I help?"

"You know Ida Lou Besco, the new lady at church whose husband just died?" Elizabeth slowed for pedestrians approaching the crosswalk.

"Of course. I'm meeting with her this afternoon before the memorial service."

Elizabeth glanced in the rearview mirror before making a left-hand turn. The tan Taurus was a safe distance behind her, leaving plenty of room for the short turning lane without fear of getting rear-ended. "Well, I believe I may know her daughter."

"Daughter? Only Betty was with her at the hospital."

The light at the intersection went from yellow to red quickly, and Elizabeth had to slam on the brakes. Once safely stopped, she sorted out how to explain the developments. What would be the best short version to tell the pastor about Sarah?

She gripped the steering wheel. "Ida Lou hasn't seen her daughter in three years. But Letitia saw a photo of the girl and thinks one of the women who came into the shelter Saturday might be her."

"Betty mentioned last night there might be a family connection. If so, wouldn't that be wonderful! The Lord moves in amazing ways. He does like bringing people hope in the middle of tragedy."

He might not be cheerful when he heard the rest. "The problem is, we don't know if this mother and daughter will forgive each other after years of silence—assuming we're right about the connection in the first place." And how would he feel about Sarah leaving her marriage?

"I see."

The light turned green, and Elizabeth made her turn.

"Have you talked to Ida Lou about this?"

"I haven't, but Betty did this morning. Ida Lou wrote a note and gave it to Betty to be delivered. Betty brought the message to me for Sarah."

"Does Ida Lou want to reconcile?"

"She asked Betty to tell her daughter that she loves her unconditionally and wants to see her as soon as possible." Elizabeth picked up speed, hoping to make up time on the straightaway before the turnoff.

"How did the daughter respond?"

"I haven't seen her yet. I'm on my way to Solutions. But I don't know how to handle the situation. On top of everything else, if this is indeed the right young woman, I need to tell her that her father recently died."

"I see your point."

Elizabeth checked the rearview mirror. That tan Taurus followed at a distance. Odd. "Could I bring Sarah to your office in about forty minutes?"

"Certainly. I can skip the gym today. Instead, I'll head to the church and ask the Lord what He wants us to do."

"Thank you, Pastor James. You're a good man." Maybe he could ask the Lord to deliver her from the sheriff's attack. Later. After Sarah and Ida Lou were cared for.

She disconnected the call. Would Pastor James feel obligated by Scripture to tell Sarah she must forgive her husband and honor the covenant vow? Few seminaries addressed how to handle cases of domestic violence.

Couples counseling didn't work if there was a power imbalance between spouses. The worst thing Sarah could do would be to run home to her husband without resolving the severe underlying issues regarding her safety.

Elizabeth turned at the hedge onto the shelter's gravel driveway. She paused and looked in her rearview mirror. The tan Taurus eased by on the main road. Good. At least no one followed her down the lane. She parked, exited the car, and rang the front doorbell. Through an intercom system, a metallic voice asked, "Who's there?"

A moment after identifying herself, there was a click, and the door swung open. The manager stood beside Sarah, who had Ricky on her hip.

"Good morning, Mindy. Sarah, could we talk for a few minutes?"

"Yes, ma'am." She handed Ricky to Mindy. "You be a good boy till Mommy gets back, okay?"

He kissed his mother's cheek, leaving a smudge of maple syrup. "I be good." He slipped down and took Mindy's outstretched hand.

"I'm going to show you all the toys we have in the playroom," she promised with a big smile.

"Trucks?"

"Lots of them!"

Sarah smoothed down a tuft of red hair at the back of his head. "Take good care of Miss Mindy, honey."

"She's my friend." The little guy trotted off, seemingly oblivious to the turmoil around him.

Sarah blew him a kiss, then looked at Elizabeth. "What's going on that you need to see me? Have you heard news about Charles?"

Elizabeth took a deep breath. "Wilma says he's been showing your picture around Summit and offering a reward for information of your whereabouts."

Sarah leaned back against the entry wall.

"But that's not what I wanted to talk to you about." Another resident walked down the hallway toward the bathroom. "Could we step outside?"

They walked toward an azalea hedge in the side yard. "Elizabeth, what is going on?"

Unable to contain herself any longer, Elizabeth blurted out, "Some friends of mine might have found information about your parents."

Sarah steadied herself against an oak tree trunk. "What?"

"I'd like to take you to see my preacher." Elizabeth traced the tip of her shoe on the grass.

"That sounds serious."

Elizabeth pursed her lips. "Pastor James could fill you in on the details better than I can."

Sarah plucked at a tear in her worn jeans and stared at her old tennis shoes. "I'm not dressed nice enough for church."

Would Sarah balk and decide not to talk with Pastor James? She'd better reassure her. "Don't worry about that. We're only going to his office."

Sarah's brow creased with worry. "What information did your friends find?"

"First, I need to ask you a question." Elizabeth looked up at the sky for a moment. "What are your parents' names?"

"Richard and Ida Lou Besco."

She exhaled. That eliminated one obstacle.

Sarah shifted her weight to one leg and set the other foot behind her as she leaned against the tree. "Are my parents okay?"

Elizabeth didn't want to lie, but she also didn't know how to deliver the crushing truth. "Pastor James has met with your mom."

A flash of eagerness lit Sarah's face.

"Your mother lives nearby."

Sarah pushed off the bark and stood up straight. She took a few steps away toward the flower bushes. "She probably doesn't want anything to do with me."

"Honey, your mom wants to see you as soon as possible. I am happy to drive you now. Do you want to go?"

A range of emotions traveled Sarah's heart-shaped face. "Yes, ma'am. I've waited too long to tell them how much I love and miss them."

CHAPTER FORTY-ONE
WHAT FORGIVENESS IS NOT

Sarah stared at the minister's bushy eyebrows and kind, hazel eyes. He wore a buttoned shirt and khaki slacks.

He smiled at the mayor, then greeted her. "Hello, Sarah. My name is James Sebastian, but everyone calls me Pastor James. Won't you sit down and get comfortable?" He extended his arm toward the interior of his office.

Taking a seat, she felt as if she was waiting to see the principal. Would he judge her for abandoning her husband? Shelves lined his study with all kinds of Bibles and other reference books. She would walk out if he started quoting Scripture about wives submitting to their husbands.

Elizabeth took the armchair beside Sarah, facing Pastor James across the study. Sarah fidgeted, waiting for someone to break the awkward silence.

"Could I offer you coffee or water?" Pastor James paused at the door.

"No, thanks." Sarah slumped in her chair and tugged a lock of hair over to cover her bruised face.

"Not for me either." Elizabeth folded her hands in her lap.

The pastor shut the door to the study and sat in a worn leather recliner facing them. "Sarah, I am glad you felt comfortable coming today. I am here to help however I can. Elizabeth said a lot is going on in your life. Would you like to talk about any of it?"

No. She didn't. She didn't want to be here at all. And if not for desperation, she wouldn't be. But her child deserved more than hearing her getting thrown around. If she was going to make anything better, she had to have help. "Sir, I am having difficulties in my marriage. My husband gets violent."

His eyes didn't look off. Nor did he appear horrified. How much more should she say? She glanced at Elizabeth for help, but the other woman remained like a statue.

"I understand the ladies at Solutions are helping you?" He leaned forward in his chair.

"Yes, Elizabeth risked her well-being to pick up my son and me from North Carolina and drive us here. My husband's a police officer."

"Oh. That certainly complicates matters." The pastor drummed his fingers on the armrest. "Elizabeth said you also are worried about your parents and haven't been in touch with them in three years. Is that correct?"

Sarah's shoulders hunched forward. "I eloped after my graduation ceremony from college. I never told them goodbye and haven't seen them since."

He turned to Elizabeth, who leaned over to her large handbag and removed a stack of ribbon-bound letters. "Mrs. Robinson, why don't you tell Sarah about that bundle of mail you have there?"

Elizabeth had said nothing to her about mail. Were they bills or what?

"My friend Betty gave me these letters this morning. She got them from Ida Lou Besco."

Sarah's heart raced. "That's my mother!" What in the world was going on?

"And who were the letters sent to?" he prompted.

Elizabeth untied the navy ribbon and held the envelopes to Sarah.

Sarah's stomach turned into a cannonball. She rifled through the stationery. Postmark after postmark told a story of heartache. "These are addressed to me. But they all have 'Return to Sender' written on them."

Each envelope revealed her husband's scrawling script of rejection. She tossed the stack of letters onto the desk as if it were a lit match about to burn her fingers. How could he have done that to her? He lied! And she'd lost precious time with the only people who loved her. Covering her face with her hands, she wept.

Elizabeth left her seat and wrapped an arm around her. A slight fragrance of talcum powder made her think of Ricky. Was he okay? Maybe now he could meet his grandparents.

"If you want tissues, I put some on the table beside you." Pastor James broke the silence.

"I'm with you," Elizabeth murmured, keeping a secure hold around her back.

"I can't believe he'd . . . hide these from me." Heaving sobs made it hard to talk. "How could my husband let me think"—she hiccupped—"that my dad and mom didn't love me anymore?" She blew her nose into a tissue, then reached for another.

Elizabeth patted Sarah's shoulder. "Honey, your mom hasn't stopped loving you. As a matter of fact, when Betty went to see her this morning to tell her we thought we'd located her daughter, she wrote a note for you and gave it to Betty. Would you like to see it?"

Sarah wiped away tears, straightened her shoulders, and reached for the note. She read it. Hope mingled with horror. Her mom loved her, but what about her dad?

Elizabeth stepped back, hovering near her chair.

At the bottom of the page, she skimmed four words over and over. They didn't make sense. They couldn't be true. Her dad was dead.

She bit her lip and tasted salty blood. She'd never see him again. Never get to tell him how sorry she was. Never see him take Ricky for ice cream or a ball game. Her dad was gone—forever.

"Sarah," the pastor's gentle voice brought her back to the moment. "Would you like to see your mother?"

Elizabeth moved back to her chair. That gesture indicated she would give Sarah space to decide.

Did she want to see her mother? Of course. She'd already lost one parent. Her mom needed her. "Yes, sir. I just don't know how to go about doing that."

Elizabeth passed over a wastebasket for the wet tissues. "Don't worry, honey. Betty said your mom couldn't wait to see you."

Running hands through her hair, Sarah took a deep breath. Then she stacked the letters with great care, placing the note on top, and retied the ribbon with a bow. "If my parents can forgive me, I guess that means I should forgive my husband."

Elizabeth gasped, then swiveled her head toward the pastor, expecting words of wisdom to come from his lips.

Too much guilt piled up. She'd hurt her dad, and now she never could apologize. What if she'd burned the bridge with Charles prematurely, too? Sarah rubbed the naked ring finger on her left hand. "You're probably going to tell me we're supposed to forgive not only seven times but also seventy-seven times."

Pastor James leaned toward her. "God wants us to forgive. But He also said wrongdoers should take responsibility for their actions."

What did he mean? Focusing was difficult. Too many things were hitting at once. It was like a carnival ride spinning faster and faster, making her feel sick.

He reached for a Bible on the shelf behind him and flipped it open. "This is from Luke 17. 'If your brother or sister sins against you, rebuke them; and *if they repent*, forgive them.'"

Looking up from the page, he said, "*Repent* means to change, to stop acting in unacceptable ways. Has your husband expressed genuine sorrow for harming you?"

Sarah shifted in her seat. "He's apologized a couple of times."

"Actions speak louder than words," Elizabeth muttered. She crossed her legs.

"Sarah, God doesn't want your husband to continue bullying you. Jesus showed His love for His bride, the Church, not by demanding subservience, but by sacrificing Himself in loving service."

"Pastor James is right," Elizabeth blurted. "Forgiveness doesn't mean rolling over and playing dead."

And death could be a real possibility if Charles found her and got crazy again.

James closed his Bible. "As a mother, you must protect your son and yourself."

Sarah plucked at the hem of her t-shirt. She didn't know what to do. She didn't trust herself because she'd made too many mistakes.

"Although I pray your husband will choose to mend his ways, until you have proof of that decision—over a long period—no one, including the Church, should put you under any obligation to remain in a dangerous situation."

"That's right." Elizabeth clapped her hands.

Sarah pushed a strand of hair behind an ear. "So, you don't think I was wrong to leave him?"

James set the Bible back on the shelf and returned to his chair. "Quite the contrary, actually. What you did was an act of great courage and resourcefulness."

Maybe she could put things right. This was an opportunity to set a new course. She didn't have to let mistakes hold her back. Ricky needed her to find a better future for both of them. "Thank you, Pastor."

She stood and gathered the letters to her chest. "Elizabeth, could you please take me to see my mom?"

Elizabeth leaped to her feet. "I'd love to."

James opened the door for the women. "I'm available anytime if you want to talk."

"I appreciate that." Sarah paused in the doorway and faced him. "You know, if God is half as kind and loving as you are, Heaven must be a glorious place."

CHAPTER FORTY-TWO

STAKEOUT

Traveling in a rented gray Sonata Sarah wouldn't recognize, Charles made good time getting across the state line. With the address from the obituary announcement, GPS made locating the Besco residence a piece of cake. He parked at the end of the street and looked for Sarah and Ricky.

He couldn't very well walk up to the door without spooking her, so he'd wait and watch. That way, he could see if she were with another man. Several of her high school beaus had pursued her at college.

The neighborhood looked decent. A brick sign with fresh flowers at the base announced Horizon Vista. Dumb name for a flat subdivision. All he wanted to see was his family. He'd load them up and have them back in Summit before anyone could say a word.

Two hours later, he re-evaluated his strategy. His father-in-law's funeral was in the afternoon. *Good riddance.* But where was Sarah? Maybe the funeral home. Should he drive there? But if he did, he might miss her. What if she weren't here at all? He pounded the steering wheel at the notion some sicko may be holding her hostage. She had to be alive. He wanted her back.

His bladder swelled with coffee from the trip. Not gonna be able to ignore the call of nature much longer. He looked at the empty jumbo cup lying on the floorboard. That wouldn't work. Someone might see him. Just a few minutes ago, a skinny, old lady wearing hot pink bicycle shorts and a purple top power-walked down the sidewalk.

She'd passed, misting herself with a spray bottle under her yellow umbrella hat. She had been swinging her arms in furious arcs, presumably to the beat of music on her earphones. He didn't want to risk her coming back and thinking he was a pervert. To distract himself from his discomfort, Charles took a pad of paper and studied notes from the morning's stakeout.

At eight a.m.—shortly after his arrival—a tan Taurus parked on the other end of the street. Through the tinted windows, Charles could tell a man was in the driver's seat. His lips weren't moving, so he wasn't making a phone call. Why would a guy sit in his car doing nothing on a residential street? Was he casing the retirement community? Charles scribbled down the license number, planning to ask Doug to trace the plate.

At 8:30 a.m., a fat, old lady walked from a nearby unit and knocked on the Bescos' front door. He'd strained to see the person who answered, hoping to catch a glimpse of his wife. But the only person visible was his mother-in-law. Even if Sarah wasn't here, could her mom know her whereabouts? He would pry the information out of Ida Lou if he had to. Wasn't he trained for investigation?

Fatso stayed inside the house for about fifteen minutes, then left in a hurry, carrying a bundle of paper wrapped in a dark blue ribbon. What was up with that?

At 8:45 a.m., the heavyset woman knocked on the door of another villa. A black woman answered and invited her inside. The fat lady reemerged five minutes later without the bundle. Probably scrapbook buddies.

Ten minutes later, the black woman hurriedly took off in a high-dollar Mercedes. The tan Taurus followed. What was going on in this neighborhood? No rhyme or reason for movement.

During the next hour, things quieted. The power-walking granny's return was the only sign of life.

Charles needed to take care of business. He'd spotted a fast-food joint on the way here. He could go there, hit the john, buy lunch, and be back in ten minutes. But Charles hated to leave the area for even a second. What if he missed something?

He considered ducking behind the holly bushes lining one wall of the neighborhood—until he saw a Hispanic gardener round the corner, pushing a wheelbarrow full of tools.

He could hold on a bit longer. At least he had shade from an oak. Hugging Ricky would make everything worthwhile. After turning on the ignition key, he fiddled with the radio knob. Maybe he could get a news update. He leaned back and let the headrest cradle his neck.

The fat, old lady came out of her house and walked across the lawn. She noticed the gardener shaping a vine on a trellis and veered toward him. Good. Maybe she was the talkative type. He could stroll by her and get information. His back ached from sitting in the car.

He strained to hear their conversation through his half-open window. No luck with cars going by. A tall man with a mustache approached the pair. The old woman pointed to the gardener and smiled.

They carried on a few minutes. The fat lady kept gesturing toward landscape features in the courtyard area. Maybe the gardener was getting the what-for. He almost felt sorry for him. Supervisors could be a pain. The tall man clapped the stocky Hispanic on the back. Next, he removed a wallet from his back pocket and flipped it open.

The old lady beamed. The Hispanic leaned down to rub a clod of dirt off his boot. The tall dude pulled out cash and pressed bills into his hand when the worker stood up. The gardener acted as though the money was a snake. What was going on? Surely this wasn't a drug deal in broad daylight. More likely an illegal immigrant getting paid under the table—or out in the yard, in this case.

Where were his binoculars? He shuffled through items staged on the seat. This suburban mime failed to entertain. He had more critical mysteries to solve. But he couldn't afford to tip his hand too early. No telling what Sarah might do if she saw him first.

The tall guy stroked his curled mustache. Hadn't the guy ever heard of razors? He looked like a leftover from some Western movie. He made elaborate arm and leg movements, looking like a windmill as he said something indistinguishable. What an idiot. The gardener's hand closed on the money, and then he started dancing in circles. Were all these people crazy?

The fat lady turned toward the road and stared. Uh oh. Was she scoping him out? He turned his head away as though reaching for the hood opener. Maybe he should get out and fake examining the engine. But before he could open the car door, a flash of ocean-blue metal crested the subdivision's entrance. The black lady in the pricey wheels was back. Was she the dealer?

The fat lady waved goodbye to the men and hustled toward the Mercedes. None of this made sense. It was like watching a three-ring circus. Good thing he hadn't gotten out of the car. What if Sarah were in that Mercedes? The Mercedes pulled to the far side of the subdivision, where buildings blocked his view. Of all the bad luck. Figured. He was tired of this parking spot, anyhow. He cranked the engine and put the car into gear. Time to see what was on the other side of the neighborhood.

Tires screeched as he took off to catch the Mercedes. The Hispanic peered hard as he flew past. *Yeah, buddy. Look all you want. Gonna call the immigration office after Sarah and Ricky get found.*

CHAPTER FORTY-THREE
HULA HOOP HIGH DIVE

The mirror-tiled elevator at the sheriff's office dinged as Letitia arrived on the top floor of the grand building. She marched toward Sheriff Bottoms' den of iniquity like an avenging angel. Attired in a custom-tailored, navy blue jacket and long skirt, she'd draped a bright orange scarf around her neck. After all, even business wear needed a splash of style. Her salt-and-pepper hair was swept into an elaborate French roll, and huge diamond studs glittered on her earlobes.

She rested her jeweled handbag on the reception desk in front of the attractive brunette. "Hillary, tell Junior I want to see him."

Hillary disguised a laugh with a cough, then picked up the receiver. Her fingernails sported a fire-engine red polish. "Sir, Mrs. Larrimore is here."

What needless pomp and circumstance. She could see Junior sitting with his feet on his oak desk through the half-open office door. "Never mind. I see he's in."

As she swept into the hallowed space, Thomas swung his feet off the desk and stood. He walked around the monstrous desk to greet her. "Mrs. Larrimore, what a pleasure to see you this morning."

He'd always been one to schmooze. Even as a kid, he knew how to butter up the crowd if he thought there'd be something in it for him. She stood stock-still and uttered not a word. Let him stew a minute. This was not a social call.

In the awkward silence, Thomas shifted his substantial weight from boot to boot. He seemed as nervous as a trapeze artist starting an act with a frayed rope.

"Would you like a seat?" Sweat dotted his forehead as he pointed to a plush, leather chair near the window.

She ignored his outstretched arm and sallied forth to commandeer his chair behind the desk. He sank into the smaller leather chair and gave her a weak smile.

"I'm here on business, Junior." What a delight to watch his face scrunch up whenever she used the childhood nickname he detested.

Hillary appeared in the doorway. "May I get you some coffee, Mrs. Larrimore?"

"No, thank you, dear. I won't be here long."

Hillary backed out and pulled the door almost shut behind her.

Letitia examined the sheriff's desktop with scorn. She pulled a tissue from her purse and used it to wipe donut crumbs off the surface farthest from a coffee spill. She moved aside a half-empty box with two remaining donuts, then placed her purse there.

"You always were a glutton." She shook her head. Her rage at his attack on Elizabeth burned. "I warned your mama not to coddle you."

He tugged at his tight collar. "Um. What business would you like to discuss today?"

A hopeful tone emerged in the question. He probably expected her to give him a large campaign donation to pay for red, white, and blue flyers with a large picture of him in his best suit. Or host a fundraiser on his behalf with all the movers and shakers she knew—just like she'd done before he got too big for his britches, figuratively and literally.

"Junior, when your mother was on her deathbed with cancer, I promised her I'd look after you, and heaven knows I've tried."

Thomas dropped his chin in deference.

Her blood pressure spiked as she looked at his bloated face. His ego had magnified to the point that he was probably right now rehearsing in his head a pompous speech about how hard he'd worked to keep their community safe. Time to take the boy down a notch—or eight.

"Son, this latest publicity stunt of yours is incorrigible."

He sat up straight, his belly bulging. "I don't know what you're talking about."

Letitia pointed her index finger toward the open newspaper. "That trash is why I'm here."

"You mean the scandal about the mayor stealing jewelry and selling it at a pawn shop?" A note of arrogance crept into his voice.

She locked eyes with him. "You know as well as I do, our mayor would never be involved in anything illegal. You're pursuing a trumped-up charge to grandstand for reelection."

He snatched a blown-glass paperweight off the desk and bounced it in his palm like a miniature crystal ball.

"Young man, you've gone too far. And I'll not stand for it," she said, slapping her hand on the desktop. Out in the hallway, where she had been eavesdropping, Hillary jumped. No matter. Nothing would deter her from holding Junior accountable for his bad behavior.

He set the ball down on the armrest. "Fred Nix showed me receipts totaling thousands of dollars, and the mayor can't account for them as her purchases. Don't you want to see justice served?"

Letitia clucked her tongue. "If your mama could see you right now, she'd take a switch to your backside, and you wouldn't be sitting for a week! This is worse than when you tricked your cousin into rolling in poison ivy."

She looked out the panoramic window to summon every bit of self-control she could. "How can you be so rotten as to impugn the good name of our mayor to serve your selfish purposes?"

Thomas ran a hand through his thinning hair. "You've always told me integrity is important. Or is that only true if it doesn't involve *your friends*?"

Letitia pursed her lips. "How many times do I have to tell you that you don't get taller by tearing someone else down?"

Thomas' double chin wobbled. "I'm doing my job to protect the public. That's my sworn oath."

"And you don't mind ruining someone else's reputation in your pursuit of glory?"

His casual shrug made her want to spit nails.

"Tell you what, Junior. I'll make you a deal. By the end of business today, you publicly announce that the pawn shop situation was a misunderstanding and the mayor's done nothing wrong."

"Or?" He crossed his right leg over the left knee, leaned back, and laced his hands behind his head, giving her a smug look.

"Or I go to the paper's publisher with that photo of you from the Omega Du fraternity party."

Thomas drew in a sharp breath. He knew exactly what picture she was talking about. During his senior year, he'd dumped a sweet girl to marry a wealthy socialite. The spurned girl cried on Candace Bottom's shoulder when she returned the family's prized heirloom sapphire engagement ring. The jilted girl also handed his mom a photo of Thomas Bottoms III. He stood on the high dive, ready to jump off, wearing nothing but a hula hoop and sporting a goofy grin.

Thomas dropped his forearms on his thighs. "Please, Mrs. Larrimore, let's be reasonable."

She went for the jugular. "I can see the headline now. 'Sexy Sheriff Splashes Down.'"

Thomas adjusted the belt on his trousers. "What you're suggesting is blackmail."

"No, Junior. I'm only asking you to correct the wrong you've done."

He cracked his knuckles. Letitia started methodically pushing her nail cuticles, waiting for him to see the light. Sometimes, that took Junior a while.

"Okay, you win. I'll call Bert and ask about doing an updated story right away."

Letitia dazzled him with a jackpot-winner smile. "That's one thing I like about you, Junior. You always heed good advice." She stood, slid her tote over her wrist, and swept out of the room as Hillary backpedaled toward her desk.

"Have a nice day, dear." Letitia sauntered past the reception area, whistling a little ditty.

Back in the elevator, Letitia pressed palms together and looked heavenward. "Father, forgive me for telling a whopper about having that picture. And, Candace, I hope you can forgive me, too. I've kept my promise never to tell a soul about that embarrassing moment. After all, Junior already knew."

Letitia envisioned her dear, departed friend forgiving her. Surely, she understood this was the only way to protect Elizabeth and the women at Solutions. Letitia didn't want a midnight visitation from an angry ghost.

CHAPTER FORTY-FOUR

BULLY BOUQUET

Charles' chase after the Mercedes proved fruitless. Only the black lady emerged from the vehicle. Might as well head to the rundown burger joint for a break. Once inside the bathroom, he found that the urinal's green-apple air freshener only added to the stench. He got out as quickly as he could.

Despite the diner's tattered vinyl booths and scuffed floors, the burgers sizzling on the grill made his mouth water. He could almost taste hot, salty fries. When had he eaten last?

He was too early for the lunch crowd. He saw only one customer standing in line. He could grab a quick bite and return to the stakeout in record time.

"May I help you, sir?" A teenager with a half-tucked shirt and jeans hanging around his hips stood by the register.

"Yeah. Gimme a double cheeseburger with everything and a large fry."

He reached into his back pocket while the pimply-faced kid went to bag his meal. When Charles flicked open the leather wallet, a picture of Sarah holding Ricky smiled up at him. His heart lurched.

Would he ever see them again? He counted out the money to pay the bill from the several twenties and a fifty. The last time he had checked Sarah's purse on Friday night, she'd had only eight bucks. Regret seared his gut. Maybe he should up her weekly allowance to fifteen dollars when she returned—if she came home.

The cashier handed him the order, and Charles hightailed it to the rental car. Once in the driver's seat, he opened the bag. He juggled the greasy burger in his left hand while jamming the key into the ignition with his right. He noticed a middle-aged, dark-haired man going inside a flower shop across the street behind him.

That was an idea. Delivering flowers to console his mother-in-law would be a good reason for going to the house. He could inspect the place up close for signs of Sarah and Ricky when delivering the bouquet.

That sure beat hanging around in a hot vehicle for hours on end. After three days, he was sick of not knowing where they were. He gobbled a few more bites, then wiped the grease from his chin with a napkin.

Flowers *were* the way to go. His mother-in-law had been sweet to him. She'd never given him a problem. Now that Sarah's old man was out of the way, Charles could be in charge of two households.

He turned off the car's engine. While finishing the burger, he surveyed the flower shop through his rearview mirror. A green-striped awning shaded the entry, and the large window displayed colorful arrangements and knickknacks. Charles squeezed ketchup on a few fries, then thrust them into his mouth as he considered what flowers Ida Lou might like.

Charles swiped at a dot of ketchup on his gray t-shirt with a napkin, then balled up the trash and chunked it on the passenger floorboard near the old coffee cup. He got out of the car and strolled toward the store.

Once inside the air-conditioned store, he was greeted by a heady perfume of blended fragrances. A motor hummed, and condensation clouded the interior of the glass-door cooler, which was full of arrangements.

He weaved around a gauntlet of small, black, plastic buckets overflowing with blooms and then headed toward the cashier. A young woman with a curly ponytail, no makeup, and *AnnMarie* stitched to her pink uniform top rang up the purchase of a middle-aged man Charles had seen enter.

"That'll be sixty-five dollars and three cents with tax." While the jeans-clad girl waited for him to pull out his wallet, she added, "Sure am glad everything's okay with you, Elder Stout. The prayer chain message about you having a heart attack had me rattled. Still can't figure out who made that mistake."

Stout removed a credit card from a well-worn wallet. "Who knows? But I do not doubt that Betty Herndale will make sure they never do it again."

Charles wished they'd hurry.

Stout signed the electronic pad. "It's mighty sad Ida Lou lost her husband on Easter Sunday."

"Guess it all depends on how you look at it," AnnMarie said.

Charles couldn't agree more. He hoped more tidbits of news were forthcoming.

"Would you like a printed receipt?" When he nodded, she pressed a button on the computer. "For some, death is the end. But for those with faith, it's the doorway to resurrection and new life."

Charles wasn't in the mood for religious mumbo-jumbo, but a little gossip might prove helpful. He gave a dry cough to get the cashier's attention. "Excuse me." He lowered his chin in feigned deference. "Were y'all by any chance talking about the Besco family?"

Stout turned toward him as he folded the receipt. "Why, yes. Are you in town for Richard's funeral?"

Charles pulled at his collar, aware he wasn't dressed for a funeral. Good thing he'd brought other clothes. "Just got in town to show my respects. Went to school with his daughter, Sarah. She around?"

"I didn't know they had any children." AnnMarie's forehead puckered. "No kids came by to care for Ida Lou when her husband was in ICU."

Charles gulped. If no one had seen Sarah, where was she? Surely these rednecks weren't lying to cover up. Maybe a change of subject would get him further. "Those are gorgeous red roses. Who's the lucky lady?"

Stout's chest puffed out. "My wife of twenty-eight years. Took off today to take her on a date. She's home packing a picnic basket for us while I get bait. We're going fishing at the lake."

Charles shifted his feet. He wasn't sure he and Sarah would make it to their fifth anniversary, much less twenty-eight.

A deep, masculine chuckle came from behind as Stout took the dozen buds with baby's breath and ferns. Charles whirled around as a guy with a crew cut and military bearing approached the counter from a back corner of the shop. How long had he been there?

"Good day," Stout called out as he cradled the arrangement and left.

Mr. Military walked up to AnnMarie. "Could you make an arrangement of roses like you did for Elder Stout, only yellow?"

Charles elbowed the intruder. "Hold on; I'm next."

"Buddy, I was in the store before you pulled up." He made no effort to step aside.

Charles bowed up. He could take him on if he had to, but no sense starting trouble when all he wanted to do was find Sarah. "I am not your buddy. And if you wanted to be next, you should've gotten in line."

AnnMarie looked from one customer to the other. "William . . ."

The guy held up his hand to silence her.

Charles propped his arms on the counter. "Look, honey, I haven't got all day."

William stepped back a bit. "Seems you're in a mighty big hurry, stranger. Guess I don't mind letting you go ahead."

That was more like it. Charles slid closer to AnnMarie. "I want two dozen yellow roses."

AnnMarie blinked. "Sorry. But I have only one dozen yellow buds right now. If you can wait, we should have another delivery around noon."

"I need two dozen roses, and I want them now."

The girl shrugged, but her hands shook. Good. She knew he meant business. He could throw in some charm now that he had her attention. "Can you at least give me twelve pinks and twelve yellows?"

"Yes. Do you want them wrapped or in a vase?" AnnMarie's voice trembled.

"Two vases, one for each color." That would give him an excellent excuse to return with a second bouquet if he didn't see Sarah immediately. If he did, he'd have an arrangement for her and one for her mother. "And make them nice ones—nothing wilted, okay?"

"Yes, sir." AnnMarie scurried to the workroom.

He cut a sideways glance at Mr. Military. A vein throbbed on his forehead, and he flexed his fists. No big deal. Charles could out-muscle this guy any day of the week. Isn't that why he trained in the gym almost every day? Being healthy meant life or death in his job.

Charles drummed his fingers on the counter loud enough for the florist to hear in the back. Time was wasting. What if he missed seeing Sarah and Ricky?

"So," William said quietly, "where you from?"

"None of your business," Charles snarled.

William pushed his glasses higher on the bridge of his nose. He waited until AnnMarie brought out the vases and then followed Charles outside. The bell hanging on the doorknob jangled as they exited.

See ya, old man. Better luck next time. Hate to have had to bash in your nose.

CHAPTER FORTY-FIVE

SPECIAL DELIVERY

Ida Lou nestled beside Sarah on the couch and looked at her daughter's cell phone, where a picture of Ricky smiled up at them.

"See, Mom, he has Dad's cowlick." Sarah beamed.

If only Richard could be here now. But that sorrow was offset by the joy of seeing their adorable, freckled grandson. Ida Lou couldn't wait to hold him. She gathered Sarah in a tight embrace. "Darling, I can't wait to meet him. You are a wonderful mom."

The doorbell rang. Ida Lou looked up. "Betty, could you please get that? Sarah just got here, and I don't want to leave her side for even a second."

A fist pounded on the door. "Goodness," Letitia said from the corner chair where she sat in Ida Lou's living room. "Someone's sure in a hurry."

Betty opened the door part way, keeping her hand on the knob. "Just hold on. Don't you know it takes a body time to move?"

"Sorry, ma'am. But I have these flowers to deliver, and it's mighty hot out here. Don't want them to wilt."

Ida Lou gasped and reached for Sarah's hand. Her daughter's face lost all color.

"Didn't your mama teach you manners? You can't just barge in here." Betty didn't back down.

What should they do? Could Sarah hide in the bedroom before her husband could see her?

"I apologize, ma'am. Just thought I'd bring these in. The vase might be a bit heavy for you." Her son-in-law couldn't see Sarah yet, but he loomed a few steps away. Could Betty hold him off? Did she realize the danger at hand?

Maybe he would leave after all. Ida Lou squeezed Sarah's hand. Letitia stood up and moved toward the door to help Betty. Too late. Ida Lou's son-in-law plowed forward and shoved a vase of yellow roses into Betty's chest. While she wobbled, trying to keep her balance, Charles entered the living room. He took slow steps toward the coffee table in front of the couch, his eyes never leaving Sarah's.

Oh, no. What could she do to save Sarah?

"Well, I never!" Betty sputtered as water sloshed up and soaked the front of her blouse. "I don't know who you are, mister, but you'd better get out of here this instant!"

Ignoring her, Charles stalked around the coffee table and edged along the couch. Letitia looked back and forth, trying to process the unexpected intrusion.

"Charles, I can explain—" Sarah spoke, only to end with a gasp as he grabbed her arm and jerked her up. She lost the grip on her phone, and it flew a few feet away.

Ida Lou sat in shock, watching her daughter—the one she'd thought she'd lost forever and regained only a few minutes ago—dangle like a helpless doll in the grip of the horrible man who'd kept them separated for years.

Instead of leaning into Charles' embrace, Sarah shrank back. Sweetie, who'd been snuggled on the couch, leaped up and growled. Charles knocked the dog off the couch, then screamed in Sarah's face, "I can't believe this. I've been worried sick for days, and you've been having a little get-together with your mommy?"

Sweetie nipped at Charles' heels. He cursed and kicked at the dog, but Sarah moved between the two. "It's not what you think," she whispered.

Ida Lou scooped up the trembling pet into her arms, shielding her from harm's way. She wished she could reach the phone, but it was too far away. What could three older women do to stop this violent man?

Letitia edged toward the opposite end of the couch, closer to her. If only she hadn't suggested her guests set their purses on the table in the foyer. And her phone was charging on the desk in the office. They'd all have cell phones glued to their fingers any other time. So why, today of all days, were none of them within reach? How could she retrieve Sarah's phone without Charles stopping her? Would there be a way to distract her maniac son-in-law long enough to get help?

Betty recovered balance and set the dripping vase near the purses. Maybe she could sneak out a cell phone. Betty looked outside the still-open front door. Did she see someone nearby who could help? Oh, no! What if Elizabeth returned from the shelter with little Ricky while Charles was here?

Charles dragged Sarah toward the door, which he kicked closed. Betty backed up in time to keep from being hit. The muscles in Charles' forearm corded up with a vise-grip on a trembling Sarah.

"Please don't hurt her." Ida Lou's hands shook. This young man had robbed her of so much, even what should have been a joyous reunion. She wanted to scream at him and beat his chest. But an outburst would only further endanger Sarah—and everyone else. Charles seemed unhinged. Any move on their part might make him hurt Sarah more. If only Richard were here, he'd knock Charles senseless and save them from this monster.

Letitia seemed to share none of her panic. She had taken a seat near the end of the sofa and crossed her ankles primly. She untied and took off her orange scarf, draping it over the phone. "Let Sarah go." Three simple words, but spoken with quiet authority and pronounced with icy clarity.

Charles wheeled toward Letitia, twisting Sarah's petite body at an alarming angle. "You shut up. She's my wife, and what we do is none of your business."

If a direct approach didn't work, maybe sweetness would. Ida Lou gulped. "Looks like we got off to an awkward start today, Charles. Why don't you take a seat so we can talk this out?" She patted the empty place next to her. Maybe if he sat down, he'd release the hold on Sarah so she could run.

Without taking his eyes off Sarah for a second, he shook her like a dirty rug. "Where's my son? I want Ricky—now!"

"Charles, please stop," Sarah begged in an agonized whisper.

Is this what her daughter's life had been like for the past three years? If only she and Richard had known, they would have rescued her.

Charles grabbed Sarah's chin in his large hand and forced her to look up into his blotched face. "How dare you tell me what to do."

His muscled body heaved with ferocity. "Now, I'm gonna ask you one more time. Where's Ricky?"

While Charles grilled Sarah, Letitia reached with stealth under the scarf toward the phone. Betty bellowed across the room, "Young man, this has gone far enough. I demand you let go of her this instant."

Did Betty draw attention to herself on purpose? How long would it take Letitia to dial 911?

Like a bull seeing a red cape, Charles stomped toward Betty, never loosening his grip on Sarah, who stumbled behind.

With Charles' back to her, Letitia lifted the receiver and pushed down three times, then set the phone aside and covered it with her scarf and jacket.

Ida Lou's pulse quickened. How long before the telltale beep would start?

"I'm not taking orders from you, Skinny," Charles sneered.

Sweetie yapped loudly. Ida Lou could barely keep the frantic dog in her arms.

A muffled voice sounded from the phone. Letitia jumped up and started singing "Onward Christian Soldiers" at the top of her lungs.

"What was that?" Charles whipped around.

Sarah started wailing, Betty coughed, and Sweetie yipped. Letitia grabbed two books from the coffee table and beat them together like cymbals. Her noise startled Sweetie, who howled louder.

"Are you nuts?" Charles whirled toward Letitia, an incredulous look on his face.

The woman kicked up her knees as high as her navy skirt allowed, marching in place and belting out, "Jesus, lead us against the foe . . ."

Sweetie barked. Betty stomped her boots in place, and Ida Lou thumped on the end table, all joining their voices with hers.

Their bizarre behavior flummoxed Charles. "You've all flipped!" he yelled over the din.

A tinge of color crept into Sarah's face for the first time since Charles arrived.

Outside the bay window, Juan pushed a lawnmower. The machine was barely audible over all the commotion in the living room.

Ida Lou set Sweetie down and rushed Charles. She grabbed his arm and tugged on it in hopes of limiting the pressure on Sarah.

"Like a mighty army moves the church," Betty and Letitia continued to sing, marching closer toward the trio. Sweetie charged Charles' shoelaces and hung on.

Charles slung Ida Lou away, grabbed a wad of Sarah's hair, and pulled her behind as he strutted across the room with Sweetie in tow. When Charles looked out the window at Juan, Letitia lifted her jacket, replaced the landline phone receiver, and then slumped sideways in the chair—dangling her right arm in a devil-may-care gesture.

"The gates of hell can never against the church prevail." Betty sang solo over the lawnmower. She held her purse in her hand as though it were a missile.

Charles balled up his fist and glared at Betty as if he were about to punch her. "I told you to shut up! And drop that purse."

Betty put the handbag on the table and stopped singing. Even Sweetie hushed and retreated under the couch.

"I'm going outside to see why that guy's snooping. No one better move a muscle or say a word till I get back." He pulled Sarah behind him as he stormed out the door.

Had the 911 operator heard enough before the hang-up to dispatch the police? Or would they dismiss the call as a prank? If only Letitia's quick thinking would save them from this crazy man.

Betty hissed, "Letitia, quick, dial again!"

"What can we do? I am afraid to move, or Charles will do something awful to Sarah." Ida Lou felt frozen in place. Her body failed to function under the shock.

Betty watched outside the window. "Charles is waving Juan away from your house."

Letitia said, "We could run out the back door and get help."

"Then Charles may drag Sarah away." Ida Lou couldn't think straight. "I might never see her again. I can't let that monster take her." Things were happening too fast; she'd never experienced this level of violence.

"Elizabeth might arrive with Ricky any moment," Letitia said. "I'm staying here in case they do."

"It's too late," Betty warned in a low voice. "He's back."

The noise of the lawnmower drifted away as Charles came inside, dragging Sarah by the arm. He slammed the front door behind them.

CHAPTER FORTY-SIX

CALL OF DUTY

Sarah's heart sank as Charles locked the front door. She was trapped, and her mom and friends were in danger, too. What would Charles do? He'd never acted this crazy in front of others. Maybe he thought he could get away with murder since he was outside Summit. How far would he go to get what he wanted?

"Sit on the couch by your mom," he ordered. "You, Fatty and Skinny, join them. I don't want anyone getting ideas."

What could she say to calm him? "Um, honey—"

"Shut up!" He shoved the coffee table aside and leaned in her face like a drill sergeant terrorizing a new recruit. "You speak when spoken to and not before." The sickly-sweet odor of his sweat indicated he had binged on booze.

He sat on the coffee table, crowding poor Betty, who attempted to move her legs to the side. Her mom sat stock-still. Letitia pushed back a cuticle.

"So, who will tell me where my son is?"

Sarah hadn't prayed in a long time. After many nights of terror, she had given up on a miraculous rescue from her husband. She'd made her choice, but her mom and these kind ladies didn't deserve this. If Elizabeth showed up with Ricky, Charles might drag them both back to Summit. She'd never get away again. *Dear Lord, let the traffic catch Elizabeth. Please don't let her bring Ricky into the middle of this. Please save us all.*

Looking over Charles' shoulder, a tan Taurus pulled up and parked by the curb.

Letitia drawled, "Young man, I'm sure we can work things out. Just calm down. You're scaring us to death."

"Okay, ma'am. I can be reasonable if you can. Tell me where my son is." He folded his arms across his chest.

A man with a crew cut approached the front door from the sidewalk.

Her mom spoke with gentleness. "Charles, we want to put this family back together. I assure you Ricky is fine."

The doorbell rang. "Ignore that." Charles kept his back to the entryway to stare at them on the couch. "Probably a delivery guy who can leave the junk at the door."

The man with the crew cut leaned from the side of the front window to look inside at them. *Please, Lord, have him help us!*

Letitia must know the man because she motioned for him to come inside. Where did she get such courage? Charles lurched toward Letitia as the doorbell rang again. Charles froze. The bell chimed once more.

"Nobody better move till I get rid of this joker." Charles whirled around to the other side of the coffee table and jumped up. He opened the front door a few inches. "What do you want?"

"Hello, sir. We meet again."

Sarah strained to hear what was being said.

"Yeah, my lucky day," Charles said, standing in front of the man so that Sarah couldn't see his face.

Would the man sense that something was wrong? Or would he go away, not knowing they were in danger?

"I'm Detective William Smythe, responding to a 911 call at this residence. This is 467 Begonia Lane, isn't it?"

Charles moved a step outside of the house as though to push the other man back toward the road. He pointed above the entryway. "Yeah, yeah. Must be some mistake. Everything's fine here."

Letitia started to get up but stopped when Charles glared back at them on the couch. Then, turning toward the visitor, he drawled, "You got a badge?"

Ida Lou nudged Sarah with her shoulder and whispered, "Get out of here. Run!"

But Sarah couldn't leave the other women in trouble. This was her fault.

"Sure do." The men's exchange at the doorway continued as though the women were invisible.

Charles reached for the badge.

"And you are . . . ?" The man with the crew cut peered around Charles' shoulder.

Charles handed back the wallet, then took a step backward. "Deputy Charles McAdams."

"My, my. You're a bit far from Summit now, aren't you?"

How did this guy know so much? Had Charles' sergeant called ahead to find her? If the detective knew Charles was a law enforcement officer, too, he might leave. Then what would she do?

"C'mon, man. Don't hold a grudge about those roses." Charles relaxed his stance.

She hated when Charles did his fake, good, ol' buddy routine. When had her husband met this detective? Letitia stood and moved in front of the couch. She signaled her forefinger across her throat when Charles wasn't looking in her direction.

"Mr. McAdams, step aside." The detective's tone allowed no choice.

Charles stood a little taller. "There's nothing to see here, Detective. We're just having a family reunion."

"William, so glad you came by to pay your respects to Ida Lou," Betty said. "Please do come in."

"Step aside," the detective repeated, "or I'll haul you off to jail on obstruction charges."

Charles held up empty hands. "Relax, man. I'm one of the good guys."

Thank goodness Betty spoke up, and the other man persisted. They might be okay, after all. Charles would have to respect the other's authority. Wouldn't he?

"Hey, you're not sore about those roses, are you? Look, you can have one of the vases if you want. The pretty pink ones are in my car. Just haven't had time to bring them in. I wouldn't want your old lady to be mad at you on my account."

The detective pushed the door open wide. "I'm not here for a social call. Move over and stand by the kitchen wall."

As Charles backed away, the detective looked at them on the couch. "What's going on?"

Charles backed toward Sarah. "I told you, this is a family—"

"I wasn't asking you!" The detective's voice lashed out like a whip as he cordoned Charles away from them. "Anyone else here have something to say?"

Betty said, "You sure are a sight for sore eyes. I'm a friend of Ida Lou Besco. This is her home. She's new in town."

"AnnMarie at the flower shop told me about your husband, Mrs. Besco. I'm really sorry." He cut his eyes to Charles.

Ida Lou was barely able to utter, "Thank you."

Betty leveled an accusing forefinger at Charles. "This interloper barged in here, posing as a delivery boy to harass my friend and her daughter. And they must leave for a funeral soon!"

Charles leaned against the drywall, confident he'd done nothing to warrant his arrest.

"That oaf threatened us and refused to leave. Can you handcuff him and take him to the station? He's a menace to society." Letitia snatched up her scarf and looped it around her neck.

"Mrs. Larrimore, I missed talking with you in church Sunday. Mighty crowded for that Easter service."

Charles dipped his chin toward his chest. Then he rolled his shoulders back as though shrugging off tension.

Detective Smythe pulled out a notebook from his shirt pocket. "Ladies, suppose you tell me why you're here."

"This is my fault." Sarah stood on wobbly legs. "I'm Sarah Besco. Charles is my husband. He came here looking for me."

This had gone far enough. She didn't want Charles to get in trouble. She just needed to keep him away from Ricky until after the funeral. Too much going on to make sense of what was the right thing to do.

"And if you don't mind my asking, ma'am, how did you get that injury on your face?"

Charles balled up his fist. Sarah looked away and twirled a long strand of hair between two fingers. What could she say to defuse the situation?

Her mom pulled her close. "Detective, could you please take my son-in-law out of here? My daughter and I need privacy."

CHAPTER FORTY-SEVEN
COMPLICATIONS

A distinct purring car engine caught Letitia's attention. Elizabeth's snazzy wheels coasted into view outside Ida Lou's living room window. Oh no! Elizabeth couldn't deliver that adorable child straight into this red-haired monster's burly arms. What could she do to warn Elizabeth to stay away?

Charles pushed himself off the wall he'd been leaning against, his expression smug. "I'll be happy to leave . . . just as soon as my wife tells me where my two-year-old son is."

Letitia noted the possessive pronoun "my" instead of "our." She looked at the orange scarf in her hand.

"She brought my son across state lines without me knowing anything. I could charge her with kidnapping." Charles stepped toward William.

What would William do with that challenge? How could Sarah be at fault for trying to protect herself and the child?

William turned to Sarah. "Have you been awarded sole custody by the court?"

Sarah gulped. "We're not divorced."

Letitia yanked off her orange scarf and flew up to the window. She waved it up and down several times. There must be a way to signal Elizabeth to stay away. "Stop this! This young man is out of his mind. How dare he bust in here, threaten us, and start bringing up the law. I will not have it, William."

Hopefully, Elizabeth would see the movement at the window and realize something wasn't right. She didn't know how long she could bend up and down without her back giving out. She hoped Elizabeth wouldn't think she was practicing yoga or interpretive dance, as she had been known to do on occasion.

William raised an eyebrow at her, then focused on Charles. "As a *police officer*, you should know there is no law against a mother taking her child wherever she wants, short of a court order, particularly with a family emergency such as Mrs. Besco is enduring."

Well, hurray for some sanity to arrive. The Mercedes slowed, and the brakes lit up.

Charles whined, "Detective, my crazy wife took off three days ago without telling me. I would've understood if I'd known her dad was in the hospital. But she didn't say a word, just left. I've been worried sick."

Really? What decent husband didn't know his father-in-law was critically ill in a hospital?

"He's a liar!" Letitia raised the orange flare in a fist as though she were itching to deliver a knockout punch.

"Mrs. Larrimore, let's settle down." William pointed to the vacant easy chair. "Maybe you want to take a seat and rest a spell. Dispatch has my back-up on the way." He sent a pointed look toward Charles.

Good. The more officers to contain Charles, the better. But they'd better hurry. The Mercedes inched along the street. Thank goodness there were no empty parking spaces.

"Detective," Charles said in an oily tone, "if you call my sergeant, he'll confirm I filed a Missing Person's Report."

"Well, you can see Sarah is fine here with her mom." Betty walked to stand beside Letitia in front of the window. "She'd be even better if you would leave her in peace with her mom."

Betty must have observed Elizabeth's car, too. How could they keep him from seeing Ricky without throwing Charles out the back door?

"I only want to find out where my son is and ensure he's safe." Charles almost produced a tear.

What a con artist. She'd believe him if Sarah weren't frozen in place with that bruised face.

William looked at Sarah. "Sorry, ma'am, but he does have the legal right to see his child."

Betty stamped her brogan. "You can't be serious! You'd let this insane man have access to a child when his wife is black and blue!"

A short, female deputy materialized by the open door. "Hey, Smythe."

William seemed glad for the interruption, and he waved her in. The Mercedes was gone. Hopefully, Elizabeth wasn't circling the block for another shot at a parking space.

William smiled at his reinforcement. "Dawson, can you take this man outside and ask him for details about the M/P report he claims to have filed?"

Having Charles outside with a clear view of the street was the last thing they needed. "No need to make a public spectacle of everything."

Letitia pointed toward the dining room. "Maybe Katie could take Mr. McAdams over there."

She had no idea where Elizabeth and the child were. At least if Katie had Charles occupied in the interior, she and Betty could intercept Elizabeth and redirect them away from the house. Maybe.

William didn't look happy at all, but he didn't argue. Katie and Charles moved toward the back.

Letitia pushed Betty toward the front door. "Go find Elizabeth. Hurry."

Then she walked up to William and whispered, "The mayor has the child and is somewhere outside. They just drove by. How can we protect him?"

William looked over at Sarah. "Do you have a restraining order?"

"No. I didn't want to cause problems for my husband at his job. Besides, no one on his force would have believed me."

"Do you have a separation agreement?"

"There wasn't time. I had to get out fast."

Letitia glared at William like a battleship commander preparing to ram an enemy. "Are you telling me you can't do anything to protect this young woman and her child?"

He backed up a few steps. "I didn't say that. But you must follow some procedures." Then, looking at Sarah, he asked, "Do you want to press charges for injuries you sustained from your husband?"

She looked away, wrapping her arms around herself as tears spilled down her face. "I don't know," she whispered.

Letitia stood on tiptoe and poised her patrician nose inches from his. "I want to press charges!"

"Did Mr. McAdams assault you?"

"No. But that idiot committed a felony by blocking our exit and intimidating us."

"Has he committed a crime?" Ida Lou asked, standing near the coffee table with her arms around her daughter. "This is all so confusing."

William nodded. "Unlawful restraint of a person by force, threat, or intimidation can qualify as a felony."

He looked around the room. "Anyone else have something to report?"

Betty yelled from the entryway, "Count me in on pressing charges against that brute. Somebody's got to do something to help this young woman."

William focused on Sarah. "You could file for a Domestic Violence Protective Order. That's no guarantee of safety, but most judges require it as documentation in matters like this."

Sarah blinked. "Documentation of what?"

He looked at her. "Without proof of abuse or some other 'just cause,' your husband could allege you abandoned your responsibilities as a spouse without his consent. Desertion would not be a criminal offense unless he has serious known health problems, but it could be grounds for divorce. And since you're the one who left, you could be held financially responsible for things like child support, spousal support, and property division."

Sarah's knees buckled. Ida Lou reached to keep her from falling to the floor, then helped her settle on the couch.

Letitia kneeled beside Sarah. "Honey, I know you're scared, but you're not alone anymore. We're here to help you."

Sarah's eyes wandered from face to face. Letitia's heart went out to her. No wonder people stay trapped in a bad relationship when victims often get re-traumatized by the legal system. She was going to talk with William about protocol when this was over.

Letitia gently patted Sarah's hand. "Do you want to give the detective permission to call the forensic nurse who conducted your exam yesterday?"

William latched onto the potential evidence. "Ma'am, any documentation of abuse you've got is important, especially when a judge determines custody for your son."

When Sarah looked hesitant, he softly asked, "Do you want to protect your son?"

Letitia looked toward the back room. How much longer could Katie keep Charles occupied? "We were trying to give Ida Lou and Sarah a moment to reconnect before bringing him in."

Still no Betty. Maybe she'd caught up with Elizabeth. At least they hadn't shown up on the doorstep.

"I've got to make a call." Letitia scooted toward her purse and pulled out her cell. Elizabeth's phone went to voicemail.

"Ma'am, if you want to press charges for your injuries, I'd be happy to drive you to the station."

Sarah lifted her face and stood with a grim expression. "I'll do whatever it takes to protect my son. Could you please allow me a few minutes to talk with my mom?"

"Certainly." He jotted a note on his pad, then he moved toward the back where Katie had Charles.

While Sarah and Ida Lou whispered in a corner, Letitia clutched her phone and bore down on him like a grizzly defending her cub. "You've got to keep that maniac away from this house!"

"There's not much I can do officially without a restraining order, but you have my word I'll stay on top of this case."

She sniffed. "Let's hope that's good enough."

CHAPTER FORTY-EIGHT
PROFESSIONAL COURTESY

Charles studied cracks in the ugly concrete wall of Prosper's cruddy jail. He had been stewing for more than an hour at the police station. Smythe detained him in a holding cell, telling him to "cool off." Like *that* was going to happen. He hadn't seen Ricky, and his kid had to be nearby. He'd underestimated those old women.

Sarah hadn't pressed charges, but Smythe said the old women would. Just his luck to stumble on crones in cahoots with a church connection. What was the world coming to when a hard-working dad couldn't see his son?

The search at the station enraged him. Didn't they know who he was? They took his wallet and phone and put them in a plastic bag. How ridiculous that a fellow officer also made him remove his shoelaces and belt. Standard procedure, but humiliating.

Smythe said he'd make the call for him to inform the sergeant at Summit of the detention, but he sure was taking his sweet time. Would it be worth calling Doug? Probably not. He had day shift and wouldn't be able to drive a couple of hours to help.

He'd declined Smythe's offer of free legal advice. Pro bono boys messed up. All he needed was Sarge to shut down this farce. His boss in Summit would fix these hicks. Wouldn't he? He was on personal leave and could go where he wanted. No law against that.

First Sergeant Wilson had told him to stay away from the station, but he hadn't told him not to pursue leads. He'd understand how concerned he was about his wife's well-being, particularly with her dad dying.

A drunk ranted and raved in the nearby cell. What a mess. Never thought he'd be on this side of the room. Without his watch, he had no idea of the time. Might as well plan his strategy for getting out. What was the best way to spin the conversation? Of course. Sarah needed him with her at the funeral. He couldn't let his beloved wife grieve alone.

The toilet in the small room had no privacy. Lucky for him, he'd stopped earlier at the hamburger joint. He was caged like an animal. All he wanted to do was get his wife and kid home.

Charles massaged his left shoulder. Sarah used to give the best back rubs when he came home tired. She'd have a lot to make up for with all the heartache she'd caused with this running away stunt.

He had to find a way to convince Sarge these goons in Prosper weren't on the up-and-up. His service record had no blemishes. He did his job and did it well. He'd even received recognition from the captain for preventing a suicidal teen from jumping off a water tower last year.

Smythe strolled down the hallway toward him. He'd like to knock the smirk off his face.

"About time you let me out." Charles got off the hard, metal bed.

"Don't get your hopes up, bud. We're only going down the hall for a phone call."

At least, that was something. Anything was better than lying around on that gross mattress. No telling who had been on it before him. He couldn't resist goading the detective. "I was wondering if you guys knew about the Fourteenth Amendment."

The detective's expression remained impassive. Needling him might not work. Okay, score a point for being cool. Charles matched his stride to Smythe's.

"You know, police officers aren't immune when civil rights have been violated."

Charles closed the gap between them, just short of stepping on Smythe's heels. Smythe ignored him and slowed at the corner. Charles halted so he wouldn't run into the guy.

"In here." Smythe pointed at an open door to a small conference room where a gray phone sat on a conference table.

Charles pulled out a chair. "My sarge is going to read you the riot act when I tell him everything that's been going on."

Smythe looked unfazed. "First Sergeant Wilson and I already spoke. He wanted you in here for a conference."

That didn't sound good. Now, he'd be on the defensive. What garbage had Smythe fed his boss?

Smythe lifted the phone receiver, then dialed. "Hello, this is Detective William Smythe of Prosper. May I speak with First Sergeant Wilson? He's expecting my call."

A moment passed, then the detective pushed a button. Charles pictured his boss' nicotine-stained fingers cradling the phone as he leaned back in the roller chair with cracked upholstery.

Sarge's raspy voice came on the speaker. "First Sergeant Wilson."

"Hello, Sergeant. This is Detective Smythe. I have McAdams with me, and you are on speaker phone."

"Sarge," Charles ranted, "you won't believe what these idiots are—"

"Shut up, McAdams. I want to hear what the detective has to say. Detective Smythe, please tell me what the status is."

"As I mentioned, McAdams held his wife and three other women against their will at his mother-in-law's private residence. Claimed they were having a family reunion. But the ladies say he's guilty of trespass and abduction."

"McAdams," Sarge barked, "what do you have to say?"

Time to play the injured party. "Sir, you know I've been frantic to find my wife. On a lucky chance, I saw her father's obituary announcement and decided to come and support her in her time of need. She must be wild with grief, and that's why our communication broke down."

"Sounds reasonable." Sarge left a long silence. He must be deliberating on the best way to get him out. "What'd you do to make those other women so mad they want to press charges?"

Didn't see that coming. "Aw, boss. You know how women overreact."

Smythe looked down and shook his head.

"That so?" Sarge's voice got louder. "You dummy! You should know better than to barge into someone's home unannounced. Smythe has three sworn testimonies against you, Blockhead."

"Sarge, if I can just go and get my wife and kid, everything will settle down. I'll talk to the other women and even apologize." Charles had no such intention, but he wanted to make a compelling case to get out of this station.

Smythe's following comment took hope down a notch. "Sergeant, your hothead officer likes beating his wife. You should see the marks on her face. She also has bruises starting on her arm from how he manhandled her earlier at her mom's residence. I've got enough evidence to arrest him for assault and battery."

Charles balled his fist in his lap below the table. This guy had it in for him.

"Did you say there was a 911 call recorded?" Sarge rasped.

Smythe cleared his throat. "Yes, but there was a lot of background noise. The dispatcher said it sounded like people singing church songs and a dog barking."

"See, Boss? I told you those women were crazy." Charles leaned toward the phone as though he could see into Sarge's eyes and convince him of the truth.

"McAdams, how often do I have to tell you to shut up?" Sarge growled. "Detective, I appreciate you calling. Is there any way we can let this matter drop if the women choose not to file a complaint?"

Smythe flicked a piece of lint off his trousers. "I suppose if the women are reassured that McAdams will behave himself. The wife didn't want anything to go to court."

She'd better not if she knows what's good for her. I'm the one who keeps a roof over our heads.

Sarge spoke again. "Detective, we both know law enforcement gets a bad enough rap as it is in these times. Won't do anybody any good to have more ugly headlines."

Smythe took off his glasses and pinched the bridge of his nose. Charles couldn't figure out which way he'd go, but he valued Sarge's efforts on his behalf. Why make a mountain out of a molehill? Didn't the detective have any real cases to solve?

Smythe put his glasses back on. "This is a cop-to-cop courtesy warning. If your guy's not out of my town in ten minutes—under your promise, I will never see his ugly face again—I'm going to give him an extended tour of our facility."

Charles blew out a sigh of relief. "Man, thanks—"

Smythe ignored his proffered hand to shake.

"Detective, I appreciate this very much. I'll make sure McAdams tows the line." Sarge rasped genuine gratitude.

"Sergeant, there's one more thing you need to know." Smythe glared at Charles.

"What is it?"

Now what? Charles just wanted to get out of here. He didn't want them chit-chatting all day. He had to get Ricky.

"Mrs. McAdams went to a forensic nurse yesterday."

"What!" Charles stood up. She didn't have any money for that. Who'd paid?

Violent coughing could be heard over the speaker. Smoking was going to kill the sergeant if he didn't quit. Smythe stared at Charles as though he were an insect.

"What did the report say?" Sarge finally collected himself.

"Maybe not enough to earn a conviction, but our hospital's nurses have served as expert witnesses for DV victims in the past. Our local judge is passionate about these cases. I hear she has some personal experience with domestic violence."

"Okay, okay. You can escort my deputy out of town."

Charles moved closer to the door. "Sir, I'm telling you they have blown this whole thing out of proportion. Broads get emotional, and then they later regret their vindictive actions."

"McAdams, the only reason I'm doing this is because of your stellar service. I will never forget how you scaled that tower and talked that kid to safety. When you get back, we will set up anger management sessions—and counseling, too. You don't want to ruin your life making stupid decisions because the stress from work gets to you."

Smythe stood up. "We put our lives on the line every day. That's our job. It's no good taking out frustration on loved ones at home."

Charles hung his head a moment. These veterans had served a long time. Maybe they were right about him finding a better way to handle things.

Sarge barked, "Get back here ASAP. You'd better look me in the eyeball by close of business today! Is that clear?"

"Yes, sir," Charles mumbled. "But what about my wife and kid?"

"Didn't you hear what I said? You are under a direct order to report to the station immediately. Best give your wife some time with her mom."

"Maybe if you'd treat her better, she'd be eager to go home." Smythe examined the fingernails on his left hand and didn't look up.

Took every ounce of strength he had not to deck the detective right then. The speaker rattled again.

"And one more thing, McAdams," Sarge added. "If you do anything else to embarrass this office, I'm gonna personally kick you to the street. Permanently."

CHAPTER FORTY-NINE
LEVELING THE PLAYING FIELD

Letitia surveyed the Besco kitchen an hour after Detective Smythe escorted Sarah's nutcase husband to Prosper's police station. No one had eaten lunch, and it was close to two o'clock. She kicked off her heels, wishing she could plant her foot against several behinds.

Sarah had decided to wait until after the funeral to press charges against Charles. How could she be so dumb? Her stalker husband barged into Ida Lou's house full of people in broad daylight! He'd come back. How could they protect her and Ricky?

Couldn't law enforcement be more effective? That man was wily and seemed to know how to make every formality work to his advantage. Wonder if Junior could assist at the sheriff level? Then again, what could he do? Maybe if he didn't have his entire police force tied up trailing Mayor Elizabeth, his officers would have time to corral dangerous maniacs.

With only two hours until the funeral, she opened a loaf of bread and lined up two rows of whole wheat on the countertop. She spooned mayonnaise onto each slice. She wondered if Sarah would press charges or cave. She couldn't stand indecisiveness.

She yanked slices of smoked turkey from a plastic bag and slapped them on the bread. "Who wants lettuce on their sandwich?" she called out as she peered into the adjacent room, where Betty, Sarah, and Elizabeth watched from the couch as Ricky constructed a city of building blocks beside the coffee table.

Ida Lou lay on her stomach beside her grandson, almost nose to nose with him. While Ricky made motor noises for a crane lifting a structure, she scooted blocks next to his loader. On the other side of the oak table leg, Sweetie rested her head on her front paws and watched the child's every move with avid interest. The plastic banana and red ball lay nearby.

A chorus of "I do" answered her question. Letitia returned to the kitchen and began tearing romaine leaves off the head.

Elizabeth joined her by the island. "Anything I can do?"

"Yeah." Letitia humphed. "Call the police chief and tell him to throw away the key to that red-haired devil's cell."

Elizabeth rinsed lettuce under the faucet. "I'm afraid I am not in a good position today to dictate to law enforcement."

"Yeah, I know." Letitia jerked open a drawer, then slammed it shut. "You see a cutting board anywhere?"

Elizabeth peered at Letitia. "Are you referring to the article in today's paper?"

"Yep. Saw it this morning." Letitia opened the refrigerator and hunted for pickles.

"There's more than that, isn't there?" Elizabeth turned off the faucet and wrapped the lettuce in paper towels to drain.

Letitia gave up on pickles but found a cutting board and began slicing tomatoes.

"Letitia Larrimore, don't you hold out on me. Did you talk with Sheriff Bottoms today?"

She arranged the ruby-red slices on the pieces of bread. "Don't just stand there, woman. Quarter those apples."

Elizabeth stared at the paring knife Letitia held up, tomato juice dripping down her wrist like a trailer for a suburban horror movie. "Answer my question."

Letitia snatched a paper towel and dabbed at the mess. "Okay, I had a little chat with Junior. He's going to issue a correction to that defamatory article."

Elizabeth got apples from the fruit bowl and rinsed them. "Why did you interfere? I can take care of myself, I'll have you know."

What was Elizabeth getting in a snit about? Shouldn't she be grateful that she had helped? She swiped a chunk of apple from Elizabeth's workspace and chewed on it. Speaking with her mouth full, she said, "Seems like I heard not too long ago that someone had suffered enough, and she deserved better."

Elizabeth stopped chopping. "Oh."

"None of us are perfect. Maybe the good Lord put us here to help each other."

CHAPTER FIFTY

NOT FORGOTTEN

Charles pulled into a rest area at the state line an hour after his release. That bloodhound Smythe had followed him right to the border, stared at him, and then pulled a U-turn and left.

Charles got out of the car and stretched. He opened the back door and removed the vase of wilted pink roses. What a waste of money! He'd never give Sarah another penny of his hard-earned wages.

On the way into the men's room, he tossed the spoiled arrangement, vase and all, into a trash can. After the thud and the tinkle of breaking glass, he dusted off his hands. Forget Sarah. He wanted nothing more to do with her. But he did want Ricky.

He glanced at the road just traveled. No sign of Smythe. If he hurried, he could return to Prosper, collect his son, and still be in Sarge's office by five. If the boss asked what took him so long, he could say he had a flat.

Whether his kid was at the funeral chapel or the Besco home, it should be easy enough to scoop him up while everyone was distracted with the memorial service. Since no formal paperwork had been filed against him, it wouldn't be kidnapping.

Charles returned to the vehicle and scrolled through his phone to map out an alternative route to Prosper so he wouldn't run into Smythe. He could hardly wait to get Ricky and beeline back to Summit, where law enforcement officials minded their own business and let a man run his household. He should have no trouble convincing Doug's girlfriend, Gabby, to babysit while he worked. Or played.

Sarah would beg a court to award her custody. But she didn't have residency in Prosper, much less a job that paid enough to hire a good lawyer.

Charles pressed the accelerator harder. He surfed radio stations for heavy metal to prepare himself for the game ahead. When he neared Prosper's town limits, he stopped at a gas station to fill up. He went inside the shop to pay, adding a baseball cap and teal tourist t-shirt with a newspaper to his purchase. They should hide his face and hair from anyone who'd seen him earlier.

Charles doubted Sarah would take Ricky to a funeral. She was protective that way. Wouldn't even let the kid watch TV, other than that ridiculous yellow bird show. Somebody would end up babysitting this afternoon. But who? Probably one of those two nosy, old women from the neighborhood. Should be easy enough to snatch the kid from either.

Three blocks from Horizon Vista, he parked in the crowded lot of the public library. He pulled off the old shirt and slid on the new. He put on the cap, picked up the paper, and headed toward a bench under a shady tree close to Ida Lou's unit. Using the newspaper to shield his face, he peered over pages and monitored pedestrian traffic at 467 Begonia Lane.

At 3:15, the black woman with the Mercedes walked down the sidewalk and knocked on Ida Lou's door. When it opened, Charles saw Fatty, with Ricky holding her hand and the hairy dog jumping up and down by her boots. Ricky's auburn hair shone brightly as he leaned down to pet the dog. The door closed before Charles could see more.

Maybe he should get a puppy for Ricky. He would promise him one as soon as they got back to Summit. He missed riding Ricky around on his shoulders. The poor kid had been dragged all over the countryside the last three days. He must be confused and worn out.

Charles thought about his childhood. He couldn't come up with a single happy memory. His dad rarely was around, and when he was, he created drama, not fun. After the old man had left for good, a string of pathetic losers had chased his mom. He never knew stability. He wouldn't let that happen to his son.

Charles had started a newspaper route at age ten to earn money and help his mother buy groceries. He'd sworn his children never would know poverty—and he'd worked hard to keep that promise.

Ida Lou's garage door opened, and a gold Cadillac backed out. Straining to see who was inside, he spotted his mother-in-law and wife up front, with Skinny and Fatty in the back. He set the newspaper aside and stood halfway behind the tree. Then he raised his arm to adjust his cap bill and craned to look for Ricky's little red head.

The kid wasn't in the car. Nor was the black woman. Charles smiled. Four down. One to go. He turned to pick up the newspaper, then walked a few steps to pitch it in the trash can, so his back was to the exiting quartet.

After the garage door closed and the Cadillac left, Charles waited a few minutes to ensure no one would return for some forgotten item. He strolled toward the back of the Besco residence.

Cutting across the lawn, he sidled up to the garage's side door. Then he took a credit card from his wallet, pushed the sole of his shoe against the door's bottom to force it open a crack, and slid up the thin plastic.

With a little push, he released the latch and then pocketed the ruined credit card. He could replace it later. Acting as if he owned the place, Charles swung open the door and entered the garage, leaving the door ajar for a quick getaway.

CHAPTER FIFTY-ONE
BRACE ON IMPACT

The other women hadn't been gone five minutes when Elizabeth heard Sweetie growl. She stopped pouring lemonade into the glass in Ida Lou's kitchen and listened. The dog raced to the door connecting to the garage and pawed at the metal threshold. Had the others forgotten something? But if so, why was the dog not wagging its tail? Elizabeth set the pitcher on the counter.

"Ricky, where are you?" Elizabeth whirled toward the living room where the child had been playing with new toys.

Before she could take more than a step, the garage entry door cracked open. Red hair showed toward the top third of the doorframe. She turned to run, but her shoes slid on the tile. A muscular man thrust open the door and entered.

This must be Sarah's husband. Ricky looked like a miniature copy. She didn't stand a chance. If he'd harm his wife, what would he do to her? A picture of Sarah's bruises came to mind.

Oh, no! The child. How could she stop him? She'd never overpower a man in his prime. So, why wasn't he in jail?

"Who are you?" She tried to put authority in her voice. Maybe she could talk sense in him. Sweetie crouched by her feet.

"I just want my son. Stay out of my way, and there will be no problem."

She let him pass. What else was there to do? She was a failure. All her training as an advocate for survivors of domestic violence hadn't prepared her for an actual crisis.

"Ricky! Daddy's here!" He called out with joyful expectation.

As soon as he moved to the living room, she grabbed her cell and tapped the emergency call icon. She'd never used that. How did it work anyhow? Too late to wonder. Sliding the phone in her slacks pocket, she followed him into the living room.

Ricky nestled in his father's embrace with his little arms around his dad's neck. "Hey, buddy. I've missed you. How about you and me head home?"

She couldn't let that happen. But what right did she have to stop him? She wasn't a member of the family. She couldn't reach the women at the memorial service. Their phones would be turned off. By the time she could drive there to warn them, Charles and the child would be long gone.

"Daddy, stay. We play farm." Ricky squirmed to get down, but his dad held him.

Sweetie charged up to Charles' feet and jumped like a pogo stick to get near the child. He booted her aside. When she tumbled over, Ricky cried.

"Sir, no need to be rough. Why don't you put the child down and sit on the couch for a few minutes?"

"No way. I'm outta here. Tell my wife if she ever wants to see Ricky again, she'd better come home and straighten up." Charles repositioned his son in the crook of his arm and retraced his steps to the kitchen.

Elizabeth followed at a respectful distance. She didn't want to do anything to escalate the situation and put Ricky at greater risk. Would help arrive in time? Had the emergency call even gone through?

Charles exited to the garage with Ricky staring back at her over his dad's shoulder. She trailed them. At least she could see what type of vehicle he would leave in and get the license tag. Maybe.

By the time she had gone through the garage to the outside, Charles had Ricky halfway across the lawn. Then she saw the gardener staring at them. "Stop him! she yelled, pointing at Charles.

Juan dropped the shovel in the dirt and faced off toward Ricky's dad. Charles kept moving until Juan stood in front and blocked any advance. The boy's upturned face was paper-white.

Charles set the child down behind him a few feet, turned around his baseball cap, bunched his fists, and charged Juan.

Sweetie dashed to guard the child, standing in front of him and growling toward the men. The gardener attempted to dodge Charles. Although young and fit, would Juan be able to match Charles' strength? If only she could use the distraction to get to the child first.

CHAPTER FIFTY-TWO

SPIN CYCLE

As the two men thrashed in the grass, Elizabeth hustled to pick up Ricky and move him to safety. She scooped up him and the dog. "C'mon, honey." Ricky let her hold him and didn't resist. Could she make it back to the house and lock the door?

A siren sounded. Good. The police should be here any minute. Ricky shivered in her arms. Sweetie licked his cheek.

At a run, Detective Smythe rounded the corner from the street. He assessed the action, then smiled. Juan had pinned Charles face down in the dirt. Charles pushed up with his arms and heaved—to no avail.

"Mayor, you okay?"

"Yes. Thank goodness you got here so fast." She gave Ricky a little hug. "Everything's going to be all right."

The men on the ground grunted but stayed put.

Smythe keyed his mic to report an update to dispatch. "Everyone's safe."

Charles spat grass out of his mouth and arched his neck. "Get him off me!"

"Only if you stay real still while I handcuff you." Smythe winked at the gardener.

A safe distance away, Elizabeth released Sweetie to lighten the load. The dog ran to Juan's side, circling the pair on the lawn.

Charles rocked back and forth, trying to break free without success. The gardener looked like he was enjoying himself. Elizabeth wished Smythe would hurry with the cuffs.

A glint of something silver in the crumpled grass caught Smythe's attention. After grabbing his handkerchief, he crouched down and retrieved a bent credit card.

"Well, well, well, look what I found. This your card, McAdams? I'd say we've got evidence for a case of trespassing and breaking and entering."

Beads of sweat globbed the dirt on Charles' forehead. "I . . . I found that on this illegal," he sputtered, "after he stole my wallet and tried to rob my mother-in-law."

Smythe crouched low to look into Charles' face. "You want to explain why you're here, barely an hour after I escorted you to the state line?"

"When I stopped for gas, I couldn't find my wallet. I realized I must have left it here. But when I returned, I found this *criminal* trying to sneak into the house."

"Uh huh." Smythe rocked back on his heels. "Where's your car?"

Ricky wiggled down from Elizabeth's arms and hurried to his dad's side before she could stop him. "Daddy, okay?"

Her heart sank lower than the *Titanic*. This child shouldn't witness anymore. She stepped over and reached out her hand. "Ricky, let's go inside. Your dad needs to talk to Mr. Smythe."

Ricky gave his dad a slight pat on the shoulder, and Charles' body sagged. The gardener almost fell off when the tension relaxed.

Smythe put his hand on Juan's back to steady him. *"Muchas gracias, mi amigo."*

Elizabeth coaxed Ricky to follow her, and Sweetie tagged behind as more officers swarmed the area. She entered the garage side door and locked the deadbolt behind her. She took Ricky into the living room and tried to distract him. Sweetie flopped beside him and panted.

A few minutes later, someone knocked on the front door. Elizabeth got up from her spot by the child and looked through the peephole. She didn't know if she'd ever feel safe again. Smythe stood outside.

She unlocked the door. "Come in, Detective. You are the hero for the day."

He wiped his feet on the mat before entering. "No, ma'am, Juan is the one who protected the boy."

"Juan? Is that the name of the gardener?"

"Yes, ma'am. Good thing he happened along when he did. A good kid."

Elizabeth glanced at Ricky on the floor, making the plastic horse gallop along the sofa's edge. "Is he going to be safe?"

"McAdams kept running his mouth about illegal aliens. Alleges *he* was the one to stop the gardener from stealing."

"That's the most preposterous thing I've ever heard." Elizabeth shook her head.

"I agree, but Juan's limited English would make it hard for him to testify in court. Mayor, it's a good thing you are a witness, too."

Elizabeth pointed toward an easy chair. "Would you like to take a seat for a moment?"

"Appreciate that, but I need to process McAdams at the station and give his sergeant a call in Summit. Just wanted to be sure you and the little guy are doing okay."

"Thanks to you and Juan, we are. But, Detective, I may not be the best witness for the stand." She clasped her hands together. "I assume you read the allegations in the newspaper?"

Smythe pushed his glasses up on the bridge of his nose. "Mayor, I know you help women at the shelter. Isn't that how you met Sarah? Don't you worry about a thing."

"But how—"

"Ma'am, the citizens of this town trust me to protect them. It's my job to know what's going on. Thank you for approving the budget allowing for more service vehicles. That Taurus is a nice ride. Occasionally, I may miss a thing or two, but I make it right in the end."

He headed outside. She closed and locked the door after him. Life was full of surprises. She knelt on the floor by Ricky and petted Sweetie. She needed a moment to catch her breath.

The boy looked into her eyes, his little fingers clutching a farm animal. "Daddy go bye-bye?"

Elizabeth's heart clenched. Poor kid. "Yes, honey."

The child scrambled onto the couch and gazed out the bay window at the black-and-white car with his father inside. "Kiss Daddy?"

Elizabeth wanted to cry. "You can blow kisses to your father."

"No!" The child grabbed his old teddy bear on the pillow, swung his feet down, and ran toward the front door. "I kiss Daddy."

Elizabeth met him at the entry and held him with one arm while she unlocked and opened the door. She called out to Smythe. "Wait a minute. Ricky wants to say goodbye."

He looked from her to the child, then shrugged. "Bring him down."

Smythe hollered at the policewoman in the driver's seat. "Hold on."

Elizabeth carried Ricky to the car, and Smythe walked beside them. As they neared, the driver rolled down the back window.

When she stood a step away from Charles, Ricky leaned forward and pressed his little lips to his father's stubbly cheek. Then he raised the teddy bear and rubbed his dad's face with the stuffed animal's silky ear.

"Here, Daddy. You take Boo." His little arms extended as far as they could reach.

Elizabeth took the bear and offered it to Charles, who had trouble grasping it because of the handcuffs. The officer in the passenger front seat set the toy beside Charles.

"I love you, Son." Charles looked sad, and she almost felt sorry for him.

"Mr. McAdams, you need to get your act together. Your boy deserves better." She hugged the child as though she could shield him from more of life's heartaches. Ricky stared at his dad, his little chin trembling.

As the cruiser departed, Elizabeth recalled a passage from Isaiah in the Bible. "And a little child will lead them."

Dear Lord, please give Sarah wisdom about how to secure little Ricky. May You intervene in his daddy's heart so he will be willing to leave behind violence and show true love. Amen.

CHAPTER FIFTY-THREE

I IN THE STORM

Sarah tiptoed out of the guest bedroom at Ida Lou's house. She left Ricky sound asleep. He cuddled a new, black teddy bear Elizabeth had brought over after dinner. Sweetie lay beside him—snoring with her feet splayed against Ricky's back.

Sarah strolled into the family room. She wore a yellow nightgown and robe belonging to her mother, who lay curled up on a corner of the sofa in a too-large terry cloth housecoat embroidered with RSB. Her mom patted the cushion beside her. Settling in, Sarah sighed. A glow flickered from a beeswax candle on the coffee table.

Finally, an opportunity to be alone with her mom. But all the words she'd rehearsed over the last three years refused to come out. Nothing she could say would bring her dad back. Or make up for the lost time. How could her mother forgive her for what she'd done? What could she say to express her appreciation—and regret?

Her mom yawned and stretched. "I'm exhausted, but I don't want to go to bed yet." She took Sarah's hand. "Time with you is precious."

The signature fragrance of rosewater brought back childhood memories of snuggles. "Oh, Mama, I'm sorry for what I did."

"Honey, that's ancient history. What's important is that we're together. Let's treasure what we have instead of feeling sorry for what we have lost."

Time to tell the whole truth and explain why she made the choices she had. "Mom, remember how, on the morning of graduation, you told me to explore options with my new degree?"

"Yes, honey, I've regretted interfering many times."

"No, you were right. I'd just found out I was pregnant." Sarah twisted the afghan in her hands. "I didn't want you to be ashamed of me."

"Oh, sweetheart. I am sorry you went through that without me. But Ricky is a wonderful gift. Having him is a blessing."

Sarah gulped back tears. How had she let Charles convince her that her parents would control and manipulate her?

Her mom reached over to smooth a lock of hair on Sarah's forehead. "How's your cheek healing?"

"Haven't noticed it much lately with everything else that's been going on."

Sarah's mother smiled sweetly as she pulled a crocheted throw over her. Despite her loss, her mom worried more about her than herself. Sarah hoped she could be that considerate of Ricky's needs in this time of change.

A sleepy Sweetie staggered into the room, jingling dog tags. She stopped by the couch and waited for Sarah to pick her up. After setting the pet between them, Sarah looked out the window into the night. "Do you think Charles will be able to sleep in jail?"

"I hope not," she muttered, rubbing Sweetie's tummy.

"Mom, I still love him."

Saying the words out loud surprised Sarah. How could she care about a man who'd lied to her, beat her, and tried to kidnap their child on the day she buried her father?

Her mom stopped petting Sweetie and hugged Sarah. "I don't think I'll ever stop loving your dad, either."

Sarah closed her eyes and recalled the moments of romance when Charles had courted her. He'd danced barefoot with her on the sandy beach the night they eloped, then snuggled next to her in the lifeguard's chair, giving her his shirt to keep her warm.

"Do we have to stop loving?" Sarah didn't know how to divide her heart between hope and reality.

Her mom leaned back on the sofa. "Well, if we do, I don't know how. But caring for someone is different than allowing yourself to be mistreated."

Sarah fiddled with the blanket, weaving her fingers in and out of the looped pattern.

"Mama, I don't know how to move forward. There are many obstacles. How am I going to take care of Ricky?"

"You aren't alone. I am here, and we have found wonderful friends in Prosper. I am learning God will help us find a way if we trust Him."

Maybe something would work out with that church daycare position Elizabeth had mentioned. If so, she could earn income and be with Ricky. But if that didn't pan out, she didn't know what to do. She sure didn't have much of a resumé.

Sarah tugged on the blanket's trim. "Do you think God loves me after what I've done?"

"I know He does." Her mom leaned closer to her.

"I'm not so sure." She hadn't been to church in years. Was it too late to start?

"Then ask Him to show you. He will—in His own special way." She pointed toward her purse on the coffee table near Sarah. "Get my hairbrush, okay?"

Uncrossing her legs to lean forward, Sarah dug in the bag and handed over the brush.

"Sit here in front of me." She motioned to the floor. "I used to brush your hair when you were little. You said it helped you think."

Sarah moved to the floor, settled her back against the couch, and rewrapped the afghan around her. Sweetie crawled from under her mom's arm and swiped Sarah's cheek with her rough pink tongue.

"Mama, she smells!"

Her mom leaned over to sniff, then wrinkled her nose. "Oh, dear, you're right. Things have been crazy around here. Why don't you put her in the tub with Ricky in the morning?"

"Those two will get bubbles everywhere!" She imagined Sweetie shaking and sending soapy water flying all over the bathroom, with Ricky laughing and trying to catch the iridescent bubbles.

Her mother made slow, gentle brush strokes along her hair. "When Ricky makes a mistake, do you stop loving him?"

"Of course not." She redirected her mom's hand away from a delicate part of her scalp—courtesy of Charles' rampage.

"Is there anything he could do to make you stop caring?"

Sarah looked over her shoulder at her mom. "No. He's my child, and I'll always love him."

"Baby, that's how God feels about you."

The rhythmic brush strokes came like steady waves kissing the shore. "Mom, do you think Daddy knew I loved him?"

Ida Lou's hand paused midair, then slid forward to tap the bundle of letters on the coffee table. "When things settle down, you can go through those again and see how much your father loved you. He knew you would come home one day, and we never gave up hope."

Sarah nestled Sweetie against her cheek. "What if Charles won't change?"

Her mother resumed the tender brushing. "Your husband has to make his own choices. And while I hope he'll turn his life around for you and Ricky, if he doesn't, you'll need to stand strong and give my grandson a safe and happy upbringing."

The candle's flame wavered, and little puffs of smoke swirled around the dwindling wick. "Charles has been the breadwinner. If he goes to jail, I won't be able to pay the bills."

"You can live with me." Ida Lou set down the brush.

"Mama, I'm twenty-four years old. I don't want to be a burden." Sarah stood and moved to the easy chair by the couch.

"You'd be the one helping me."

Sarah's heart wrenched. "Oh, Mama, I'm sorry. I've been busy thinking about myself and didn't consider your grief. You've always seemed strong."

"Thank you, darling, but I don't feel strong. Your dad took care of many things. I don't know how to turn on the irrigation system or check our online bank balances."

Sarah straightened her shoulders. "Mom, together, we can make it!"

Ida Lou smiled. "Of course, we can. God will help us rebuild. And each of us will discover how much we can grow with His help."

There was hope after all. Time to celebrate. "And I seem to recall a Besco family tradition. Do you have any ice cream?"

"Are you kidding? Your dad keeps at least two flavors in the freezer. Right now, I think we have mint chocolate chip and butter pecan."

Sarah's eyes welled up with tears. But she refused to let them fall—not now. If her mom could be strong, so could she. "Which flavor do you like better?"

They walked to the kitchen, arguing about the merits of chocolate chips versus roasted pecans. Sweetie trotted after them, expecting a dollop or two for herself.

CHAPTER FIFTY-FOUR

ADROIT REDIRECTION

The toaster seared one side of the bread more than the other as Betty took the jar of peanut butter from the pantry. Then, settling onto a kitchen chair, she shed the newspaper's plastic skin and snapped open the front page. She grinned at the *Herald Constellation's* banner headline: "Mayor's Charity Efforts Benefit Survivors of Domestic Violence."

> Prosper—Sheriff Thomas Bottoms III concluded investigation into allegations Mayor Elizabeth Robinson stole jewelry and sold it to pawn shops.
>
> "The mayor is cleared of any shadow of wrongdoing," the sheriff said in an interview last night, stating the items sold to Fred's Pawn Shop were not stolen property.
>
> He added that he appreciated the public monitoring activities in the community and encouraged citizens with concerns to call him anytime. "But they should leave the interpretation of such information to law enforcement experts."
>
> Further investigation by *Herald Constellation* reporters uncovered the jewelry in question came from women staying at a shelter for victims of domestic violence, who used the proceeds to support themselves. (The name and

location of this shelter is being withheld out of concern for the safety of the residents.)

An employee of the shelter gave the mayor high praise. "Mrs. Robinson has a generous heart. She picks people up, dusts them off, and helps them get back on their feet. Our shelter couldn't go on without her support."

The mayor was unavailable for comment.

In a follow-up interview, Fred Nix, the pawn shop owner who initially reported concerns about the mayor, said, "Me coming forward to tell the sheriff about suspicious activities shows our industry is self-policing. We already work with cops on a regular basis. We don't need the government telling us what to do."

What a rat. But at least Elizabeth's name was finally cleared. Betty read on.

"Domestic violence is a terrible issue in every part of US society," said Letitia Larrimore, a volunteer with an agency that helps survivors.

According to statistics released by the National Coalition Against Domestic Violence, "On average, nearly twenty people per minute are physically abused by an intimate partner in the United States."

Larrimore added, "The mayor donates her time and gasoline to assist people fleeing domestic violence." Anyone interested in donating items to the shelter, such as toiletries, fresh food and pantry items, gift cards for clothing, and bus tokens, may contact Women United for Him at 555-697-4459.

"Mayor Robinson heads up many efforts to help people in the community, and we're lucky to have her in Prosper," Larrimore said.

Sheriff Bottoms agreed. "The mayor cooperated to the fullest in this investigation. Just goes to show you what an outstanding place Prosper is. We keep watch 24/7 to keep our community respectable."

During budget talks at next week's city council meeting, Councilman Bobby Ward plans to propose the town subsidize some of the shelter's operating expenses. "I understand the shelter is filled to capacity, with no place other than hotels to put more people."

The sheriff said he is researching options for auctioning unclaimed stolen property confiscated from criminals and using the proceeds to benefit survivors of domestic violence. "Wouldn't it be great if this abandoned stuff sitting in storage could be used to replace items victims have lost due to violence?"

Anyone needing more information about domestic violence and sources for help may contact the National Coalition Against Domestic Violence at 800-799-SAFE (7233). Callers are cautioned to protect call history from abusers. There also is an online site at www.thehotline.org. Users are advised to protect search history.

Betty didn't know what Letitia had done to change the sheriff's outlook, but her friend was a genius. Who else could redirect public opinion with such cleverness?

Betty spread peanut butter on her burned toast and munched it with satisfaction. Now all she had to worry about was how to protect the Besco family from further attacks by Charles. Ida Lou and Sarah had enough to deal with in their grief; they shouldn't have to worry about anything else.

The WUFHs discussed setting up an anonymous fund for legal aid for clients of Solutions so that survivors could get good counsel. Letitia also wanted to organize a community workshop with art therapy to help children cope with the trauma they'd experienced. She'd phone Detective William Smythe after breakfast to get updates.

There also was the matter of the prayer chain mishap to rectify. She would call AnnMarie after talking with Smythe. She didn't want Pastor James to doubt her ability to lead the team.

CHAPTER FIFTY-FIVE
CAGE MATCH

Charles approached the jail's visitation room with a confident step. He wasn't about to show fear in this joint. That could cost him his life. He slumped into a plastic chair and rested cuffed hands on the table.

He looked at the slender man across the clear screen from him. The guy had ridiculous bushy eyebrows over hazel eyes. "By the looks of that tacky, old suit, you must be my public defender."

"Nope." The other man didn't act offended.

"Then who are you?" Was he on public display, or what? What he needed was a kick-butt lawyer. Hopefully, Doug could come up with a quick loan.

"My name is James Sebastian, but most folks call me Pastor James."

"You here to give me my last rites or something?" Might need them if the other inmates found out who he was. So far, they had kept him in isolation.

"I'm a minister, not a priest." James glanced at the guard, who stood close by, keeping an intimidating presence.

Charles leaned forward and spoke in a calm voice. "The guys in here are gonna kill me when they find out I'm a cop."

"Maybe." James shrugged.

Charles' stomach spasmed. He had no idea how to get out of this fix. He sure couldn't ask Sarge to vouch for him. For that matter, he may not even have a job to go back to. "What am I gonna do?"

"For now, you're going to answer a few questions." Pastor James patted the worn Bible in front of him. "And you need to tell me the truth. Why did your wife leave?"

"I don't know. She's always whining and nagging about one thing or—"

"Time to come clean, buddy." His stern tone left no room for deception.

"All right." Charles looked off to one side. "I lost my temper because she hadn't answered my call. So, I . . . I banged her up a little bit."

"A little bit?" James thumped his hand on the table. "The hospital's forensic report indicated near-lethal strangulation."

Charles' head snapped up. "No way."

"You almost killed her."

Charles recalled the bloodied nightgown. "I didn't mean to hurt her. I love her."

"I believe you do." James kept the tone neutral.

Well, that was something. At least, the holy man wasn't raging at him. He needed somebody in his corner. "As a kid, my old man lost his temper and beat up Mom. I never thought I would do the same thing."

"Suffering violence as a child causes great trauma. Is that what you want for your son?"

What was up with this guy? One minute, he was sympathetic; and then the next, he slam-dunked him. "Look. I don't know what to do. My wife left; my kid stays with strangers; and my boss will probably fire me after the fiasco here."

"Charles," James said in a gentle voice, "you can't deceive and mistreat people and expect them to keep letting you wrong them."

"Hey, I thought you preacher-types were all about forgiveness."

James laid his hand on the Bible. "Forgiveness isn't about whitewashing problems. It's doing the tough work of helping someone see his wrong behavior and encouraging him to make amends."

"And what about the wrongs done to me?"

"Such as?" James tilted his head and raised one thick eyebrow.

Charles clenched his fists. "If Sarah hadn't taken off, none of this would've happened."

"Man up, Charles!" Pastor James shouted so loudly, the guard cocked his head.

That was unexpected. The church types were weaklings, weren't they? But this guy had about blasted him into the next room. How should he respond?

"Charles, you've misused your God-given authority as a husband to injure the person you vowed to honor and cherish. You're also neglecting your responsibility as a father to guide your son in honorable ways."

Who was this guy to talk down to him? Charles clenched his fist. Since his hands were cuffed, he swiveled his head to the guard, wanting him to deal with the insult.

"The preacher's telling the truth, McAdams. You're an embarrassment to every honorable officer in law enforcement." So much for moral support.

Charles covered his face with his hands, the cuffs sliding down his wrists. "You know what my little boy did yesterday?"

"Tell me." Pastor James leaned forward on his elbows.

"Ricky gave me his favorite stuffed teddy bear while I sat in the back of the cruiser." Charles' voice broke. "And you know what he did then?" The words caught in his throat, but he forced them out. "He kissed me."

James remained silent. His head bowed as though in prayer.

Charles held up his hands in a gesture of surrender. "I want my son to have what I never did. Including an honorable father."

James lifted his head and smiled. "Now you're talking!"

"But how can I do anything about that if I'm locked up?"

"God has used prisons to forge many of His strongest leaders."

No idea what that meant. Sounded crazy. Most inmates got hardened from what Charles had seen. He didn't want to serve time for trying to be with his kid.

James looked at the guard. "May I have permission to show Charles something in the Bible?"

"Go ahead. That book's been inspected."

He flipped to a marked page. "In Genesis, the first book of the Bible, there's a story about a man named Joseph. Although how he landed in jail differs from your circumstances, God can redeem this time away from your family and bring about good in your life, just as He did for Joseph."

"How?" None of that made sense. Staying in jail would ruin his career and do nothing to put his family back together. Would Sarah wait? Most wives of guys who served time didn't.

James ran his finger along the page and read. "While Joseph was in prison, the Lord was with him. He showed him kindness and granted him favor in the eyes of the prison warden."

Charles knew a few stories of criminals who had turned their lives around. But he was the good guy, wasn't he? "Is that why you came here? To read me some fairy tale?"

James pushed the Bible toward Charles. "Read it yourself."

The guard cleared his throat. "Time's up, Pastor. But if you want, you can let him borrow that Bible."

"I'd like that very much." He turned to Charles. "Your Heavenly Father loves you. And He has big plans for you." He stood. "Let the guard know if you want me to come back and visit."

Now what? The last thing Charles wanted to do was read an old book. But maybe he should look at it. About the only thing he had was time.

CHAPTER FIFTY-SIX

QUIET SANCTUARY

Ida Lou sat with Sweetie in the quiet sanctuary of First Church, hurling questions at God. Hard to believe that only one week had passed since Richard's collapse, when she'd come here for the Good Friday vigil. She'd lived decades in the last seven days.

Refusing to wear widow's black—Richard said that color depressed him—she crossed her legs and shook out her ankle-length plum skirt. She stared at the red-velvet-draped altar in front of the sanctuary.

"God, I don't get it. Why did You let Richard die when You knew Sarah was coming home?" Her legs bounced up and down, making the pleats in her skirt sweep open like an angel's wing preparing for flight.

Sweetie tried to crawl off her lap, but Ida Lou blocked her with her hand. The dog licked it.

Ida Lou stared at the wooden cross mounted on the wall. "Fine. You don't want to talk, but I've got to, or I'll go crazy with grief. Every song I hear makes me think of Richard. I miss his strong hand holding mine and how he put his arm around my waist and brushed his lips on my forehead."

Sweetie managed to escape, and Ida Lou didn't have the energy to go after her. The poor little thing sniffed along the blue-carpeted aisle.

Ida Lou dabbed her eyes with the blouse sleeve. Why hadn't she put tissues in her purse? "God, are You here? I'm not asking for a burning bush or anything, but could You at least let me know You hear me?"

The only sound was muffled traffic on the road outside.

"All right. Have it Your way." Dust motes traveled a corridor toward the stained-glass window behind the wooden cross.

"I am grateful You sent Sarah, despite the timing. And little Ricky looks just like my Richard, except for his hair. Please protect them both, Lord. And help them find their way."

The stained-glass image of Jesus seemed to reach into her soul. "I even pray for Charles. Lord, I hope You knock some sense into him. Help him become the man You've created him to be."

Recrossing her legs, Ida Lou fanned the skirt with an impatient tug. "I need to thank You for Betty, Letitia, Elizabeth, and Juan, too. Those amazing people have been incredibly kind to me—and my whole family."

Sunlight diffused through the window and warmed the pew where she sat. Fidgety, she reached for the little, yellow pencil in the wooden holder on the back of the pew. Unfortunately, its lead was broken, and it had no eraser.

"God, I just want to erase all the pain from my heart, but I don't know how."

Sweetie returned from investigating the sanctuary and curled into a ball by her feet. Ida Lou toyed with the tiny pencil. "I can't write any more happiness into life without Richard." She dropped it back into the holder.

Leaning her head against the hard pew, she gazed at a massive beam supporting the roof. She pictured the men of Prosper's founding congregation working hard to construct the sanctuary a century ago. She wondered if they knew their faithful labor would one day shield her.

God did have a way of putting provision in place decades before a person needed it. Seemingly random circumstances reunited her with Sarah. She shivered to think about what might have happened to her daughter and grandson without intervention from Betty, Letitia, and Elizabeth.

The women had invited her to join them in charity work yesterday while Sarah and Ricky toured the church's preschool. Her neighbors had made a difference for her daughter and grandson. Shouldn't she also invest in others' lives? That's what Richard would tell her.

She sat up and concentrated on Jesus' face in the stained-glass window. "When the ladies started telling me about WUFHs, I thought they were talking about a dog group for Sweetie."

Sweetie sat up on her haunches and cocked her furry little head at the sound of her name.

"Hello?" a male voice boomed in the empty room.

Ida Lou froze. *God? Is that You?*

A pudgy, acne-scarred face appeared in the doorway from a side hall. Terrence from the funeral home entered the sanctuary.

Ida Lou leaned down, scooped up Sweetie, and crouched on her hands and knees on the floor. She hoped Terrence couldn't see her. How embarrassing if he had heard her talking alone out loud in the sanctuary. Maybe if she hid, he wouldn't notice.

Slow, heavy footsteps trod down the aisle, stopping at the end of her row. Her eyes traveled from polished, black dress shoes to black trousers, a ghastly red tie, and then Terrence's concerned face. "Mrs. Besco? Are you all right?"

She released Sweetie. Then, she crouched, steadying herself on the pew in front of her like a runner preparing for a race. The dog jumped up and down, whimpering to be picked up.

Ida Lou nearly burst out laughing at her ridiculous situation. She breathed deeply. "I'm fine, thanks. Must have dropped my earring." She patted the floor for effect.

"I can help you look." When he leaned over, Sweetie leaped into his arms. His clothing had a faint, acrid, smoky smell.

"No need. I found it." She rubbed her right ear, feeling the diamond stud still in place.

She hoped Terrence would have the decency to get the hint and leave. He didn't.

"Mind if I sit down?"

"Of course not." But she did. He probably wanted to offer sympathy. She'd had enough of that to last a lifetime. But, unfortunately, none of the mourning lessened the raw ache in her heart. The last thing she wanted was to melt into another puddle of tears.

He extended a hand to help her, his other arm encircling Sweetie's belly. Ida Lou accepted his assistance and rose as gracefully as possible under the circumstances. She sat on the pew, then scooted down several inches.

Terrence lowered his large body onto the bench seat, settled Sweetie on his lap, and pulled a handkerchief from his coat pocket. He blew his nose, sounding like a trumpet.

He folded the cotton cloth, then gripped it in his hand. "You in here talking with God?"

How much of her tirade had he heard? Would he report her to Pastor James for being disrespectful in the sanctuary or crazy?

She lowered her head. "Yeah. I've been trying to get Him to explain why He let my husband die."

Terrence nodded as though he understood. "A stroke took my mom when I was seventeen. I'm thirty-two years old now and still asking God about that." His matter-of-fact tone removed any awkwardness she felt.

"I'm so sorry." Now she didn't know what to say to comfort him.

"I sit on this pew weekly to talk with her and tell her how things are going." Terrence scratched behind Sweetie's ear. "She always sat in church right about where you are."

"Oh." Embarrassed, Ida Lou started to get up, but Terrence held out his hand for her to stay.

"It's okay. Mama always was one to share."

Ida Lou ached for the loss he'd suffered. She thanked God for the twenty-five years she'd had with Richard, as well as her reunion with Sarah. Maybe she should reach out to Terrence the way the WUFHs cared for Sarah. On second thought, she wasn't sure how much more stress she could handle. Didn't she need time to grieve without other burdens?

He sniffled, and his head sank onto his chest. Sweetie licked Terrence's chin.

"You know, I'm having a taco party at my house tonight to thank Juan for everything he does in the neighborhood. Would you like to join us?"

The man's face brightened. "I'd love that." His gaze lowered. "Most folks tend to shy away from morticians."

"I'd be honored to have you come to my party." Although she did hope he wouldn't talk about his work at dinner. "You stood with me in my time of need."

"That's my way of giving back. I don't want anyone to feel as lonely as I did when I had to tell Mama goodbye." He tickled under Sweetie's chin.

As she pictured how many tears Terrence must have shed over the years in this place, the blue carpet along the aisles seemed to undulate like water trickling from a hose. The sound resembled rain pitter-pattering on a tin roof, and a vision of crystal water flowing from the aisles made Ida Lou lift her feet so her sandals wouldn't get wet.

She lowered them immediately. *I must be hallucinating. Does grief cause this?* She closed and rubbed her eyes. When she peeked again, roiling streams collided in the center of the church and tumbled in waves toward the altar.

Sweetie sat upright and swiveled her head from side to side, trying to locate the source of the sound. Finally, she jumped out of Terrence's lap and paced on the pew.

Ida Lou turned to see if Terrence reacted to the phenomenon, but his eyes remained shut and his head bowed in prayer.

No rainstorm outside. Only sunshine. Odd. Across the pews, see-through shapes of people materialized in every seat in the sanctuary. A melody of weeping voices cascaded like a river pounding downstream toward the altar.

Sweetie sailed off the bench and raced toward the center aisle. She darted back and forth, snapping as though she were trying to catch something. Ida Lou pinched her left forearm. Nope, she wasn't dreaming. So then, what was going on?

Terrence's lips moved, but no sound came from them. Should she poke him to make him look up?

The wave of tears terraced upward to fill a silver urn large enough to hold four grown men. Ida Lou sat perfectly still, but Sweetie cavorted around the urn in circles.

If I've lost my mind, my dog has, too.

A voice like white-water rapids thundered, "'I keep track of all sorrows and collect tears in My bottle. Each drop is recorded, and no pain goes unheeded.'"

Ida Lou gasped. Sweetie ran at full speed back to her, leaping into her lap. There was no logical explanation for what had just happened. However, no way she could deny the clear impression God had answered her unspoken question that He did see her pain and cared tremendously.

She wanted to cry out and tell Terrence about the miracle unfolding around them. But her lips remained sealed. What if he didn't see what she did? Would he think her insane? Eager for him to know God wasn't immune to their suffering, she tore her attention away from the coursing streams and tapped Terrence's arm.

With his head bowed, he said, "God, thanks for my new friend. And thank You for giving me a special place to go for company tonight. Amen." Terrence turned to face her, his eyes puffy and red.

Before she could say anything, the vision of people praying and waters tumbling vanished. Peacefulness settled on her. The vision, along with Terrence's simple prayer and example of perseverance, had given her a glimpse of glory. How could she explain this? She needed to think about what to say before speaking. Maybe she'd be able to talk with him tonight after supper.

Terrence stood and placed the handkerchief in his back pocket. "Reckon I need to be on my way to the office to finish up, so I won't be late for your dinner. What time should I get there?"

"Come around six. And bring a big appetite. You know where I live?"

"Yes, ma'am. Your address is in our records." He began to shuffle down the aisle.

"Of course. I look forward to seeing you tonight."

After he left, she waited to see if the images would reappear. Nothing did. The stained-glass image of Jesus stared into an otherwise empty room. Looking upward, she remarked, "You sure do work in surprising ways."

The black Bible in the pew rack in front of her beckoned, and she lifted it with reverence. Pages fluttered open to Hebrews 4:16: "Let us then approach God's throne of grace with confidence, so that we may receive mercy and find grace to help us in our time of need."

A warm calm cloaked her. "Thank You, Lord, for reassuring me."

She closed the Bible and returned it to the wooden holder. Then she slid to the edge of the pew and stood, with Sweetie right at her heels. "Richard, I love you and miss you very much. But I know God is going to take good care of me."

She walked toward the cross—her movement billowing the accordion skirt. Then she knelt at the altar. "God, I'd like to start a college fund for Ricky. Do You think You could help me find where Richard put the passwords for our online banking account?"

If the good Lord could send her a miraculous vision, a request like that shouldn't be complicated.

CHAPTER FIFTY-SEVEN

KEY TO THE KINGDOM

Prosper's faithful filled the pews the Sunday after Easter. Betty noticed a few people seated on the front row. Those spots usually remained empty, as some of the more zealous choir members were known to accidentally spray spittle during moving renditions of their favorite hymns. But today, there weren't other seats available.

Seeing no alternative, Betty walked down the outside aisle toward the first pew. When she reached the edge of the row, she saw Ida Lou near the center. She wore a midnight blue sheath with red heels and held the little Yorkie in her lap. Betty stopped suddenly, and Letitia ran into her and kicked the heel of her brogan.

"Ouch!" Letitia leaned down to massage her big toe, unprotected in a sandal.

"Be careful," Betty fussed.

Sarah and Ricky sat to the right of Ida Lou. The young woman looked pretty in a new yellow dress, chatting with her mother over the head of her little boy, who wore a white shirt and navy trousers. Even the dog was dressed up, sporting a bright yellow ribbon tied to her topknot and a doggie coat with "Security" embroidered in red. Letitia's handiwork, no doubt.

Three spread-out bulletins on the pew to their left saved seats for them. Betty hadn't taken antihistamines this morning. Big mistake. Afraid of getting too close to the dog, she waved Letitia to go in first.

Her friend hesitated. "No, no. Age before beauty, I always say."

"Ha ha." Betty refused to budge.

Betty shook her head at Letitia's bold outfit, styled after a Nigerian coronation ceremony. The get-up featured an apricot blouse tucked into a checked wraparound skirt. A huge, black, cloth hat sat on her head, mushrooming up like a cheese soufflé that had started rising but collapsed halfway. What that woman wouldn't do to get attention.

Betty stood by the window, adjusting her plain, floral muumuu. Letitia swept past and settled on the bench beside Ida Lou.

Hoping for more breathing room—literally—Betty checked out the other latecomers, who milled about and looked for seats. Elizabeth entered, wearing a white, embroidered, organza dress. Betty caught her eye and pointed toward the space on the front row. The mayor nodded, then headed toward them along the exterior wall. Juan followed a few steps behind her.

When Elizabeth neared Betty, Sarah put Ricky on her lap to make room. Then Letitia and Ida Lou scooted toward the pair, leaving space for the others. Betty turned to the side and waved the mayor to go past her and sit by Letitia. She wanted to keep as much distance as possible from that dratted dog.

Juan sat at the end of their row. He wore a blue, cotton work shirt, stretched to the full by his broad shoulders. Although his jeans were clean, there was a rip over the knee. Maybe that was all he had to wear. Betty patted the empty spot beside her.

Everyone in the row greeted Juan with smiles, waves, and welcoming words—in English, of course. He sat beside Betty. He must dry his clothing outdoors on a clothesline because his shirt smelled like sunshine.

She explained in limited English how pleased they were that he'd come. Then she showed him her cell phone, where she'd pulled up a translation app from English to Spanish.

A young father in the row behind them portioned out snacks to entertain his three wiggly children. Sweetie put her paws on the back of the pew, wagged her tail, and begged for a handout.

"Ida Lou should keep that mutt off the upholstery," Betty muttered to Elizabeth. But inwardly, she smiled, thinking about the Good Friday prayer vigil. A pang of guilt hit her for being judgmental. Hadn't they all been learning to look beyond external appearances to see the heart as God did?

Pastor James stepped to the podium to deliver his message. "Welcome to First Church. 'This is the day the Lord has made. [Let us] rejoice and be glad in it.'"

Betty typed "Hello" on her phone to practice translating for Juan, then she noticed as she looked to Juan that the poor congregant behind Letitia kept moving her head back and forth to see around the two-tiered headpiece.

"Today, we'll start with Isaiah 16:5 if you want to get your Bibles out. The passage will also be up on the screen." The pastor paused.

Soft thumps of Bibles being taken from the pew racks alternated with the flutter of pages. Several people scrolled down cell phone screens. Had Juan read a Bible before? Betty wasn't sure how much background knowledge he had.

"'In love, a throne will be established; in faithfulness, a man will sit on it—one from the house of David—one who in judging seeks justice and speeds the cause of righteousness,'" Pastor James read.

"The most important thing to know about Jesus is everything He does is motivated by love. He shows love to us in tender mercy, and He shows love to the Father with obedience."

Betty wasn't sure how to unpack that for Juan, so she simplified as best she could and typed key phrases.

"Jesus' kingdom is not about gathering titles or worldly wealth but showing devotion to our Father." His white, collared shirt peeked up from under the black robe.

Pastor James scanned the faces of his flock. "Jesus did nothing from selfish ambition. Instead, He descended to lower earthly regions to walk with us."

Betty glanced at Elizabeth. The mayor modeled a quiet service to others.

"The first point to know is that love is what motivates Jesus. The second point is that Jesus' sacrifice on the cross is what saves us. In Revelation 1:18, Jesus said, 'I am the Living One; I was dead, and now look, I am alive forever and ever! And I hold the keys of death and Hades.'"

Betty's fingers stumbled on the screen, trying to keep up. Finally, she rested a moment and tilted the phone for Juan to see.

Pastor James took keys from his robe pocket and jingled them. "Jesus is willing to go into the darkest places and most fearsome dungeons to free us captives from sin."

The room got quiet as people shifted in their seats. "We have all done wrong at one time or another. And we have been made clean only by God's grace through His Son's obedience. Jesus' faithful service at Calvary paves the way for us to enter God's presence."

Letitia peeked over and pointed to herself, indicating she could sit by Juan to take a turn translating. Betty shook her head, though the woman behind Letitia may have been grateful not to stare at the oversized hat.

The pastor continued. "We want to be full of faith. But life has a way of knocking the stuffing out of us."

That got a few nervous chuckles from around the room.

"Maybe you've endured the loss of a loved one. Or perhaps you faced bankruptcy, divorce, or some other tragedy and didn't know where to go for comfort."

Betty missed the weight of Donovan's arm around her shoulder during church. Even crammed in with all of her friends, loneliness crept in.

"We ask ourselves, especially during this Easter season, 'Why hasn't God performed a miracle for me?'" The pastor lifted his arms, and the robe resembled wings. He seemed to look at Ida Lou and Sarah. That man sure liked to tread where angels feared to go. "We can trust God has a plan—even if we can't see all the details right now—to bring fullness to our lives and restore what we have lost."

Believing God would someday reunite her with Donovan was the only thing that held her together at times. Juan seemed to notice her distress. He closed his right hand with gentle pressure over hers so she could stop typing.

Jingling keys drew her attention back to the minister, who held the ring again. "Jesus is the Key to the Kingdom. He unlocks God's mercy toward us. On our own, we never can do or be enough to approach God's throne with purity."

Betty wished an angel from the stained-glass window could whisper everything she needed to know. But then again, when Ida Lou confided what she'd seen in the sanctuary on Friday, Betty's first reaction had been to make sure the restrooms outside the sanctuary didn't have leaky plumbing.

Pastor James turned over a sheet of his sermon notes. "In times of great sorrow, we also might wonder where our Lord is. Where is He when we lose a job, a marriage fails, or someone betrays us?"

Would Sarah forge ahead on her own or run back to her husband? Against everyone's advice, Sarah had refused to press charges against Charles, stating she wanted him to be able to return to Summit and keep his job. However, she heeded the advice the team at Solutions and Pastor James gave to put precautions in place.

Through connections at Solutions, Letitia paid a retainer to hire an attorney to represent Sarah and fill out paperwork with the clerk of court for Sarah to get temporary custody of Ricky. They added a request that Charles complete counseling for batterers and that any visitation would be conducted in Prosper under supervision. Sarah agreed to attend a support group at Solutions to address her issues.

Smythe informed Betty that since First Sergeant Wilson planned to suspend Charles for thirty days with administrative sanctions and counseling, the local prosecutor deferred criminal charges. Would showing Charles mercy encourage him to mend his ways or cement his sense of impunity?

Sarah's head was down, and a few tears dripped off her chin. Betty dug out the tissues from her purse and passed them down the row. Ricky put his arms around his mom's neck and kissed her cheek.

Pastor James stepped around the podium to move closer to the congregation. "Rest assured, Jesus is standing right beside you. He promises to walk with us every step of the way on this journey. And He will be with you in every circumstance."

"Mommy," Ricky piped up loud enough for the congregation to hear, "I'm hungry."

Everyone laughed, including Pastor James. "We all ought to be hungry for the Lord and His Good News."

Behind them, the father in the pew tapped Ida Lou's shoulder and handed her several animal crackers. She mouthed a thank you.

Sweetie tiptoed across the laps toward Juan. Betty reached for a Bible and used it as a barricade. The little mutt jumped to the floor, then bounded onto Juan's chest. No way could she get up and leave from the front row. She'd have to stick it out.

"The third point is this: we show *our* love to Jesus by helping others. That's what living as a community is all about. Seeing each other as we are, with our imperfections, and loving anyway. That's how we demonstrate our love for God."

Ida Lou linked her elbow with Sarah's. Letitia grabbed Elizabeth's hand. Juan smiled at Betty.

"How often do we miss an opportunity to serve Jesus? We might overlook a neighbor, a coworker, or gardener because we are too busy with our agendas." Pastor James paused to let this call-to-action register. "In Matthew 10:42, Jesus says, 'If anyone gives even a cup of cold water to one of these little ones who is my disciple, that person will certainly not lose their reward.'"

The woman behind Letitia tapped her on the shoulder, using mime to show her lack of visibility due to the bouffant hat. Letitia leaned toward Elizabeth's shoulder, finally giving the poor woman a glimpse of the pastor's face. The tall gentleman beside her didn't seem to mind. Betty took shallow breaths as Sweetie panted on Juan's lap next to her. She needed tissues to cover her nose.

The preacher pointed to his heart. "We are the living places where Christ continues His work. Each day begins a new sequel in which God reveals His everlasting love. Someday, we will see Him face to face."

Along with all of our dear, departed loved ones.

Pastor James held up his open Bible. "Are we willing to be messengers of hope and reassurance to a world filled with cares?"

Betty planned to learn more about Juan this week. Maybe there would be a way she could help.

The pastor pointed toward the back of the sanctuary. "As you leave today, please stop by the tables in the foyer. We have sign-up sheets for volunteers to help with a clothing drive for women and children at a shelter for survivors of domestic violence. Today's love offering will go to support that group. You can place your cash or check donations in the baskets on your way out. You also can give online if that is more convenient."

The woman behind Letitia opened her purse and pulled out her wallet.

"Also, if you have experience teaching English as a second language or know a foreign language well, please fill out a connect card or go online to our website and add your contact information. We plan to start offering free classes one night a week on our church campus."

Hmm. Betty had never done that. But when she saw Juan sit up straight when he heard "free classes," she felt a strong tug on her heart to get involved with this new ministry.

"And members of the prayer chain, we'll have an important meeting in my office at ten o'clock Tuesday morning. I hope to see you there."

Betty shot a reproachful look toward Letitia, sure she had a pretty good idea what the topic of that meeting was going to be. Her friend adjusted that abomination of a hat, pretending not to notice Betty.

"John 3:17 tells us 'God did not send His Son into the world to condemn' but to save us. Please bow your heads for the closing prayer."

Juan watched what the others did. He stopped petting Sweetie's back and lowered his head.

"Lord," said Pastor James, "please teach us how to use whatever gifts we have received to serve others. And in every word we speak, help us bring hope and comfort to those in pain. Help us see with Your eyes and let us serve in the strength You provide so that in all things You will receive praise. To the risen Jesus Christ be the glory and the power forever."

When Pastor James said, "Amen," Sweetie stood up in Juan's arms and barked. Many in the congregation laughed. What a fitting way to end this busy week in Prosper.

After church, Betty wanted a nap at home. She had a feeling she was going to need strength. There was no telling what the WUFHs might get involved with next.

AUTHOR'S NOTE

Domestic violence is a cancer eating away at many families. On the outside, things look fine. Couples even go to church. But behind closed doors, a power imbalance shatters hearts.

I became more aware of these concerns after completing training as an advocate at Empowerhouse in Fredericksburg, Virginia, in 2011. Empowerhouse is a non-profit organization providing confidential domestic violence assistance.[1] The accredited program is funded by state and federal grants, localities, donations, and fundraisers. This organization serves the community well, and I wanted to do something to help others.

The statistics shared in training staggered me. "In the United States, more than ten million adults experience domestic violence annually," according to a summary of a U.S. national survey.[2] Domestic violence is defined by the National Coalition Against Domestic Violence as "the willful intimidation, physical assault, battery, sexual assault, and/ or other abusive behavior as part of a systematic pattern of power and control perpetrated by one intimate partner against another. It includes physical violence, sexual violence, psychological violence,

---

1   https://www.empowerhouseva.org/?page_id=2
2   M.C. Black,, K.C., et. al., 2011, The National Intimate Partner and Sexual Violence Survey (NISVS): 2010 Summary Report, 2011 (Atlanta: National Center for Injury Prevention and Control, Centers for Disease Control and Prevention), https://www.cdc.gov/violenceprevention/pdf/nisvs_report2010-a.pdf.

316 WHO BROUGHT THE DOG TO CHURCH?

and emotional abuse."[3] This may happen at your neighbors' house. It may occur in yours.

In my capacity as an advocate, I heard voices shaking with terror when people phoned for help. I did intake interviews with perpetrators and assessed the likelihood of repeated offenses and the risk of lethality. I delivered personal items to the hidden shelter and drove victims to appointments. Listening to these stories revealed that DV haunts all ages, socioeconomic groups, and ethnicities. I wanted to write how to identify problems, as well as solutions.

I felt a novel may allow people to experience the concerns in a way that was nonthreatening, while still offering practical advice and bringing awareness about resources. Providing a safe forum to discuss suffering done in secret may free others from harm.

Another strand of the story weaves in with my involvement as a Stephen Minister and facilitator for GriefShare. Standing with people during crises brought home the importance of compassion when we are at our most vulnerable. My prayer is that the fictional events in Prosper remind us to show mercy and support each other with the love of Christ.

3   "Domestic Violence," [Fact Sheet], Domestic Violence National Coalition Against Domestic Violence, 2020, https://assets.speakcdn.com/assets/2497/ domestic_violence-2020080709350855.pdf?1596811079991.

BOOK CLUB GUIDE

1. Think about a time you made a snap judgment based on someone's appearance that was later proved wrong. What happened to change your opinion?

2. Have you been around anyone involved in an abusive relationship? What can be done to help those trapped in domestic violence? A resource can be found online at the National Coalition Against Domestic Violence. Be sure to have a victim log into a device the abuser cannot track. You may also donate a phone for a victim to NCADV.[4]

3. Women tend to define themselves by their relationships. So why did the author leave out a romantic love interest in this story?

4. What are the pros and cons of current legislation affecting immigration?

5. What has to happen for true reconciliation in estranged relationships such as Sarah's with her mom and husband?

6. Have you ever had to face the death of a person you loved? What helped you cope with the grief? If you need support or know someone who does, view online GriefShare resources at https://www.griefshare.org.

7. What end-of-life issues have you had to face and/or plan for, such as what Ida Lou had to decide with Richard's Do Not Resuscitate order (DNR)?

---

4   https://ncadv.org.

8. Residents of Prosper struggle to maintain a close-knit community. Do you feel connected in your neighborhood or city? If not, why? What can be done to make the group closer?

9. "Power tends to corrupt, and absolute power corrupts absolutely." John Emerich Edward Dalberg Acton wrote this in a letter dated 1887.[5] Have you ever had to deal with a corrupt official? What did you do?

10. How does adversity affect religious beliefs?

11. When was the last time you had a really good belly laugh? What happened?

12. Do you have a pet? How does Sweetie impact the story?

13. According to The American Pets Products Association, U.S. consumers spent more than $103.6 billion on pet industry expenditures in 2020. How do you feel about that?[6]

14. How did Pastor James inspire his flock to live out faith by doing good?

15. Discuss this Bible passage from James 2:16: "Suppose a brother or a sister is without clothes and daily food. If one of you says to them, 'Go in peace; keep warm and well fed,' but does nothing about their physical needs, what good is it? In the same way, faith by itself, if it is not accompanied by action, is dead."

---

5   "The Meaning and Origin of the Expression: Power Corrupts; Absolute Power Corrupts Absolutely," The Phrase Finder, Accessed August 1, 2022, http://www.phrases.org.uk/meanings/absolute-power-corrupts-absolutely.html.

6   "Pet Industry Market Size, Trends & Ownership Statistics," American Pet Products Association, Accessed August 16, 2022, http://www.americanpetproducts.org/press_industrytrends.asp.

PRACTICAL IDEAS FOR OFFERING COMFORT

- Phone to check on the person, then say, "I am available if you would like to talk."
- Go visit and greet the person, saying, "It is nice to see you!"
- Ask about the person. What is a favorite memory, favorite silly story, or treasured photo? What is something they love? Give them a positive avenue to share.
- Offer to chauffeur the person to appointments or business places to lessen their stress.
- Join the person on the couch, watch a movie, and eat popcorn without bringing up heavy issues, unless the person wants to talk. Don't try to "fix" anything. Just be present.
- Invite the person to dinner for company or prepare a meal to bring over and share to lessen loneliness.
- Say, "I have no idea what things are like for you right now, but I love you and am here for you."
- Ask for permission to give a hug and provide a gentle embrace.
- Don't be afraid to mention the name of someone who is gone. Sometimes, just hearing the beloved name gives comfort to those left behind.
- Do you feel like talking or want to do something fun?

- Inquire if there is a household chore that the person would appreciate help with doing.
- Consider donating to a cause to honor the memory of the person. For example, gifting books to a library or a tree to beautify a community establishes tangible legacies the family can cherish.
- Remember to follow up weeks after the loss to continue support after the immediate crisis. Mark birthdays and anniversaries on your calendar to remind you to reach out at peak times of someone feeling loss.
- Ask if the person grieving would like someone to go with them to the cemetery on birthdays or holidays to acknowledge their loss.

Thank you to members of the grief support group
who provided these suggestions!

ACKNOWLEDGMENTS

The idea for this book began in 2011 when I trained with Empowerhouse in Fredericksburg, Virginia, as an advocate for survivors of domestic violence. Thank you to the staff there who provide help for many who are suffering.

GriefShare is a wonderful organization that offers comfort for those who lose a loved one (https://www.griefshare.org).

Members of the Riverside Writers in Spotsylvania, Virginia, gave terrific support and insights on early drafts.

Kathy Ide is an amazing writing tutor and editor.

Julie Gwinn was the first to suggest the manuscript may have broad appeal as a novel.

Word Weavers International sponsored the October Florida Christian Writers Conference in 2021 that launched the revival of the work.

Rhonda Rhea, Athena Holtz, and Dori Harrell shared wisdom on improving the text.

Kaley Rhea took the story to the next level with meticulous and deep insights.

Samuel Lowry believed in a new voice and made time to mentor. Much gratitude also to editor Martin Wiles and the rest of the Ambassador International team who brought the book to life.

Pastors Steve Hay, Keith Boyette, Doug Kokx, and Dawn Carter secured me in times of trial and covered my life with prayer.

Family and friends supported me for more than a decade as I kept telling them I was writing a book, but nothing seemed to happen. They did not discourage me from chasing the dream, anyhow.

Thank you all for sharing this journey to bring hope to those who are hurting.

ABOUT THE AUTHOR

A native of Florida, Tracy L. Smoak grew up near Orlando, riding horses and climbing citrus trees. Her passion is to encourage others in their faith journey.

In writing her debut novel, Tracy utilized experience as a trained advocate for survivors of domestic violence at Empowerhouse in Fredericksburg, Virginia. She also relied on insights from GriefShare at Wilderness Methodist Church in Spotsylvania, Virginia. Tracy holds a master's in education with fifteen years of experience teaching English in public high schools. She is a member of Word Weavers International.

Tracy loves photography and avoids boiled asparagus like after-school detention but will walk long distances for Cadbury Fruit and Nut chocolate bars.

For more information on Tracy's book *Break the Cycle: Healing from an Abusive Relationship*, please visit her website at www.tracysmoak.com.

CONTACT INFORMATION

Email: tracysmoak6912@gmail.com

LINKS TO SOCIAL MEDIA AND SITES

Website with weekly blogs about hope

www.tracysmoak.com

Facebook

www.facebook.com/tracysmoak2

LinkedIn

www.linkedin.com/in/tracy-l-smoak-author-1421308a

Instagram

www.instagram.com/tracysmoak_findinghope

YouTube

www.youtube.com/channel/UCTt_2ua49dUvqrAPqyzCP8A

OTHER WORKS BY TRACY L. SMOAK

Arranged with Love with photographs by Tracy Smoak (Redemption Press)

Living Water to Refresh Your Soul with photographs by Tracy Smoak

Refuge of Grace: Finding Your Safe Place (Bold Vision)

A devotion in *Pray a Word a Day Volume 2 (Guideposts)*

Employed by God: Benefits Packaged with Faith (available on Amazon)

Break the Cycle: Healing from an Abusive Relationship (available on Amazon)

Ambassador International's mission is to magnify the Lord Jesus Christ and promote His Gospel through the written word.

We believe through the publication of Christian literature, Jesus Christ and His Word will be exalted, believers will be strengthened in their walk with Him, and the lost will be directed to Jesus Christ as the only way of salvation.

For more information about
AMBASSADOR INTERNATIONAL
please visit:

www.ambassador-international.com

Thank you for reading this book. Please consider leaving us a review on your favorite retailer's website, Goodreads or Bookbub, or our website.

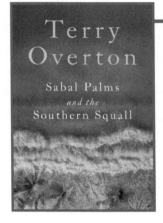

Elaine Smith is content with her life as a widow in the small, coastal town of Sabal Palms. She enjoys her time with friends, and she enjoys writing stories and devotionals, despite the advice of her friends. When a southern squall hits the coast, Elaine's abandoned writings start showing up in the most mysterious places. Can God actually use Elaine's trash to become someone else's treasure? Is there more to her writings than she even realizes?

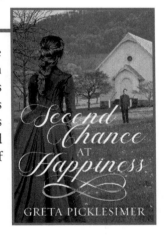

After Catherine Reed's husband dies, she moves back home in order to accept a new position as the teacher for the town's one-room schoolhouse. Samuel Harris has suffered his own loss and guilt has burdened him ever since. When his old flame comes back to town, he wonders if they can find healing together . . .

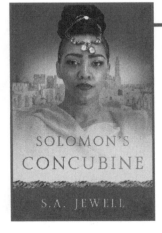

King Solomon is well-known as a wise man and the wealthiest king to have ever lived. But with great power often comes great corruption, and Solomon was no exception—including his collection of wives and concubines. But who were these women? What was life like for them in Solomon's harem? S.A. Jewell dives into a deeper part of Solomon's kingdom and shows how God is always faithful, even when we may doubt His plan.

Made in the USA
Columbia, SC
10 July 2023